E.R. PUNSHON
THE CONQUEROR INN

ERNEST ROBERTSON PUNSHON was born in London in 1872.

At the age of fourteen he started life in an office. His employers soon informed him that he would never make a really satisfactory clerk, and he, agreeing, spent the next few years wandering about Canada and the United States, endeavouring without great success to earn a living in any occupation that offered. Returning home by way of working a passage on a cattle boat, he began to write. He contributed to many magazines and periodicals, wrote plays, and published nearly fifty novels, among which his detective stories proved the most popular and enduring.

He died in 1956.

The Bobby Owen Mysteries

E.R. PUNSHON

THE CONQUEROR INN

With an introduction
by Curtis Evans

DEAN STREET PRESS

INTRODUCTION

DETECTIVE NOVELS by E.R. Punshon have long been greatly prized by collectors of vintage mystery fiction, not only because of their high quality but because of their plain scarcity. One reason the books so often have been difficult to find (until the recent Punshon reprint revival) lies in the fact that historically Punshon's publication record--like that of the author's exuberantly imaginative Detection Club colleague Gladys Mitchell, another leading Golden Age British crime novelist highly sought by collectors--was rather spotty in the United States. Only a dozen of Punshon's nearly three dozen Bobby Owen detective novels were published in the US, six of them from the 1930s and six from the 1940s.

Information Received and *Crossword Mystery*, the first two Bobby Owen detective novels which appeared in the US, had major American publishers (Houghton, Mifflin and Alfred A. Knopf respectively), but the four later Thirties Punshon titles--*The Bath Mysteries, Mystery of Mr Jessop, The Dusky Hour* and *Dictator's Way* (retitled *Death of a Tyrant*)—were issued by Hillman-Curl's "Clue Club" imprint, a short-lived concern which during its brief time in existence aimed squarely at the American rental library market. Assuring readers that the death's head logo emblazoned on every Clue Club book served as a guarantee of originality and good writing, the Clue Club published 44 mystery novels between 1937 and 1939, the most distinguished of which, in my estimation, are the four Punshon titles. After the Clue Club went defunct on the eve of the Second World War, Punshon had no publisher in the United States until his detective novels were picked up by Macmillan, who in 1944 published *The Conqueror Inn*, which in the UK had been issued the previous year by Punshon's longtime English publisher, the highly-regarded Victor Gollancz. (On publisher Hillman-Curl and its Clue Club imprint see Bill Pronzini, "Hillman-Curl [1936-1939]," in William F. Deeck, ed., *Murder at 3 Cents a Day: An Annotated Crime Fiction Bibliography of the Lending Library Publishers: 1936-1967,* 2006).

An important American publisher, Macmillan already included several notable British mystery authors in its stable, including a promising new writer, George Bellairs; Punshon's Detection Club colleagues G.D.H. and Margaret Cole, prominent Socialist intellectuals; and Eden Phillpotts, who though primarily a mainstream regional novelist produced a sizeable body of crime fiction over his very long life. (Among mystery fans he is best known today for having encouraged a young Dartmouth neighbor, Agatha Christie, to write fiction professionally.) Additionally, Macmillan had recently scored great successes with *Who Killed Aunt Maggie?* and *Blood on Her Shoe*, two regional mystery novels set in the American Deep South (both of which were later adapted to film) by Atlanta journalist Medora Field, a close friend of Margaret Mitchell, author of the massive bestseller *Gone with the Wind*, which also had been published by Macmillan.

Publishing not only *The Conqueror Inn* but Punshon's next four Bobby Owen detective novels (as well as a slightly later Bobby Owen title, *So Many Doors*), Macmillan--in contrast with Gollancz, then laboring under severe government restrictions owing to wartime paper shortages—did full justice to their prestigious new English mystery author, issuing books of good production quality with attractive dust jackets illustrated by first-rate cover artists like Arthur Hawkins, Jr., modernist designer of jackets for William Faulkner novels, and H. Lawrence Hoffman, some of whose artwork was shown in 2015 at an exhibition, "Mystery, Murder & Mayhem: The Paperback Book Cover Art of H. Lawrence Hoffman (1940-1948)." Macmillan boosted *The Conqueror Inn* as a "meaty, satisfying mystery for readers who like a real puzzle," and American reviewers concurred. In the *New York Times Book Review* Isaac Anderson praised the novel as an "extremely intricate crime puzzle with an equally intricate solution," while in the rival *New York Herald Tribune Book Review* Will Cuppy lauded it as an "impressive baffler by one of the better English practitioners."

Meanwhile, out west, Anthony Boucher--who was soon to replace Isaac Anderson at the *NYTBR*, where until his death two decades later he would reign as the leading American mystery critic (the Anthony Awards are named in his honor)--made note in the *San Francisco Chronicle* of the "solid construction" and "distinguished characterization" which he discerned in *The Conqueror Inn*; and in Tucson, Arizona, a book reviewer for *Hoofs and Horns*, an idiosyncratic but popular American rodeo magazine, enthusiastically took up Punshon's cause, lavishing *The Conqueror*

Inn with a veritable encomium: "One of the foremost British thriller-writers here gives us a first-class mystery, replete with creeps, thrills and tingles of foreboding as one grim scene builds into another and suspicion is expertly thrown in turn against each actor in this sinister drama of greed and hate couched in wartime datelines. ... A better tale of dark deeds would be hard to come by." This latter review likely would have particularly pleased the 72-year-old Punshon, who in the 1890s had partially spent several vagabond years of his adventurous young manhood punching cattle in the American West.

In Golden Age British mystery the pub often is portrayed as a place of good cheer and hearty fellowship, despite the inconvenience of a little local murder or two; yet Punshon's lonely moorland public house in *The Conqueror Inn* is anything but a cheerful abode, being rather a forbidding locus of desolation, deception and death. At the beginning of the novel Inspector Bobby Owen--whose superior, Colonel Glynne, chief constable of the Wychshire County Police, is "growing more and more used to leaving everything to the young man already recognized as his successor"—is driving though the "fresh, clean autumn air," grateful for any excuse to get out from behind his desk, to investigate a report concerning the discovery of an abandoned box of banknotes a couple of miles distant from the isolated Conqueror Inn (so named because of a tale that William the Conqueror had been served with wine at the inn "when he and his men were on their way to lay the north country waste"). Bobby soon finds, however, that there is much more than a matter of lost banknotes at hand. Near where the box was discovered lies a newly dug grave that when disinterred gruesomely reveals the naked, mutilated body of an unidentified—and seemingly unidentifiable— man. "[C]oldly, deliberately, almost scientifically, the dead man's face had been battered out of all resemblance to human features," writes Punshon. "Bobby ... had seen many strange and dreadful sights, but nothing, he felt, quite so shocking as this careful disfigurement of the dead, this refusal to allow to a dead man in his grave even a semblance of humanity."

Once again Punshon insightfully explores ageless human passions which can lead to violence, but he also for the first time in the Bobby Owen series draws significantly and fascinatingly on topical wartime questions, concerning which I will leave readers of *The Conqueror Inn* to discover for themselves. Punshon also enjoyably develops Bobby's relationships both with his subordinate Sergeant Payne--"young and intelligent, with a first-class education--he had gone from a Midwych elementary to a Midwych secondary school," the egalitarian author notes pointedly—and the woman who is very much Bobby's equal, his wife Olive, who now routinely discusses Wychshire's invariably fiendishly perplexing murder cases with her spouse, gently upbraiding him when she sees fit. "I don't ... call that deduction," she challenges him at one point. "I call it guessing." However, Punshon readers can rest assured that the tenacious Inspector Owen will, with an occasional nudge from Olive, get there in the end.

Curtis Evans

CHAPTER I

PLAYING TRUANT

INSPECTOR BOBBY OWEN, of the Midwych County Police, chief indeed of the Midwych County C.I.D., doubling with that office the post of secretary to the chief constable, Colonel Glynne, had an uneasy conscience.

Because he was playing truant.

He knew very well that this errand he was on should have been confided to a subordinate. He knew very well that at this moment he ought to be sitting in his office, before a paper-strewn table, dealing with all that flood of orders, instructions, regulations, counter orders, instructions, regulations, that the bureaucratic machine turned out day by day; calm, regular, and unceasing, as the procession of the seasons. Not one of all of them, of course, but its issue could be reasonably defended. None the less Bobby was inclined in his more rebellious moments to wonder if a severe rationing of such activities, every government office limited strictly to such or such a number each month, would seriously impede the war effort.

However, for the time he had left all that behind. Sergeant Payne, young and intelligent, with a first-class education—he had gone from a Midwych elementary to a Midwych secondary school—could deal for to-day with the paper stuff. Meanwhile, in spite of the murmurings of a dissatisfied conscience, Bobby was thoroughly enjoying his drive through the fresh, clean, autumn air.

It was weeks, and it seemed like years, since he had spent a day away from the office. He wished he had been able to bring Olive with him. But a policeman on duty has to be careful, and the company of a wife would have made this trip look too much like what it really was, a mere pleasure excursion.

The road he was following was one he did not know well, even though his duty took him so often to and fro in the county, deputizing for the Colonel, who was growing more and more used to leaving everything to the young man already recognized as his successor. Driving had to be done with caution for the surface was bad—a second-class road the county surveyor had been inclined, in the stress of war time, to neglect of late. Then it had a good many sharp corners and awkward hairpin bends. It left the main Midwych and Scotland road some miles north of the city, served occasional small villages, isolated farms, country mansions, and then divided, one branch running on to join the Holyhead road, the other turning back to meet again the main Scottish route, having thus made a detour of about thirty miles or so.

A little-used road then and less used than ever in these days of war with pleasure motoring nearly at a standstill and none of the new factories, airfields, camps, in the district it served before its division. To the east, as Bobby drove northward, lay in the distance Wychwood proper, a dense vast mass of woodland, where trees had grown and flourished, decayed and fallen and died, since times beyond the memory of man, before perhaps man was. Further on, east and south, lay the vast industrial district of which Midwych city was a centre. On Bobby's other hand, to the west lay the bare uplands of Wychwood forest, waste land, thin and hungry, swept by every wind, giving scant sustenance to a few flocks of sheep, though bearing still the name of forest from that vast antiquity when 'forest' meant merely beyond the bounds, the desolate, outside lands.

'Outside' indeed all that lonely country seemed, with no hint anywhere of human life or habitation. It was this enormous loneliness that helped to give a touch of the bizarre to the odd story Bobby had managed to persuade the chief constable and himself ought to be investigated, as the message over the phone had requested, by an 'experienced officer.'

It was almost like driving through an uninhabited land, he thought, and he supposed that ancient Briton and Roman soldier, Norman knight and Tudor gallant, Roundhead and Cavalier, Georgian dragoon and the Home Guard of to-day, all had passed this way and would none of them have seen change or alteration.

An ancient land and a lonely, and it was something of a relief when he saw in the distance a building that must, he supposed, be his destination.

The Conqueror Inn.

He paused to draw up for a moment to consult the large-scale map he had brought with him. No other building shown near, so this must be it, and who, he wondered, wanted an inn in so desolate a spot? And how did the innkeeper manage to make a living?

The inn stood high, at a point whence the road descended in both directions. It had a grim, bare, weatherbeaten appearance, a defiant aspect to it somehow, as if it challenged the elements to do their worst. Behind it were a few outbuildings, and on the southern slope of the rising ground, whose height it crowned, were a few cultivated acres. On them a cow or two, some sheep, and a few pigs were visible. A farmer, or smallholder rather, was then apparently the tenant of the Conqueror Inn, as well as landlord, and that probably explained how he was able to achieve the difficult feat of continuing to exist.

Outside the inn, Bobby drew up and alighted. He noticed that already, though it was barely closing time, the inn doors were shut. Somewhat cynically, he wondered if such strict obedience to the licensing laws was always practised, or whether an expected visit from the police had anything to do with this admirable adherence to the law. He sounded his horn. Nothing happened. So he went through the proscribed motions for immobilizing the car—pedantic perhaps out here in this wilderness, but officials must needs be pedants—and walked round to the rear of the building. A man carrying a pitchfork came from one of the outbuildings and stood watching him gravely. He did not speak and Bobby said:

"Mr. Christopherson?"

The other nodded. He was a big man with a big square head, and his enormous hands held the pitchfork like a weapon. More of a farmer than an innkeeper in his appearance, probably more in his element behind a plough than behind a bar, Bobby thought. He showed his card and said:

"There was a 'phone message late last night. It was from you?"

Mr. Christopherson nodded again. He seemed a man of few words. He glanced at the card, glanced at Bobby, and said in a deep, slow voice:

"You're young for an inspector. Come into the house and I'll show you."

He moved towards the inn and Bobby followed him, slightly offended. He didn't feel at all young. He doubted if he was really much younger than Christopherson himself, even though about this farmer-innkeeper there seemed to hang something of the ageless past of the lands in which he lived. A fantastic notion came into his mind that perhaps this man had always been here, and himself had watched the passage of Briton and Roman and knight and cavalier. An ageless man in an ageless land. He gave himself a little angry shake to get rid of such fantasies. Through a door so low both his guide and himself had to stoop to pass beneath, they entered a long, low kitchen, stone floored. A bright fire burned in a fireplace almost as big itself as many rooms in modern houses. It was of peat and it was bright because a woman was blowing it with a pair of long-handled bellows. She was tall and square and elderly. Bobby could not see her face clearly as her attitude hid it from him. She took not the least notice of their entry. She did not even turn round. At a table near the window a girl was kneading dough. She was tall and strong and young and the rhythmic movements of her arms and body as she worked had a kind of solemn grace and beauty of their own. She looked at the two men as they came in but did not speak. It was as though the eternal silence of the moors had penetrated here, too, and that here, too, things happened as they happened without need for comment or chatter. Hardly a pretty girl, for her features were too large and too irregular, but impressive in her way all the same. And slightly disconcerting, Bobby found the utter indifference with which her eyes, dark, sombre and hidden, swept over him and left him and returned to her task. It seemed to convey to him the message that war or no war the fundamental task of all was the making and baking and breaking of bread.

Christopherson ignored the two women as completely as they ignored him and Bobby. He walked on through the room and Bobby followed. A short passage, stone flagged, led into a small room. Another door opened from it into the bar. The room seemed to be used as an office. Christopherson unlocked a cupboard and took out a wooden box or small packing-case, such as wholesale dealers use for deliveries to retailers of what are called packed goods. The lid had been nailed on but now was loose. Christopherson lifted it and showed it was filled with tightly packed bundles of one-pound notes. He made no comment but stood waiting and Bobby said:

"Was the lid like that when you found it?"

"No. Nailed," Christopherson answered.

"You opened it, then?"

Christopherson let this go unanswered. He gave the impression of considering the question one that so obviously carried its own answer that no reply was necessary.

"How much is there?" Bobby asked.

"I don't know," Christopherson replied. "I've touched nothing."

"We must count it together and I'll give you a receipt before I take it," Bobby said.

He was experiencing some surprise at finding that the tale told over the 'phone had been in no way exaggerated. The report received by 'phone that a wooden case full of bank-notes had been picked up by the roadside, had not sounded very convincing. A practical joke had been suspected, and there had been a certain amount of chaff about the probable size of the 'case.' The general feeling was that the 'case' would turn out to be a small box wherein some motorist had placed a few notes for convenience and that somehow or another it had fallen from his car. A routine matter really. One for the nearest constable. There had been no opportunity to ask for further information for after giving his name and message and where he was speaking from, Christopherson had rung off. The inn itself had no 'phone. He had spoken from a roadside A.A. 'phone cabin, so once he had left it there was no way of communicating further.

The usual thing would have been to ring up the nearest constable and order him to report. But there was something rather queer about this story of a case filled with bank-notes having been picked up in so lonely a spot and Christopherson himself had seemed to think so, for he had asked that an officer of experience should be sent. Besides, decisive factor, Bobby, with a flash of lightning insight, had seen that here was a chance to get away from his eternal office work for an hour or two in the open air.

"I had better spare the time to run out myself and see if there's anything in it," he had said with an air of annoyance and impatience that deceived no one. "Not likely, but you can never tell."

After all, these are strange days when strange things happen. And when someone suggested that perhaps the bank-notes had been dropped by parachute, Bobby nodded gravely and promised that that possibility would not be forgotten.

Now looking at that not so small box stuffed with those neatly packed bundles of bank-notes, Bobby was thinking to himself that certainly it had been worth while to come in person. People don't usually carry about wooden boxes stuffed with bank-notes. If they do, and if the box is lost, one would expect them to be prompt to report the fact. Few would be careless about keeping an eye on so valuable a package or in noticing its disappearance.

"Where exactly did you find it?" Bobby asked.

"Two miles south, near the road, in a dry gullet," Christopherson answered and went on: "Near by there's what looks like a grave—a new dug grave."

CHAPTER II
THE GRAVE

THE WORDS CAME SO slowly, so quietly, almost so indifferently from this big, slow, tranquil man, that for a moment or two Bobby could only stare blankly, hardly knowing what significance to attach to them. Then he said questioningly:

"A grave?"

Christopherson did not answer. It seemed that having said a thing once, he saw no necessity to repeat it.

"Why do you think it's a grave?" Bobby asked.

"It is long and narrow and newly dug in a hidden place," Christopherson answered. He paused, seemed to hesitate, and continued: "After dark yesterday, about seven or eight, I think, Rachel heard something that may have been a pistol shot. At the time she thought it was a lorry backfiring. She thought she heard voices, shouting. She told me when I came in. I took a lantern and went to see if help was needed. A breakdown or an accident, I thought. There was no one, but I found that." He lifted a hand towards the box of bank-notes and resumed: "When I saw what was in it, I went to the road 'phone box to let the police know. It must have been nearly ten by then. This morning I went to look again. There are marks on the road and on the turf near."

A good witness, Bobby thought. Able both to observe and to describe. All the essentials given and nothing omitted. Or—was nothing omitted? A policeman learns to accept no story at face value and Bobby had not yet made up his mind what to think of this quiet, slow-moving man. 'Still waters run deep,' he remembered, and difficult to know what such 'stillness' may conceal in its depths. He said:

"What sort of marks do you mean?"

"Confused. Footprints. Tyre tracks. But it rained in the night and they are hard to make out."

That much was true anyhow, for Bobby remembered having been wakened by the heavy pelting of the rain. For a little he had lain awake listening to it and then had slept again.

"Is Rachel your daughter?" he asked. "Is she the young lady I saw as we came through the house?"

"She is my daughter, she is young, she is not a lady," Christopherson answered.

"I suppose," commented Bobby, "that in the Brains Trust Professor Joad would say that depended on what you mean by a lady. Anyhow, she was doing a lady's job—lady means kneader of bread, you know."

Christopherson received this piece of information in silence. Bobby, who had spoken while trying to make up his mind what to think of the landlord of the Conqueror Inn and of what he had just said, fell silent too.

"I think first of all we had better count this money," he said finally. "I'll give you a receipt for it and then I'll get you to show me where you found it and what you say looks like a grave."

"I will be in the yard when you are ready," Christopherson said. "I have work to do."

"I think you had better stay till the money's counted, hadn't you?" Bobby suggested.

"Why?"

"Well, for one thing, to make sure that it is counted correctly."

"That is your business, not mine," Christopherson answered.

"The receipt I shall have to give is very much your business, isn't it?" Bobby asked, but Christopherson shook his head, and turned towards the door.

"There is no need for a receipt," he said. "You have the money. What else is necessary?"

Bobby, faintly puzzled, looked again at the big, quiet man. He could not decide whether such apparent simplicity was genuine or whether it was a pose assumed for some hidden purpose. Yet what that purpose could be, he was unable to imagine. He said:

"Suppose there's a thousand pounds here—and I should guess there's all that, perhaps more—and I said there was only nine hundred, you might be asked what had become of the other hundred when we find the owner."

"I could only say I did not know," Christopherson answered. "If you mean, as I think you do, that I should protect myself against your cheating, how can I help what you do? It is you who must answer for your actions, not I." He opened the door and on the threshold turned to repeat: "I shall be in the yard when you are ready."

Bobby listened to his slow, firm step retreating along the whitewashed stone passage towards the kitchen.

"What are you to make of a chap like that?" Bobby asked himself doubtfully. "Either too simple and too innocent for this world or too deep and too cunning for any world whatever."

He set himself to his task of counting the notes and presently made the total an even £2,000. He replaced the lid, nailed it, wrote out the receipt Mr. Christopherson had scorned and left it on the table, and then went into the kitchen. The bread-making had progressed. The loaves were nearly ready for an oven heated by the peat the elder woman had worked to a glowing mass by the aid of her bellows. Bobby said:

"I am sorry to trouble you, but could you give me some cord or stout string to tie round this?"

He had spoken to the girl, Rachel. She lifted her eyes from the dough she was shaping to a loaf and for the first time, from eyes dark and deep as the night, looked at him steadily and long, and though he was not sure he thought there was both fear and challenge in her gaze. He returned it with one as steady and as searching as her own, and when presently she looked away he felt somehow as though issue had been joined between them. If that were so, then he felt, too, that such an issue whatever it might be, for whatever cause, would not be lightly fought or swiftly won. Turning her attention again to the dough on the board before her, she said to the older woman the one word:

"Mother."

Apparently between themselves this family practised the same economy of words. Mrs. Christopherson put down the bellows, went to a drawer, came back with a length of cord and put it down by Bobby's hand. He said "Thank you" and just caught the glance she gave him as she turned away. No mistaking what that quick look signified. A passion of fear and dread and anger, so great he wondered how she could control it, so great he was certain it would burst forth immediately. He waited, expectant; and Rachel looked up quickly and seemed to understand, for, again beyond doubt, there was quick and urgent warning in her voice when she repeated the one word she had uttered before:

"Mother."

Strange to see how utterly, how completely, that fire of dread and passion in the older woman seemed to die down and vanish at the sound of the girl's warning voice. As instantaneously as the glow and fire of an electric furnace dies when the current is switched off. But that, as with the electric furnace, it could be switched on again as swiftly, Bobby had no doubt. He noticed that she had not returned to her bellows but now was fumbling among some knives that lay on the kitchen dresser. She selected one and went out of the room. Bobby tied the cord given him round the box of notes. Then he said to the girl:

"You are Miss Rachel Christopherson, are you not?"

She made a slight affirmative gesture, without ceasing her work. It was the last of the dough she was busy with now, shaping it in her strong brown hands. Bobby watched the lump of dough taking its final form. Rachel seemed to be paying him no attention. She might have forgotten he was there for all the apparent notice she took of him. Yet none the less, he thought he could perceive a certain tension in her, an acute awareness of his presence. He wondered why. Already, by the habit of his profession, he had tried to notice everything in the room and so far had seen nothing out of the way. Now he looked again, searching, inclined to believe there must be something somewhere to explain the sense of strain he was so conscious of. His glance rested on the window. He went across to it. Rachel had just that instant put the last of her loaves in the oven. She stood up sharply and said as sharply:

"What are you looking at?"

"At this," he answered and pointed to the window pane. A small piece of the glass had been cut out just above the catch and had been as carefully replaced. Looking more carefully and closely he could see traces of a sticky substance on the glass and guessed the old trick had been played of placing in position a strong piece of paper smeared with some adhesive, so as to avoid the risk of the cut out piece falling and breaking with resultant noise. He said: "It looks as though someone had cut a hole there. You could put your hand through and release the catch. I've seen that trick played before now. In London. Skilled burglary. An old hand's work. Have you had a burglary here?"

She stood tense and upright and did not speak. More than ever those great eyes of hers seemed dark pools of night against the pallor of her face, a pallor that showed even beneath the wholesome tan of wind and rain. She did not speak. Watching her, and more and more puzzled, he repeated:

"An old hand's work. Have you had a burglary here?"

"What is that to do with you?" she asked, and her voice was low and harsh and indistinct.

"Well, I'm a policeman, you know," he answered mildly.

"That's no reason for peeping and prying," she told him.

"When people complain of police peeping and prying, it generally means they have something to conceal," he answered. "Have you something to conceal?"

She came towards him, came quite close. Upright, pale, controlled, intense, she stood and faced him. For a moment they stood thus, like two duellists. A moment of strange and silent drama, instinct with a sense of mystery and passion of which Bobby at least understood nothing, nothing at all. She said in the same low, half-strangled tone:

"You have no right to ask me questions. Will you please go?"

"I am here by your father's request and on public duty," Bobby told her.

"Your duty," she flashed back, "is not to meddle with things that don't concern you."

"Well, that's the whole question, isn't it?" he retorted in his turn. "You see, what does not concern me as a man, may be very much my concern as an officer of police. And when strange things seem to be happening, they may turn out to be connected." He put his hand on the box of bank-notes he had just corded up. "There's this," he said, "and I understand you heard a pistol shot last night."

He had the impression that this slight change of subject relieved her considerably. She answered in a more normal tone:

"I heard something. I thought it was an engine backfiring. That is all."

"Very well," he said gently. "All the same I think you are in trouble and I think it has something to do with that window and I think you would be wise to tell me what it is. Because, you know, that's what police are for. To help, to protect. Our job."

She shook her head.

"God may help us," she said very softly, "but not you, not police."

CHAPTER III
HISTORY AND PHILOSOPHY

When she had said this she gave him a startled look as if both surprised and alarmed at her own words, and turned and went suddenly and quickly out of the room. It seemed she felt she had said too much and that she was afraid of saying more. Something not far removed from despair had sounded in that last cry of hers. Yet it seemed to Bobby difficult to associate her with hidden secrets that would not bear the light of day; so fresh, open, and candid was the impression she had made on him. Experience reminded him though that the most unlikely people may be betrayed by passion or by circumstance into strange paths, and that if a woman's affections or her sympathies are engaged there is nothing she will shrink from.

It came into his mind that if this story of a grave were true, and if murder had been done, then possibly Rachel might know the murderer's identity, might even have consented to give him 'aid and comfort.' He might even be concealed somewhere beneath this very roof.

But at this point in his meditations Bobby checked himself. He was letting his imagination run away with him. If murder had been done and the girl—or her parents—knew it, and had given the murderer shelter, was it conceivable they would have called in the police and started an investigation obviously certain to include themselves? Besides, if it were like that, how to fit in that forcible entry of which the patched window bore witness?

Bobby rubbed the tip of his nose as if he wanted to rub it clean away. He abandoned that pastime, picked up his precious box of bank-notes, and went into the yard. No one was visible; but almost at once Mr. Christopherson appeared from one of the outbuildings, and Bobby noticed, too, that someone was watching from behind the curtains of one of the upper windows of the house. Mrs. Christopherson, he thought, not Rachel. He said to Mr. Christopherson:

"If you are ready we might as well go now. Perhaps we had better take a spade if you've got one handy."

Christopherson went back into the shed he had just left and came out with a spade and a pick. Bobby said:

"Your place faces east, doesn't it? And your kitchen due south?"

Christopherson nodded an affirmative. Bobby continued:

"The heavy rain last night came from the north, I believe? A driving rain with a strong north wind?"

Again Christopherson, now looking a little puzzled, nodded in agreement. He said:

"It is high open ground where I found the box. Spigot's Slope it's called."

"Get the full force of the gale," Bobby observed. "Bad enough to call a gale?"

Once more Christopherson nodded agreement, but his eyes had grown not only puzzled but wary. Plainly he guessed there was some hidden reason for these questions and he was uneasy. Bobby tried the direct approach. He asked:

"Who is the man who broke into your house the other night and what did he want?"

The effect on Christopherson of this question reminded Bobby of that seen in the boxing ring when a sudden and unexpected blow gets well home. Christopherson, that calm, tranquil, self-reliant man, who seemed as elemental and eternal as the earth and sky, took a staggering step back, changed colour, stammered in a voice entirely changed:

"Who told you? How do you know?"

Questions Bobby had no intention of answering. As a judge should give his decisions, which may be right, but never his reasons, which are probably wrong, so a detective should state his facts, when he has them, but never his methods, which may be inexcusable or worse. So all his answer was to ask again:

"Who is he? What did he want?"

Christopherson had recovered now—and recovered quickly—from the shock of that unexpected question. He began to move away, spade and pick over his shoulder, towards the front of the house where the road ran. He said as he went:

"We don't know."

"One moment," Bobby said sharply. "What do you mean? You don't know who he was or you don't know what he wanted?"

"I mean both," Christopherson replied. "We don't know who it was and we don't know what he wanted."

"Isn't that rather strange?" Bobby asked and got no reply. He asked: "When was this?"

"We noticed it Sunday morning. Rachel saw it as soon as she came down and she called me."

"Forty-eight hours before Miss Rachel heard the shot and you found the bank notes," Bobby reflected. "You didn't report it. Why not?"

"What was there to report? That perhaps someone had got into the house and then got out again? Nothing was taken."

"Nothing?"

"We have missed nothing. Is an offence committed if nothing is taken?"

"Breaking and entering," Bobby said briefly.

"Breaking perhaps. A broken window. That has happened before. Entering. We don't know. Nothing to show."

"Was nothing heard during the night? By none of you? Was nothing displaced? Nothing moved or touched?"

"We heard nothing," Christopherson answered. "We noticed nothing. There was no sign anything had been touched. All we can say is that a small square of glass was cut out of the kitchen window. A neat job. The glass was lying on the window ledge outside. I put it back. It fitted perfectly. That is all. I saw no reason to say anything. Nothing to say anything about. How do you know?"

"Oh, police know a lot," Bobby answered.

Christopherson looked at him thoughtfully.

"I suppose you mean," he said slowly, "you noticed the window and guessed the rest?"

"Well, let's go," Bobby said, slightly disconcerted, and feeling he might as well have said as much at first.

Christopherson was not a man easily impressed—or easily frightened for that matter. All the same a queer business, and Bobby felt very sure that both Christopherson himself and Rachel knew more than either of them had seen fit to say. But for the moment he had neither reason nor authority to press the matter further.

They walked on together to Bobby's car. As they went Bobby said:

"I noticed you had your doors shut when I got here though it was some minutes before closing time. Are you always so prompt?"

Christopherson did not answer at first. Bobby had the impression that he was considering how to reply. Perhaps wondering, too, whether this question also had a hidden significance. Then he said:

"You notice a good deal, don't you?"

"It's my job," Bobby answered.

"Even little things?"

"Especially little things. It's the little foxes that destroy the vineyards, you remember. Besides, little things are sometimes less little than they seem. And sometimes little things lead to big."

"I did not know policemen could be so philosophical," Christopherson remarked.

"I did not know that was philosophy," retorted Bobby. "I should have called it observation and common sense."

Other words for the same thing," Christopherson answered.

They had reached the car now. Bobby put the box he was carrying under the driver's seat. Christopherson found a place for spade and pick. Anxious to keep his companion chatting, for he knew well that no man may speak a word but in it he shows forth his mind and character for those who have the skill to read aright, Bobby said:

"Are you interested in philosophy?"

"One has to read something in the winter," the other answered apologetically.

"You choose philosophy?"

"It is as full of strange fancies as poetry and as full of imagination as fiction," Christopherson explained. "Takes you out of yourself and out of the commonplace world of everyday fact and need. Escapist stuff, in fact. Amusing to be told that the spade you find so useful for digging potatoes has nothing to do with the spade-in-itself. Following an argument of Spinoza's is as exciting as trying to track the vermin that's raided your hen run."

Bobby reflected that some teachers and writers of and on philosophy might take a hint from this farmer-innkeeper and try a little harder to relate the questions that interested them to the common things of life. But then he wondered if all this had been an attempt to divert his attention. A drawback of the policeman's life that he is so apt to grow suspicious. He said:

"You didn't say if you always closed before time. Wouldn't it be awkward if a customer turned up? You would be bound to serve him, wouldn't you?"

"Yes, but not when it's impossible. I've nothing to serve. There isn't a drop in the house. Brewers give their own houses preference. This is a free house. It has been in my family a long time—'the memory of man runneth not to the contrary' as they used to say in the old days."

"The building doesn't look so very old," Bobby remarked, turning to look at it.

"It dates from 1750. It was burnt down in the '45, when Highlanders came this way. There was a skirmish with dragoons and the inn was burnt. It had been burnt down before. That's one reason why we have nothing to show to prove our claim to be the oldest licensed house in England. It is called 'The Conqueror Inn' because of a story that William the Conqueror was served with wine here when he and his men were on their way to lay the north country waste."

"History, too, as well as philosophy," Bobby said smilingly. "Well, a plain cop has enough to do without meddling with either. But this seems such a lonely sort of place, I wonder it pays you to keep open."

"Lonely the way you've come from Midwych," Christopherson admitted. "But we are not far from the main road—only a little more than a mile, a mile and a half perhaps. Further on, there's a fair sized village. Even if the moor looks lonely, there are farms on it and cottages. Before the war we depended a good deal on visitors. Hikers, cyclists, motorists. Fishermen, too. There are two good trout streams running down the valley."

"Is that where the 'phone box is, on the main road, I mean?" Bobby asked. "The one you rang up from?"

Christopherson nodded an assent. Bobby went on:

"You've no 'phone here?"

This time Christopherson shook his head, and then, as if he felt some explanation were needed, he said:

"Perhaps I agree with the French duchess, wasn't it? who did not wish to be like her own footmen and have to answer the bell whenever it rang. And then, before the war, some who came here for a rest and the fishing seemed to like the idea of being out of reach of the 'phone. They said they had enough of it in business. As a matter of fact, the road box is near enough if it is really needed, and I've an arrangement with the woman who keeps the post office in the village to send up any message she gets for us."

"I see," Bobby said.

They were both in their places now. Before Bobby started the car, he asked:

"Most traffic takes the main road, I suppose? You don't have much by here?"

"No," Christopherson answered. "Recently we've had more. One or two lorry drivers think they gain time coming this way. It's a longer way round but they can go all out. There's so much traffic on the main road, they have to drive carefully on it. Breakdowns, too, sometimes. That may mean a big traffic block. A man named Micky Burke started using it and others like Loo Leader followed him. We hear them at night sometimes going by much faster than they ought to—forty or fifty miles an hour sometimes."

"They don't stop at your place?"

"Very seldom. The two men I mentioned do sometimes. Not so much lately."

"I must get in touch with them," Bobby said, "and see if they can tell me anything. Anyone else you can think of likely to have been by here last night?"

"I don't think so," Christopherson answered. "I haven't seen Burke for some days. He may have gone by at night or without stopping. I saw Leader pass this morning, going north."

"Any private cars?" Bobby asked; and when Christopherson shook his head and said they were rare, Bobby added: "Had any visitors staying the night recently?"

There was a moment's hesitation before Christopherson answered. Bobby had the impression that this question was unwelcome and that the greater readiness the innkeeper had shown to talk during these last minutes had been in part at least because he had foreseen this question and had wished if possible to avoid it. But a reply could not be refused, since an inn's register must be open to inspection, and he said:

"There have been one or two. The only one for some time is Captain Peter Wintle. From the training camp south of Ingleside."

CHAPTER IV
NAKED HORROR

THE RUN ALONG the road to Spigot's Slope took only a few minutes. A touch on Bobby's arm told him where to stop. He and Christopherson alighted and took out the spade and pick. Bobby, as again he went through the proscribed motions to make his car immobile, was still wondering whether he had been right in thinking that the name of this Captain Wintle had been mentioned only with hesitation and reluctance, would probably not have been mentioned at all but for the fact that it was on record in the inn register.

The slope of the land was fairly steep here, showing a drop of perhaps fifty feet from west to east. Down the slope ran a gully that still occasionally in the spring carried a running stream. A culvert took it beneath the road. Eastward, the gully, still fairly deep near the road, gradually flattened out till it lost itself on a stretch of level ground. It was in this gully, close to the road, that Christopherson had found the box the previous night, a stray gleam from his lantern chancing to catch it as he swung his light to and fro. He pointed out the exact spot. Further on and lower down he showed the freshly dug ground he had spoken of.

There was no mound. Only the freshly disturbed appearance of the earth showed that here recent digging had been carried out.

Such earth as had been displaced had been scattered loosely about in a thin, unnoticeable layer. Bobby stood looking at it thoughtfully. Someone had taken pains, taken precautions. A lonely spot, a lonely grave, if grave it were. That must be determined now. Yet the reason must have been urgent that had set unknown hands digging here. He said:

"It might very easily never have been noticed."

Christopherson did not reply. He seemed lost in his own thoughts. Bobby went back to where they had left the car and spent a little time examining the road. There were faint marks of tyres. An oil stain, too. By the roadside were marks on the turf. Trampling, he thought. But all too confused and indistinct, especially after a night of wind and rain, for him to be able to read in them any tale of what there had taken place. Nor for that matter do the tufts of the short, coarse, moorland grass, or the surface of a road, take passing impressions easily or clearly. To Christopherson, still standing upright and quiet by the side of that sad patch of disturbed earth, he called down the slope:

"Can you make anything of these marks?"

"I think no one could," Christopherson called back, but the wind blew away his words and Bobby had to go nearer and ask him to repeat them.

Christopherson did so and added:

"You can see a lorry stopped there. I think two lorries, but I am not sure. A light car, too, I think. There's been a lot of rain. You noticed there are cigarette ends? As if someone had been waiting there and smoking to pass the time."

Bobby nodded. He had collected them, half a dozen or so. Nothing to distinguish them from any other cigarette ends so far as he could see. But as Christopherson had remarked, they did suggest an interval of waiting; though whether the light car for the lorry or lorries, or the lorries for each other or for the car, or whether there had been an interception or a rendezvous, there was nothing to show. Carrying spade and pick, he joined Christopherson and they began work. Two lorries, one coming from the south, from the Midwych direction, one from the north, from beyond the Conqueror Inn, went by; each having to swerve a little on the narrow road to pass in safety where Bobby had left his car. Not long or deep had

Bobby and Christopherson to dig before they came to the horror the kindly earth had hidden.

It was the body of a man, stripped of every shred of clothing. Directly over the heart was a bullet wound. But the horror lay in this, that coldly, deliberately, almost scientifically, the dead man's face had been battered out of all resemblance to human features. As carefully, as gently as might be, Bobby cleared away the damp, surrounding earth. Christopherson, evidently deeply affected, moved a few steps away. He turned his back to where Bobby was still busy at the open grave, for Bobby at least had his duty to do, however shocking. Then he came back and looked long and hard at the thing lying there, that Bobby had now completely uncovered. He said:

"Why have they done that? Smashed his face, I mean. Why should they?"

"To prevent identification," Bobby answered. "All his clothes taken, too. That means they couldn't afford to let it be known who it was. All the same there must be someone missing, somewhere. That's a starting point, for all the beastly care they've taken."

"Another lorry's coming," Christopherson said.

"Don't take any notice," Bobby said.

But evidently they had been seen; and the spectacle of a car standing by the roadside and of two men digging in that lonely spot, had aroused curiosity. The lorry stopped. The driver stood up in his place, and, focusing binoculars, looked at them. Bobby hoped they were good glasses and would show clearly the angry and, he trusted, forbidding scowl he had assumed. Possibly, however, his angry frown only intensified curiosity. Anyhow, the driver got down. His companion remained seated. The driver began to walk down the slope towards where Bobby and Christopherson were standing. Bobby went forward to meet him. He noticed the newcomer still had his binoculars in his hand and that they looked in fact as if they were a good make. Bobby was half inclined to suggest that they should be handed over as a gift to the army, as had been publicly suggested should be done. Possibly, however, this was not a propitious moment for such a suggestion. Instead he said authoritatively:

"We don't want any help. Nothing for you to do. You can get along."

"What's up, guv'nor?" the other asked. He was a tall, thin man with long, sprawling limbs and a long, narrow head, his huge protruding beak of a nose and small bright eyes close on either side giving him somewhat the look of a bird of prey or rather of a spider on the watch for a heedless fly. "You're police, aren't you?" he went on as Bobby did not answer. "Anything wrong?"

Bobby was annoyed. He was always annoyed when he was in plain clothes and yet immediately recognized as a policeman. He said sharply:

"Nothing to do with you. You can clear out."

"Free country, ain't it?" the other retorted. "How do I know what you're up to? Perhaps you aren't a policeman. Perhaps you're a couple of blooming parachutists burying a secret wireless set?"

"Don't try to play the fool," Bobby said angrily. He produced his warrant card. "There you are," he said. "Now clear off."

"Not me," the lorry driver answered with a defiant grin. "I've as good a right here as you. This isn't Germany."

Deliberately he walked past Bobby. Christopherson, who had been watching, said:

"I wouldn't come any nearer if I were you. It's not a thing to see unless you have to."

"Think I've never seen a stiff before?" asked the lorry driver. He came nearer and looked and when he saw he gave a cry and almost ran a few steps back. He had become very white, he looked as if he were going to be sick. "Who did that?" he gasped. "Did you do it digging?"

Christopherson did not answer. He never did answer unnecessary questions, and it was very evident that that dreadful mutilation had been purposed and deliberate. The lorry driver went a few steps still further away and sat down. It was rather as if he did so because his legs had failed him. He took out his handkerchief and began to wipe his face which had grown damp with perspiration.

"It turned me up," he muttered. "Shooting's one thing but that's another."

His companion had apparently perceived now that something was amiss. He jumped down and began to run towards them.

He was a short, thickset man who looked exactly what he was—a former pugilist. He had the bony brows that are so useful to protect the eyes, the 'cauliflower' ear, the generally battered countenance that proclaim one of the 'fancy.' Past his prime now, and showing signs of an over-indulgence in food and drink that strict training had formerly forbidden him. Formidable still, with his long arms and fine chest and shoulders, though loose living had begun the physical ruin another decade or less would certainly complete. To the lorry driver Bobby said:

"It's your own fault. I told you to keep out of it."

"I didn't know," the man muttered. "I didn't know it was like that."

By now his mate had come up.

"What's up with you?" he demanded. "Never seen a deader before. What's a deader anyway?"

"He's got no face," the lorry driver said. "It's all bashed in."

"What do you mean?" asked his mate and made a step towards the open grave.

But the driver called him back.

"Naked and his face isn't there any more," he said. "Gave me a turn. No clothes and his face done in. That's so no one can tell who he is."

"Have you any idea?" Bobby asked. "Have you heard of anyone being missing?"

They both shook their heads. The lorry driver got to his feet, though he still did not seem too steady on them. His mate was looking very blank and bewildered and was giving suspicious glances all round him, as if suspecting something fresh and unexpected and uncomfortable was about to happen. They were both plainly badly shaken. Nor was that, Bobby supposed, anything to be surprised at. Bobby, in the course of his experiences, had seen many strange and dreadful sights, but nothing, he felt, quite so shocking as this careful disfiguring of the dead, this refusal to allow to a dead man in his grave even a semblance of humanity. The lorry driver said again:

"I never looked for such a thing as that. Not that. No."

"A dirty trick," his mate agreed. "It never did ought to have been done." He paused and said: "It'll bring bad luck to them as done it."

"You had better get along," Bobby told them. "I'll take your names first though, please."

"Mine's Leader," the driver said. "Loo Leader. Loo for Lewis."

He added his address in Midwych. Bobby put it down in his notebook and said:

"Occupation, lorry driver, I suppose. Who do you work for?"

"Me own self," Leader answered. "Lots of jobs these days for a bloke with a couple of lorries. I'm taking a load of stuff to Ingleside camp. This bloke," he indicated his companion, "works for me—Alf Hall, he is. Used to be Midlands middle-weight champ."

"Would have been world champ only for not having the right backers," asserted Mr. Hall, scowling at the thought of what should have been but never was.

Only for running into the business end of a better man's glove," grinned Leader, who by now had recovered himself. "I've another bloke working for me as well. He drives my second lorry. Alf takes over when we lay off. Branching out I am. If the war goes on like the last one, I'll have a fleet on my own before it's over."

"Often take this road?" Bobby asked.

"All depends. When it's quickest. Sometimes it's quickest even when it's furthest. Not so crowded, see? You can put speed on a bit. Longest way round may be quickest way there."

"Were you on the road last night?"

"Running back from Preston. Empty."

"What time?" Bobby asked.

Leader took off his cap and scratched his head and looked at Hall, who took off his cap, scratched his head, and looked at Leader.

"Now that's asking," he said.

"So it is," agreed Leader.

"You keep a road log, I suppose?" Bobby asked.

"Well, I won't say same as the blokes do what work for the big firms," Leader answered. "Being my own boss I'm not too particular with myself. Book myself out and book myself in and that's about all." He asked Hall: "You didn't take notice what time we left the Ritz, did you?"

"The Ritz?" Bobby repeated, sharply, suspecting ill-timed jesting.

"Pull up place," Leader explained with a faintly irritating grin, as if he felt he had scored by puzzling Bobby for the moment. "Us chaps on the road call it the Ritz because it's sort of swanky. It's Mrs. Rogers keeps it. Flowers on the table. Style to it. So we got to call it the Ritz and now she's got the name painted up. Alf, what time was it when we got there?"

Hall took off his cap, scratched his head, replaced his cap, said at last:

"Now that's asking, that is."

"Before or after lighting up time?" demanded Leader.

"Now you're talking," said Hall. "I mind now. We switched on the headlamps at Backstairs Corner. That's ten minutes run the other side the Ritz."

"That's right," agreed Leader. "So we did. We had tinned eggs on toast and coffee and squashed fly afterwards and a smoke as well. I reckon we were there all of an hour."

"There or thereabouts," agreed Hall.

"Ten or twelve miles from here," Leader went on. "We didn't speed, having no call to. Counting getting started it would take us all of half an hour to get here. Make it," said Leader concentrating, "two hours from lighting up time or thereabouts, not more."

"Did you notice any other traffic on the road or see or hear anything out of the way?"

"Not a thing. There was a car drawn up by the roadside, a bit further on from here I should judge, towards Midwych. You remember, Alf?"

Once more Hall took off his cap, scratched his head, replaced his cap, operations he seemed to think necessary before answering any question.

"Necking," he said finally.

"That's right," agreed Leader. "Common that is. We see lots of it. Chap and a girl drive out where it's quiet and start necking." He stopped and bestowed a wink on the irresponsive Bobby, or the even more irresponsive Christopherson. "Does it stop at necking?" he inquired. "Ask me another. We don't take no notice. Mind you, if there was anything drawn up by the side of the road on the turf with lights out, we mightn't have seen it. Good and dark last night before moon up."

Bobby asked one or two more questions but gained no further information. He made a note of the time Leader said he had left Preston and of the name of the firm to whom he had made delivery. Leader guessed that his statements were to be checked, grinned, assured Bobby he never told lies to cops. It didn't pay, he said, and then he volunteered the additional information that now he thought of it he remembered looking back and noticing a light on the road like that given by a lantern a man was carrying. He suggested that perhaps it was when the burying was being done or—he broke off with a faint shudder as if at the memory of the mutilation that had been so brutally carried out.

Nodding sympathetically, apparently guessing what Leader was thinking about, Hall said once more and as if the thought pleased him:

"Bring bad luck to them that did it, that will."

Bobby had no more questions to ask. He told them though that he might have to see them again, and Leader grinned and said it was always a pleasure to see a cop. Then he and his mate climbed back into their lorry and went on their way, and Bobby asked Christopherson to remain on watch while he himself drove back to the A.A. 'phone box on the main road and rang up Midwych for help.

CHAPTER V

THE K. AND K.M.T.C.

THERE WAS SO much to be done, so much photographing necessary, so many sketches to be made, such a wealth of detail to be thought of, that it was a considerable time before Bobby could return to the Conqueror Inn, which had become a sort of temporary police headquarters.

A disappointment, though, to his various assistants when they found that its cellars were empty and that tea was the only beverage available. The inn larder, too, was nearly as badly furnished, though Rachel—her mother remained very much in the background—did manage to produce some sort of a scratch meal. Bobby, coming late, had for his share to put up with what was left, which was not much.

"They have cut our supplies down," Rachel explained in her grave, quiet way, "now we have so few visitors. We aren't allowed much more than our ordinary rations and a reserve of tinned stuff. It has all to be accounted for, too."

However, Bobby had gained in that high keen air an appetite not much disposed to find fault with any provender set before him. In any case, there were plenty of potatoes, though a total absence of butter made even those roasted in the peat fire less enjoyable than are roast potatoes generally. His hunger satisfied, Bobby asked for the guest register and found that the only recent visitor who had stayed the night was the Captain Peter Wintle already mentioned by Rachel's father. Bobby asked about other customers, those who came for a casual meal or drink. Very few, Rachel insisted again. The two or three other licensed houses in the neighbourhood were owned by brewers who not unnaturally perhaps, gave them preference so that they got first such supplies as were available. Bobby once more questioned Mr. Christopherson about this and received the impression that for some reason the claims of the Conqueror Inn had not been pressed very strenuously by its landlord, either with the brewers or with the local food authorities. When Bobby said something to this effect, Christopherson admitted as much.

"It hardly seemed worth the time and trouble," he explained. "Making a fuss, I mean. If you write to the food office you get an acknowledgement and that's about all. If you go to see them it means a day wasted, hours of waiting, and no result. They remind me I admit two or three weeks may go by without our even seeing a customer. After the war, when the motorists and the hikers and the fishermen come again, it will be different. Or we might as well surrender our licence. If it wasn't that we've always done a little farming, we should have been hard put to it to carry on."

"Isn't there a certain amount of traffic along this road—lorries for instance?"

"Two or three a day perhaps," Christopherson answered. "Sometimes more. More often none at all."

Bobby wondered if Christopherson wished for reasons of his own to emphasize the loneliness of the place, the lack of customers, the absence of traffic. Still, most people are more willing to talk of their drawbacks, difficulties, bad luck, than of any advantages that may have come their way. Yet one has to remember that these are strange days, days when melodrama has become the stuff of everyday life, and an inn so lonely as this might be a convenient centre for many activities.

A secret place, Bobby was beginning to think it. By paradox the more secret, the more hidden, by reason of its conspicuous, open position on this crest of the high moor, a landmark for miles around and thereby able itself to watch and receive warning of any approach. Christopherson said suddenly:

"Why have your men taken away a pane of the kitchen window?"

"They have replaced it, haven't they?" Bobby asked. "I told them to. I suppose they did. You have a sound pane now instead of a patched one. They asked your permission first?"

"They made it plain that was merely being polite," Christopherson answered. "Wouldn't it have been all the same if I had refused?"

"Oh, well," Bobby answered, "I'm glad you didn't. After all, Mr. Christopherson, police have a right to expect the assistance of all citizens—especially in the case of a brutal murder like this. I am sure I may rely on any help you can give to bring whoever is guilty to justice?"

"I might reply, what is justice?" Christopherson said. "It is a question that has been asked. You have not answered me. Why should you want that pane of glass? Is it for fingerprints?"

"Everyone knows all about fingerprints nowadays," Bobby remarked. "There's been an attempted breaking and entering here. There has been a murder not far away. There may be some connection. My job is to try to find out. Gloves may have been worn. If so, there will be no dabs. But gloves are clumsy things to work in. That square of glass was cut out very neatly. It had been smeared with some adhesive substance. It faces south so it was sheltered from last night's rain. I am quite hopeful dabs may be found. Whether they will help us is another matter. But if they are there, I want them on record."

"You are thorough," Christopherson said, as if he admitted it reluctantly, and he frowned, looking away from Bobby.

Bobby told himself that Christopherson did not like this idea of police thoroughness. It would be necessary, he decided, to find out the reason, if any. Though one had to remember there might be no substantial reason. Merely prejudice perhaps, and dislike of any risk of interference with the normal routine of life. Bobby said:

You have seen or heard of no strangers in the neighbourhood. No other passers by of any kind?"

"No," answered Christopherson, "except the Home Guard patrol, if you count them. They used to stop here every evening at one time but now they use the 'Black Bull' on the main road. I had no beer to give them once or twice and they were annoyed that I couldn't get a new dart board. The old one wasn't much good, I know."

Bobby made no comment, though he had not known that the general shortage extended to dart boards. He had a feeling that no great effort had been made either to procure one or to retain the patronage of the Home Guard patrol. More evidence that Christopherson was less eager for custom than is the normal innkeeper.

"I suppose Home Guards still patrol this road?" Bobby asked.

"Yes, but they changed their times and now it's late when they go by, after we're in bed, so we see nothing of them."

"Can you tell me what motor traffic passed yesterday? Both the dead man and his murderer must have got here somehow and most likely by car."

"We don't always know what does pass," Christopherson answered. "If I happen to be at the back and my wife and daughter are in the kitchen, we might not hear anything, or, if we did, we might not notice. I didn't see any private car. If I had done I should have remembered it. We don't see many private cars now. There were a few lorries. One was a brewer's. That was about dinner time, soon after noon. I noticed it because I thought it might be our supplies coming at last. But it didn't stop. Going on to the 'Black Bull' in the village most likely. They could tell you there. Later on a K. and K. lorry went by. Burke was driving, the man I told you about, the one who started using this road to escape the highroad traffic. He waved and I waved back. He was running light and he would have clocked in most likely before the shot Rachel heard—that is, of course, if he went on without stopping. There may have been other lorries, too, but those are the only ones I noticed."

"What are the K. and K. lorries?" Bobby asked.

"The Kram and Kram Midwych Transport Company," Christopherson explained. "A man named Kram runs it—he and his daughter. Micky Burke says Miss Kram is more the boss than her father. When Micky started coming this way, Mr. Kram came out to have a look. He asked me a lot of questions. About road conditions and so on. He seemed to have some idea of using my outbuildings as a kind of entrepot, he said. I didn't see much sense in it. The idea was that his lorries were to store stuff and change loads here. It didn't come to anything. Only a passing idea probably. Anyhow, I heard no more about it. For a time the K. and K. lorries used us as a stopping place. They don't now, except Micky Burke now and then."

"Any reason for stopping coming?" Bobby asked.

"An inn that is short of beer is soon short of custom, too," Christopherson answered, and Bobby had to admit that this was an aphorism of undeniable truth.

"You said something about Leader, too," Bobby remarked. "I suppose that's the same man we saw just now. Know anything about him?"

"He is in a small way," Christopherson answered. "Owns a couple of lorries, I think. He went by here earlier this morning, going north. I think I told you, didn't I? He told me once he had heard about the K. and K. lorries coming this way to save time, and what was good enough for them was good enough for him. I believe he does fairly well. Road transport pays in these days."

It was late now and as there seemed for the present no more either to be learned or to be done, Bobby departed. At headquarters there was still, however, much to be seen to, so that it was late before he got home for a short night's rest. He was up early to be back in good time at his office where he found waiting for him three reports, all of considerable interest.

CHAPTER VI
THREE REPORTS

OF THESE THREE reports, over which Bobby sat and brooded long, the one which surprised him least was that from the fingerprint people. For when two strange things are closely connected in time and place, they may well be connected in fact as well. So it had already seemed likely to Bobby that fingerprints, found on the kitchen window of the Conqueror Inn, might turn out to be those of the dead man. That that was so, here was the proof set out in dry official language with photographic reproductions added to show the many points of resemblance making the fact certain.

Was then the cause and origin of the crime to be sought in this attempt, successful or not, to break into the inn? Bobby asked himself the question, staring blankly before him, remembering the pale, still face of the girl Rachel, the tranquil countenance of the big innkeeper-farmer. Not the faces of common criminals, he was sure. Yet murder is no common crime. The fascination that it has for us lies not only in the nature of a deed so terrible and so irretrievable, in which mere man takes upon himself the right to act as God in cutting short the tenure of another's life; but also because in that it may be committed for strange reasons, throwing strange lights upon the human mind; committed, too, sometimes by those who but for some twist of circumstance would have led the quiet and normal existence of ordinary folk.

Again if the Christophersons, father and daughter, had some secret to hide they valued above the shedding of blood, why had they chosen to call in the police? And what part was played by the box stuffed with bank-notes and left derelict by the roadside?

There was the time factor, too, to remember. According to the story told by Christopherson the cutting of the kitchen window pane had taken place forty-eight hours before the murder.

Facts impossible to bring into relation at present.

Bobby laid down the first report and passed to consider the second. This was medical. With a wealth of professional detail it confirmed the cause of death as a bullet that had pierced the heart—enclosed, the bullet referred to—gave the probable time of death as agreeing with the time when Rachel said she had heard the pistol shot, described the injuries to the head and face as inflicted after death by means of a heavy blunt instrument, such as a hammer, an iron bar, or even a large stone. There was added to this, which Bobby had expected, the unexpected and surprising information that the body, that of a young, healthy and well-nourished man, showed a number of bruises and weals, probably inflicted about forty-eight hours before death. Apparently two days before his murder the dead man had received a severe thrashing—the weals suggested a stick or cane of some sort had been used—whereto he had offered a strenuous and not ineffective resistance, since the knuckles of both hands showed abrasions and on one hand a finger was broken.

Bruised knuckles must mean that bruises had been administered as well as received. Christopherson had shown no visible signs of conflict, but then they might not be visible. He was a man no longer young but he was of powerful physique, his work on the land kept him in training, he was probably capable of holding his own with most, even with those younger than himself. Nothing to show, though, that Christopherson was the man involved.

"Got, I suppose," Bobby told himself gloomily, "to look out for someone with a black eye. What a hope!"

The third report dealt with the wooden box and its contents. A preliminary examination of the bank-notes had been without result. They were all notes that had been in circulation and there were no consecutive numbers. No possibility of tracing them, though they would each be examined again and separately, on the chance of some useful discovery being made. The rough wood the box was made of had taken no impressions but there were minute traces both of coal dust and of fish scales. Though caused before or after it had been used for packing bank-notes, there was nothing to show. The interior of the box had produced only such non-committal dust as could and might be accumulated in any place at any time.

Nothing, it seemed, in these reports to narrow the field of inquiry or to provide a starting point.

Routine inquiries were naturally already in progress. A man was dead and therefore somewhere someone must be missing from his circle of acquaintances and work. In some public house a regular customer might be missed, or a landlady might be wondering what had become of her lodger, or a tradesman be noticing with surprise that one registered customer was drawing no rations. Every constable in the district was already on the look-out for some such hint and soon every police force in the country would be asked to report at once any unexplained disappearance they might hear of.

"We shall get something soon, sir," Sergeant Payne declared with confidence. "Young fellows don't vanish without somebody knowing. Well nourished, too. Must have fed somewhere. Ten to one there's a girl asking herself why her best boy hasn't turned up lately. The clothes, too. We may find them stuffed down a drain or something."

"They may have been burnt," Bobby said. "Make a note for all men to be asked if they've noticed or heard of any smell of burning cloth or anything like that. Clutching at straws, I suppose. Our job's like that. Blundering about in the dark till at last you stumble on something. Or else you don't. Or else you don't realize it counts till it's too late."

"Yes, sir," agreed Sergeant Payne, "only all the same no one can just drop out without someone knowing."

But Bobby was not sure. He remembered the Rouse case. A dead man there of whom nothing was ever known or will be either, who he was or whence he came.

"I think," he told Payne, "I'll drive over to Ingleside camp and try to get a talk with this Captain Wintle. He seems to have been the only recent visitor to the Conqueror Inn. I would like to know if there's any reason for his visits. He may have seen or noticed something. I don't know how I am going to spare the time but I'll have to manage it somehow."

"Why not ask him to call here?" suggested Payne, not altogether unaware that his superior officer's absence would most likely mean a good deal of extra work for Sergeant Payne and no chance of getting home in time to take his wife to see that picture she had been talking about.

"Army captains in war," Bobby pointed out, "are important people. As likely as not he wouldn't come, couldn't spare the time. On duty or something like that."

Payne looked slightly shocked. To his mind an inspector of the county police, more especially an inspector who was also head of a C.I.D. that but for the war would by now have been a model for Scotland Yard itself instead of being, as it was, in a state of sketchy and suspended animation, more especially still an inspector marked out to be a chief constable some day, was much more important than a mere captain of infantry.

After all, he reflected, an army captain is small fry to a major, hardly exists in the sight of a colonel, is not even perceptible to a general, whereas a chief constable has no superior save God and the King. And some chief constables are not even very clear about that.

In peace time Bobby would have taken a companion. No telling on such an errand when help or a witness may not be required. Not, of course, that this was to be a formal interrogation. Merely a kind of friendly, informal inquiry. But police work has been doubled, and police staff halved, since the beginning of the war, and Bobby had to go alone.

It was growing late when he reached Ingleside camp, and there was more delay while he explained his errand and while efforts were being made to find Captain Wintle, who was in the camp somewhere though no one seemed to know exactly where. However, presently he was discovered, and into the mess ante-room where Bobby was waiting came a broad set, good-looking youngster, young for his rank in an army in which opportunities for promotion had not been numerous, with a scar on his left cheek that was a reminiscence of Dunkirk, a broad forehead, a thrusting nose, and bright, quick, blue eyes, one of which, Bobby noticed with interest, was in that stage of returning to the normal a badly bruised eye might be expected to show after an interval of some forty-eight hours.

CHAPTER VII
EVERYTHING HAS A MEANING

CHEERFULLY WINTLE APOLOGIZED for having kept Bobby waiting so long.

"I was with the CO.," he explained. "Police, aren't you? None of our men been getting into trouble, I hope?"

"Oh, no, no, nothing like that," Bobby answered and paused, looking pointedly at that eye now recovering from a bruise which might well be of rather more than forty-eight hours' standing.

"Well, what is it, then?" Wintle asked sharply, as if aware of and not much approving the direction of Bobby's gaze. He added: "Result of a collision with a doorpost in the blackout the other night."

"Oh, yes," Bobby said, wondering if it were not an uneasy conscience that had produced so prompt an explanation there had been no obligation to offer. "Oh, yes," he repeated and added smilingly: "I was thinking perhaps there had been some sort of scrap going on here—or even perhaps a mutiny in the camp."

Captain Wintle gave Bobby an extremely unfriendly glare, the one Bobby suspected he kept in store for the slackers of his company.

"Did you?" he snapped, making it sound as if he thought it like Bobby's cheek to think anything at all, and a pity he couldn't be given three days' 'C.B.' on the spot. "Well, what is it you want?"

"I think you know the Conqueror Inn," Bobby said; and when Wintle only stared again, but this time with evident surprise, Bobby added: "You have stayed there two or three times, I believe?"

"Suppose I have?" Wintle retorted, and now his eyes had grown alert and wary. "What about it?"

"Well, you see," Bobby explained, "we are anxious to get all the information we can. A murder has been committed near by."

"A murder?" Wintle repeated, and now he had become suddenly very pale. "Good God, man, what do you mean?" And when Bobby did not answer instantly. "Who?" he almost shouted. "Who?"

"We don't know," Bobby answered.

"What do you mean? Don't play the fool with me," Wintle said angrily. "Murder? What murder?"

"A murder," Bobby repeated, "but that is all we know at present. The body of a young man shot through the heart has been found only a mile or two from the Conqueror Inn."

Wintle sat down abruptly. So far he had neither seated himself nor offered a seat to Bobby. He was evidently greatly disturbed, greatly shaken, and yet, Bobby thought, oddly relieved as well. It was almost as though at first he had feared something worse than merely murder, though what that worse could be, Bobby found it difficult to imagine. Looking up at the still standing Bobby, he muttered:

"A young man? Are you sure? Who is it?"

"That is what we are trying to find out," Bobby said.

"What is he like?"

"Impossible to say," Bobby explained. "The features have been deliberately mutilated so as to make recognition impossible."

Wintle made no comment on this. He got to his feet again and went to the window and stood looking out, his back to Bobby. Bobby wondered if this was to keep hidden any emotion his features might show. Presently he turned and came back to where Bobby was standing waiting by the fireplace. He said:

Well, there's nothing I can tell you. I know nothing about it."

Oh, well, you see," Bobby explained, "it often happens that people who think they know nothing at all, can in fact give very useful information. It seems that what was almost certainly the murderer's shot was heard at the Conqueror Inn by Miss Rachel Christopherson."

Wintle went away to look out of the window again. When he came back he said:

"It's a most extraordinary story. Miss Christopherson? Yes, of course." He stared hard once more at Bobby, a little as if conveying some mute challenge or defiance. "She heard the shot?"

"So it seems. She told her father. He went to have a look round. He noticed recent digging. He told us. We found the body of a young man. He had been shot. His features had been destroyed. All clothing had been removed."

"A queer business," Wintle said, frowningly. "You mean there is nothing to show who he was?"

"Nothing," Bobby said. "The bullet had apparently been fired from a point four five service revolver."

He paused. Wintle seemed about to say something but then changed his mind, and remained silent. Bobby continued:

"There's something else that seems curious. The medical report says that the body shows recent bruises. They suggest that the dead man had been recently mixed up in some—" Bobby paused and deliberately used the word 'scrap' he had employed before. "In some scrap," he said. "In fact, that he had had a good thrashing about forty-eight hours ago."

Wintle said nothing. His features had become wooden, expressionless. But his eyes were attentive. One had the impression that so he always looked when danger threatened, that so perhaps he had looked on the beaches at Dunkirk. What danger threatened now, Bobby wondered. He waited, hoping that Wintle would speak. But the young soldier remained silent. Apparently he understood that speech offers openings that silence denies. But that is a reflection likely to occur only to those who have reason to fear where an opening may lead. A thing to remember, Bobby told himself. He said:

"A coincidence." When Wintle was still silent, Bobby added: "I mean, that the dead man should have been injured in some sort of—scrap—about the same time I should judge that you had your collision with the gate post—was it? You agree?"

"I agree," Wintle answered steadily, "that I see what you are attempting to imply. I suggest that if you want to make any direct accusation, you know, I suppose, how to go about it. In the meantime I can only tell you that I know absolutely nothing about the dead man, neither his name, nor where he came from, nor who murdered him. What connection is there between the fact that he had a thrashing—if he had one—a day or two before his death with his being shot later on?"

"I don't know," Bobby answered. "Evidently there may be such a connection. Captain Wintle, I am afraid I must now go so far as to warn you that while you are not obliged to answer any questions, and while you are entitled to legal assistance if you wish, yet refusal to answer questions is likely to give rise to certain conclusions and to certain suspicions it would be very easy to avoid."

"Is this," demanded Wintle, "the classic warning before making an arrest?"

"No," Bobby answered at once. "There's nothing to make me even think of such a thing. But I do not think you are being entirely frank. For an officer holding the King's commission not to be entirely frank when asked for help by an officer of police, seems to me very unfortunate. You will allow me to remind you that such an attitude may have grave results?"

"I don't think the reminder is necessary," Wintle answered quietly. "I have told you already, I know nothing about it. So there is nothing I can say that could help you in the slightest."

"Apart from knowing, is there anything you suspect or guess or believe—or even imagine?"

Wintle looked slightly disconcerted.

"You know all the questions, don't you?" he muttered. He hesitated a moment and then said: "If I did, I should think a long time before saying things very likely all wrong, quite unfounded, likely to upset and distress other people for no reason."

"I won't press you any further at present," Bobby said, "but I hope you will think it over and possibly change your mind."

"There's one thing I will tell you," Wintle said. "You would most likely hear it anyhow. Christopherson lost a son at Dunkirk. He was in my platoon. I was platoon officer. He saved my life during the retreat. I was in a bad fix. Young Christopherson helped me out—at the risk of his own life. At the cost of it for that matter. He was hit by a bomb a Jerry plane dropped where he was standing after helping me and then there was no trace of him. Or his lorry or the men with him. That's why I went there—to the Conqueror Inn, I mean. To tell them about their boy. Of course, they knew, but it seems to help people if they can talk a bit and ask questions. More personal than just merely an official notice. And, of course, if it hadn't been for their boy, I shouldn't be here to-day."

"Thank you," Bobby said. "It may be a help knowing that."

Wintle, who had spoken with some emotion, at that gave Bobby a hard look, much as if saying that if he had thought it would help, he would not have told it. He went on:

"I have been back there several times. It helps. They haven't much custom now. It's quiet, too. A change. One gets sick of the sort of community life you lead in a camp. A change," he repeated. "But I don't suppose you can realize what the quiet of the high moors means after hours of shouting and being shouted at on the parade ground."

Bobby was inclined to deduce from this offer of a multiplicity of reasons that there was another one—the real one—which Captain Wintle did not wish to tell. He got to his feet.

"I won't keep you any longer," he said. "In a case of murder one has often to ask many questions that must seem impertinent—in both senses of the word. I can only hope that if on reflection you feel inclined to say anything more you will let me know and I think I ought to say that most likely I shall find it necessary to come to see you again."

"I have told you all I know," Wintle said briefly. "Wait here a moment." He left the room and came back, bringing with him his service revolver. "Better test it," he said, "and make sure the bullet wasn't fired from it. As a matter of fact it hasn't been fired for some weeks."

"Thank you," Bobby said, taking the weapon. "I will have it examined and returned to you at once. Of course, I am quite sure it isn't the one the bullet came from. If it had been, you wouldn't have given it me." He added: "We may think it necessary to ask for permission to examine all service revolvers in the camp."

"Good Lord, there are dozens of them, hundreds," Wintle exclaimed.

"That would make no difference," Bobby explained. "We have gone to a good deal more trouble than that at times."

"Thorough, aren't you?" Wintle muttered.

"It's the only way," Bobby said. "In everything. Wasn't there someone once who took 'Thorough' for his motto? It has to be the police motto anyhow. And I do hope, if there is anything at all that occurs to you, anything you remember in thinking it over, even the merely trifle, you will let us know. The tiniest detail may be a pointer in the right direction. A casual remark that didn't seem to mean much at the time. Or for that matter, even a silence."

"You mean," Wintle said slowly, "that everything has a meaning?"

"You could not," Bobby told him, "put it more clearly."

CHAPTER VIII
DEEP WATERS

LATE AS IT had now become, Bobby drove from Ingleside Camp not home, but to the company headquarters of the Home Guard acting in the Conqueror Inn district.

There the cautious inquiries that he made confirmed him in the belief that no great effort had been made by Mr. Christopherson to retain the patronage of the Home Guard night patrols.

"They're a good bit too independent there," declared the Home Guard lieutenant to whom Bobby was talking. "Why, the landlord—Christopherson's his name—wouldn't take a delivery from one brewery because it wasn't the special stuff he wanted. You can't pick and choose like that in war time, you know. Consequence was, he got none at all. In the end we made up our minds to use the Black Bull instead. Much more obliging there. No one wants to go back to the Conqueror Inn, though it's much handier for some of our chaps. Lies higher, too. Good observation."

"You still keep an eye on the road there, though?"

"Oh, yes, rather. Just the place for air-borne troops. Or spies. Drop a spy there and he could be in Midwych in a few hours. We are by there every night—rather late at night now."

"Have you ever had any report of any unusual incident?" Bobby asked, and explained why he put the question.

The Home Guard lieutenant was very interested. Never before in his life had he been in such close contact with anything so startling and so sensational as a murder. He referred to reports. He rang up one of his platoon sergeants. All he could find to vary a monotonous succession of 'Nothing to report' was that once nearly a month previously a light had been noticed at the Conqueror Inn. Two men had had to be sent in a motor cycle and sidecar. The light, shining from an attic window, had been visible for miles, and Mr. Christopherson had been lucky to escape with a severe warning.

The explanation he offered was that he had fallen asleep while reading in bed and that a gust of wind, which had risen during the night, had blown down a black-out curtain too heavy for the bamboo pole supporting it. The two Home Guards had been invited to verify this for themselves. They had done so; and as it was certainly true that the force of the wind had increased suddenly and violently about midnight, it had been decided in the end not to issue a summons.

"Partly," explained the Home Guard lieutenant, "because he lost a son at Dunkirk. Promising lad. Musician or something. Played the violin. Had a job with the Midwych Philharmonic. Everyone knew how proud the old man and the family, too, were of the boy, and there was a lot of sympathy when he was reported killed. Personally," added the lieutenant thoughtfully, "I never cared much for the violin. Give me a good accordion and you can keep your scratchy stuff."

Bobby uttered a few platitudes about war being like that. It was always the best and most talented who went the first. To himself, he was thinking that this story presented some curious and possibly even significant facts. Two details at least, he decided, it would be well to keep in mind, even though, as was very probable, they turned out to be entirely irrelevant and unimportant.

"But all that happened a month ago," the lieutenant pointed out, "and there's not been a shadow of a complaint since. So there can't be any connection with a murder this week."

Bobby, preferring agreement to argument, said he supposed not, and asked what traffic there was on the road by the inn. The lieutenant said there was very little, though more lately. Congestion on the main road, the more direct route, had induced some drivers to make use of this secondary road. If that grew more common, something would have to be done about maintenance which had been neglected of late. Only in exceptional circumstances would a lorry be challenged. Pedestrians, at night after dark, would very likely be asked to show their identity cards. Patrols were apt to be zealous in the discharge of their duties, zeal being often a product, said the lieutenant, of monotony and boredom.

Bobby thought this was very true, and, encouraged, the lieutenant declared that the most boring job imaginable was to mooch along a deserted country road in the dark. Rarest thing in the world to meet anyone. It had happened though, he remembered now, last Saturday night. The patrol corporal had mentioned an encounter with a young woman near the Conqueror Inn. But as her identity card had been in order and she had given an address near the village on the main road, there had seemed no reason to question her further. Her name was recorded as Emma Jones. The address was Wayside Bungalows, known to some of the patrol as a cluster of bungalows recently erected and now occupied almost entirely by Midwych evacuees. The young woman had been out on an egg-hunting expedition round the neighbouring farms and cottages, and had succeeded in obtaining two she displayed with some pride.

Bobby surprised the lieutenant by showing some interest in this incident. The report did not include any description of the young woman's personal appearance, but the lieutenant thought the corporal in charge of the patrol might remember something about her, if the inspector thought it worth while to go round to see him. Bobby said he supposed he might as well. 'One never knew,' he said vaguely, and so the lieutenant gave him the corporal's address and Bobby expressed his thanks and departed.

Bobby was fortunate in finding the corporal at home, but the description he received was extremely vague and would have fitted a very large proportion of young women. For one thing it had been dark; and the patrol, though zealous, wished also to be polite, and had not cared to shine a torch in the girl's face so as to see her more clearly. On the small side, the corporal thought, and spoke with a pronounced London accent the patrol all thought very funny and that the corporal now imitated very effectively. Bobby, wishing, like the patrol, to be polite, laughed and said it was jolly good, and he ought to know because he had lived in London once. Encouraged, the corporal now recalled that one of his men had said after a time, and after much thought, that the two eggs of which Miss Emma Jones had given them such a triumphant glimpse, had looked less like the genuine article than like china eggs, such as those sometimes put in a nest in order to cajole a recalcitrant hen into rivalry and laying.

So Bobby said that was interesting, too, and thanked him and drove off back to Midwych, judging it now much too late to do anything more that night.

At the county headquarters he found waiting for him various reporters whom he got rid of by assuring them that he knew no more than they had heard already. They had, however, his full authority to assure their readers that the police were pursuing their inquiries and had every reason to hope that they would soon be in possession of an important clue. The gratitude the reporters expressed for this information was of a limited character, and Bobby, a little hurt by such lack of appreciation, pointed out that any competent news-hound could easily make two thrilling columns of two such exclusive items.

Then, declining further argument and ignoring coldly an invitation to define the word 'exclusive,' he sent them away, and sent instead for Sergeant Payne to whom he gave careful instructions for the morrow.

"I want you first of all," he explained, "to find out if Captain Wintle slept in camp or had leave during the weekend, and if it would be possible for him to get out of the camp and return without being noticed."

"Do you think it's possible he can be the man we want?" Payne asked with some excitement. "An army captain!"

"Possible," Bobby answered, "because all things are possible. I feel sure he comes into it somehow just as I am sure the Christophersons know a lot more than they've told. I must check up on Wintle's Dunkirk story, I suppose, though it's sure to be true. It gives a good plausible sympathetic reason for his stopping sometimes at the Conqueror Inn. The thing is, is there anything behind? Anyhow, mind how you go about the job. I want to know everything I can about him, ready for when I go to see him again, but I don't want to start any gossip. For one thing if we did we might get official complaints through the War Office. Have to handle army officers carefully these days. Besides, it's quite likely he has nothing to do with what's happened and there's no sense in starting stories that may damage an innocent man's career."

"Yes, sir, I see, sir," said Payne thoughtfully. "Very odd case, sir."

"So it is," agreed Bobby. "With a good deal behind it, I think. Next, I want you to find out if at Wayside Bungalows there's a Miss Emma Jones, an evacuee from Midwych, who talks, oddly enough, with a strong Cockney accent, and went egg hunting last Saturday. If you find her, you might ask her where she bought her eggs. If you can't find her, tell Smithers—that's the name of the local constable, isn't it?—to try to find out if any farm or cottage within walking distance had a visit that Saturday from an egg-hunting evacuee."

"Yes, sir," said Payne again. "Speaking with a strong Cockney accent, you said, sir? You wouldn't expect that from a Midwych evacuee, would you?"

"You would not," agreed Bobby. "Suggestive, eh?" and when Payne nodded in slow agreement, since the probable significance of this had at once occurred to him, Bobby added: "In the same way, if it's a fact that the two eggs she showed were only of the artificial porcelain variety—well, it suggests a good deal of forethought and caution, doesn't it?"

"Deep waters, in fact, sir," Payne said, and Bobby nodded in full agreement.

CHAPTER IX
SLOGANS

In the morning, first thing, before even going to his office, since a 'phone call had assured him that nothing there demanded his immediate attention, Bobby made his way to the address of the K. and K. Midwych Transport Company. Once this had been an imposing private residence, the home in bygone times of one of the merchant princes of Midwych in those spacious days of old when a dozen or so domestic servants could be had without difficulty and when their combined wages did not amount to much more than a competent cook would ask to-day. So, too, what once had been a majestic front drive for the solemn reception of the carriage and pair was now a paved forecourt where various lorries were receiving, discharging, or awaiting loads.

A busy scene, suggesting a busy prosperity, and indeed, as the man, Loo Leader, had remarked, road transport is of evergrowing importance. Among the lorries a young woman moved, her hands full of papers, giving instructions, apparently, and receiving reports. She seemed on excellent and even noisy terms with the lorry crews, laughing a good deal, exchanging with them a good deal of backchat. Bobby noticed, though, that what she said was listened to attentively, and that orders she gave were carried out promptly. At the first glance, so small and young she looked, though of a certain plump and comfortable roundness of figure, one might easily have overlooked her in that bustling scene of busy men active about the great waiting lorries. Yet a second glance seemed somehow to suggest that in some curious way all revolved about her personality, and that it was at her will and by her direction that these men toiled, that these huge lorries came and went.

One of the men noticed Bobby standing watching. He called the girl's attention to him. She came towards him and Bobby went forward to meet her. He noticed that in speaking to him she dropped the broad, even somewhat exaggerated, Midwych accent she had used in talking with the men.

"Good morning," she said. "Anything we can do for you?"

"Could I see your manager?" he asked.

"Certainly," she answered. "In the office."

She had small active eyes that he felt were examining him with close attention. Not a pretty girl, by any means. Her mouth was much too large, her nose flat with large nostrils, her other features irregular, her hair coarse and straight and not apparently the subject of much care. None the less with an indefinable air of energy and power about her, her movements swift and decided. It was as though she exhaled a sort of passionate zest of life, a kind of passionate eagerness of appetite. Bobby's mind went back to the withdrawn and tranquil atmosphere with which Rachel Christopherson managed somehow to surround herself. An odd contrast, Bobby thought, between those two young women: the one like a clear calm hillside spring, the other like a mountain torrent dashing impetuously on its way. He found himself wondering what they would think of each other, if, by any remote chance, they ever happened to meet. Not that there was much chance of that, he supposed, and then he became aware that those small active eyes of hers, which, while these thoughts chased each other through his mind, had been so busily examining him, had now abruptly changed. It was almost like a conjuring trick. Where before they had been eager, searching, probing indeed, like small points of darting light, now they seemed to enlarge themselves, grow soft and receptive. Even her voice changed. As the harsh Midwych accent had gone before, so now went the brisk business-like tone that had followed. It grew gentler, it took on what could almost be described as an accent of welcome and invitation. She surprised him still more by a girlish giggle she gave as she continued:

"It's my dad, you mean, I expect. I'm Maggie Kram." She paused momentarily as if to offer him a chance to give his name and when he did not take it, went on: "This way, please. K. and K. are always pleased to answer all inquiries."

She walked by his side, looking very small by contrast with his full six feet. He noticed that one or two of the lorry drivers were looking sideways at them and that since she had begun talking to him the rhythm of activity in the forecourt had distinctly slackened. She peeped up at him and giggled again and said:

"I wish I were tall. It's horrid to be so small. People won't take notice of you if you are small, not unless you simply make them."

It rather looked, Bobby thought, as if she were very ready to start a flirtation with him. A fast moving young woman, he told himself, with some amusement. But there are some girls, he knew, ready to flirt with anyone, anywhere, at any time, with anything that wore trousers, especially if it were six feet or so in height and possessed a good chest measurement. He was too modest to add, in this case, the further qualification of moderate good looks.

Oh, well, he said smilingly, "I expect people who aren't so very tall don't bump their heads as often as others."

Before she could answer, a small wizened elderly man, slightly bowlegged, appeared from behind one of the lorries and came towards them. She shook a small hand at him, waving him back. Bobby noticed that she had very small hands and feet, and he was inclined to guess from this and other small gestures he had noticed that she was proud of them. He noticed, too, how decisively she turned a shoulder towards this newcomer and the hard note in her voice as she called:

"Not now, Micky, wait a minute."

The man she addressed scowled but turned back towards his lorry. Bobby guessed that this might be the Micky Burke of whom the landlord of the Conqueror Inn had spoken. He said:

"One of your drivers?"

Maggie answered only by another giggle, and Bobby wondered if this giggling trick was a proof of congenital weakness of mind, her idea of being friendly to a potential client, a protective armour she adopted in intercourse with the men she worked with, or a mere idiosyncrasy. They were quite near the house now and from its front door emerged suddenly a small round man of middle age, neat in appearance and brisk in movement, and so like Maggie with his wide mouth and flat, full nostrilled nose, his small and hidden eyes, that it was easy to guess he was her father. He saw them approaching and waited at the head of the steps that led up to the door, steps that once no doubt had been scrubbed and whitened every morning to gleam impeccably in the morning sun, but that now were washed only by the rain.

"Gentleman to see you, dad," Miss Kram called.

"Good morning, sir, good morning," Mr. Kram responded. He rubbed his hands together and beamed in a manner oddly reminiscent of his daughter's trick of giggling. Again one was not sure whether that beaming smile were friendly or protective or merely meaningless. He went on: "Now I wonder what K. and K. can have the pleasure of doing for you? Move anything anywhere and the earth if required. That's our slogan, sir, and we live up to it."

"Well, I must say you look busy enough this morning," Bobby agreed. "You are Mr. Kram?"

"That's me, sir," the little round man agreed and beamed again, just as Bobby felt his daughter would have giggled. "Merton Kram, of the K. and K.M.T.C.—initials, sir, that one day will be as well known as L.M. and S. Yes, sir, the railways will always have their place, no doubt, but take it from me, sir, road transport is the transport of the future. From door to door, sir, that's our slogan, and we live up to it."

Bobby, slightly overwhelmed by so much exuberance, wondering, too, how many more slogans Mr. Kram had in stock and lived up to, produced his official card and explained that he had come to make a few inquiries.

"I don't know if you have seen the paper this morning," he said, and Mr. Kram shook his head.

"No time for the papers," he said, "not till we've got all the lorries off. Eh, Maggie? Come inside, Inspector. Some of our men been speeding? They will do it if they get the chance. Half an hour saved on the road is half an hour more in the pub. That's their slogan and they live up to it; ha, ha. No accident, though, I hope?"

As he talked he turned back into the house and led the way across a wide tessellated hall, many of the tiles badly cracked, into what once had been most probably the breakfast-room. A clatter of typewriting in the distance suggested that the former dining-room on the other side of the hall was now the general office. On a table near the window in the room into which Mr. Kram conducted Bobby, lay two or three newspapers, still apparently untouched. Maggie Kram, who had followed the two men into the room, went across to pick one up. The headlines announcing the discovery made near the Conqueror Inn north of the city were conspicuous. She did not speak, but there was a sudden stiffening of her whole body. When she turned she had become very pale and her eyes, those small and active eyes of hers, that had later become soft and receptive, showed now as withdrawn into two far-off specks of shining light.

She held out the paper to her father.

"There's been a murder near the Conqueror Inn," she said.

He took the paper from her. He spoke slowly. His face was impassive, too impassive, Bobby thought.

"Oh, yes, I didn't see that," he said.

"Who is it?" Maggie asked in the same soft low voice she had used before.

"Now, my dear, don't you see what it says?" he asked. "Unidentifiable. Injuries to the face. Anyhow, nobody wc know, I take it."

Bobby thought that this, carelessly as it seemed to be spoken, was meant to reassure the girl. She seemed to pay no attention. She came nearer to her father, thrusting her face forward. Neither of them spoke. She was shaking now from head to foot and the newspaper dropped from her hand to the floor as though she had no longer power to hold it.

"Now, now, Maggie, my dear, now, now," Kram said.

Without answering she moved towards the door. Bobby put up his arm to stop her, for he wished to question her. But as he began to speak, she, without looking at him, dashed down his arm with a strange, unexpected strength, passed, and ran out into the hall. He followed and called after her, but she took no notice and ran on, her footsteps loud and rapid on the broken, tessellated floor. She disappeared through the open front door and he did not attempt pursuit. He went back into the room and across it to the window. As he had half expected, he saw her running fast towards that lorry from behind which, a little before, had emerged the small elderly wizened man she had addressed as Micky, and whom he had in his mind identified as the Micky Burke of whom Christopherson had spoken. She disappeared behind the lorry. Bobby turned back to Kram who was now sitting at his desk. He said in the same impassive, indifferent tones:

"You must excuse my daughter, Inspector. Maggie's very highly strung, very nervous. Has been since a child. Almost hysterical at times. A bundle of nerves."

"I think there's more to it than that," Bobby said quietly. Then he asked: "Who is Micky Burke?"

CHAPTER X
MICKY BURKE

"Micky Burke?" Kram repeated. He looked mildly interested, very mildly interested. For once at least Bobby's favourite technique, that of the abrupt and unexpected question, had failed to produce results. Perhaps because there were no results to produce. Maggie Kram's behaviour, her sudden rush away to find Burke, required explanation, but the explanation of a girl's behaviour is not always known to her father. "Micky Burke?" Kram repeated. "He is one of our drivers—one of our best and the worst as well. What's he been doing now?"

"How do you mean?" Bobby countered. "Your best driver and your worst as well?"

Kram got up, produced a box of cigarettes, pushed them over to Bobby.

"Have one," he said. "Help yourself. No shortage of cigarettes here. Too bad if you've a contract for delivery from factory to wholesalers and can't get hold of a few for yourself. One of our best clients—the Blue Pencil Cigarette company. Cash and carry, that's our slogan. Ha, ha." As he talked he moved across the room to the window. "Thought as much," he said, looking out. "There's Maggie talking to Burke. Thinks it was him."

"She thinks he committed the murder?" Bobby asked, beginning to feel slightly bewildered.

"That's right. That's what's upset her so." Kram turned and smiled blandly at Bobby. "She's been telling me since I don't know when Burke would be killing someone. When you started talking about murder and she saw those headlines, she just jumped to the conclusion it had happened at last. Made sure he had run someone down and never reported it. And K. and K.M.T.C. going to be mixed up in a first class scandal."

He turned back from the window and gazed blandly and innocently at Bobby who gazed back doubtfully, even unbelievingly.

"You mean," he asked, "Miss Kram thought a man shot through the heart, deliberately mutilated, buried in secret, had been run down accidentally by one of your lorries?"

"That's right," Kram repeated. "She wouldn't notice the details. Just saw someone had been killed near the Conqueror Inn, knew Micky had hit on the idea of coming back along that road—he said it saved time—and took it into her head it was him done it. Then she panicked and rushed away like you saw to ask him about it. A bundle of nerves, that's what she is, almost hysterical at times." He turned to the window again. "There he is," he said. "Micky, I mean." He pointed to the small wizened elderly man whom Bobby had noticed before and to whom Maggie Kram was now talking eagerly. He threw up the window. "Hi, Micky," he shouted, "I want you, if Miss Maggie's quite finished wanting to know who you ran down the other night."

It had all been quite natural. Nothing, Bobby felt, he could openly object to. All the same there was Micky warned of what Miss Kram was supposed to have been saying to him. Bobby felt suspicion growing. Burke said something to the girl. She vanished behind the lorry. Burke began to walk slowly towards the house. Inside the room Kram went back to his desk.

"You would never think," he said, "that dried up little devil was the speed merchant he is, would you? Get there or bust. That's his slogan, and by gad, he lives up to it. I get a complaint about him every week pretty nearly. But nothing I can do. He always has his answer pat. Gets away with it every time. Fellow comes in boiling, fair boiling. Hair, turned white in a single night because Micky took a twelve ton lorry between a string of lorries loaded with oxygen tubes and the edge of the canal embankment without an inch to spare—I mean an inch, it was measured, apparently. What does Micky say? Swears there was yards to spare. Says the oxygen tube merchants had pulled over on the wrong side and left plenty of room. I don't believe him, but what can you do? No harm done. If you ask me, that's why Larry's gone home. Couldn't stand the pace."

"Who is Larry?" Bobby asked.

"Nephew of Micky's. Larry Connor. Came over from Ireland to enlist. Wanted to join the R.A.F. They wouldn't have him. Eyesight not up to their standard, they said. Larry sulked. Said his sight was as good as anyone's and they turned him down because he was Irish."

"They wouldn't do that," Bobby said.

"Well, that's what he said. Very sore about it, too. There was something in the paper about Southern Irish being refused for the Home Guard."

"That's been put right," Bobby said.

"Has it?" Kram said. "I don't know that I blame them for being careful. I don't know I should be so keen on employing an Irishman myself, only it's getting difficult to find staff, and a Paddy's better than no one. That's our slogan, ha, ha. Anyhow, Larry sulked, so I offered him a job. I said: When Uncle Micky kills himself, you can take over. Ha, ha. My joke. Well, I told Micky to try Larry out, show him the ropes. That sort of thing. They did a few trips together and now Larry's gone back to Ireland. Went off this weekend. And if you ask me, it was because Micky had put the fear of death in him, the way he throws that lorry about. Does tricks with it to beat those you used to see in the motor cycle races in the Isle of Man before the war."

There was a knock at the door and Micky entered. An elderly man, in the early fifties probably, small in build and with a dried up look, but strong and active still. He had thin, close shut lips, tightly pressed together, and cold still eyes that looked out mistrustfully on all the world and at the moment more especially mistrustfully at Bobby.

"Miss Kram's got hold of the wrong end of the stick, hasn't she?" he asked at once. "It said in the paper the chap they found near the Conqueror Inn was shot. Not a motor accident. Only if it's about that bloke in the Buick, ask him to show you as much as a scratch on his car. There was yards between him and me and the road as clear and clean as the soul of a saint. If he as near as the skin on an egg went over the wall of the bridge, it was his own great fault for swerving the way he did."

Kram chuckled softly.

"I've just been telling the inspector you think you can handle an outsize lorry like it was a motor cycle. The stories I hear! Why, there was a sergeant came over special from Ingle-side Camp. Said he had heard about Micky and he was the sort of driver they wanted in the Tank Corps. Nothing doing, eh, Micky?"

"I did my bit in the last war," Micky answered, indicating the faded medal ribbon he was wearing. "The young men can carry on now. I'm well over age and Irish as well, though Midwych born. They've nothing on me."

Kram chuckled again.

"I had to go out and pull 'em apart," he said. "The sergeant got peeved and wanted to know if Micky had heard the famous story about the Irishman who saw a fight going on in the street and asked if it was a public fight or could he be neutral?"

"I would have shown him neutral," growled Micky.

"He was twice your fighting weight," Kram grinned. To Bobby he said: "Micky grabbed a spanner. The Sergeant took it from him."

"All along of you interfering," Micky growled again. "That's what gave the blighter his chance."

"There's no open war on the British army in my yard," Kram declared, grinning again. "The sergeant went off with the spanner, too. Government property now, I suppose. Used for tightening up tanks or something, most likely. And the cost of a new one is going down on Micky's next wage sheet. I provide spanners for use on lorries, not for braining sergeants."

"I'll pay for no spanner," Micky declared angrily. "Charge it to the sergeant. He's got it."

"Don't know him," retorted Kram. "A driver's responsible for his tools."

"You can take my notice," Micky snapped. "I'll quit."

"Tell Miss Maggie," Kram answered indifferently. "Anyhow, I shall sleep better if I know you aren't out on the road, doing your stunts. I'm always expecting the insurance people to refuse renewing your policy."

"And what for should they?" demanded Micky belligerently, "and me with my record as spotless as the conscience of a babe born that same hour?"

He turned towards the door as if he thought the interview ended, but Bobby stopped him.

"One moment," he said. "You've heard about the murder near the Conqueror Inn?"

"It's in all the papers," Micky answered. "What about it?"

"You've been passing that way recently, haven't you?"

"That's right," Micky admitted cautiously. "Why not?"

"Every night regularly for more than a week," Mr. Kram cut in. "Coming back from up north—empty more often than not. Got done down up there and it's not so often you can say that of K. and K. Cut the rate because I thought I was sure of a return load and then got left."

"I only want to know," Bobby explained to Micky, "if you have ever seen or noticed anything at all out of the way? The murder took place apparently quite close to the inn. At any rate the body was found only a mile or two away, south. At a spot called Spigot's Slope. Know it?"

Micky shook his head.

"Not by name," he said. "I might if you showed it me, though generally it's dark when I go by."

He went on to say that he had never seen or heard anything unusual, nothing that could throw any light on what had happened. It wasn't often now that he stopped at the Conqueror Inn, though at one time he had done so fairly regularly. For a glass of beer, and a bite to eat perhaps.

"Or nothing to eat and a glass of something stronger than beer," Kram interposed jeeringly.

Micky favoured him with another angry scowl.

"You've got my notice," he snapped. "No one's ever seen me the worse for drink," he added defensively.

"Agreed," admitted Kram with an airy wave of the hand, "you can take it, as they say, when it's whisky." To Bobby he explained: "Micky is the widow's cruse the other way round. The widow's cruse was never empty and Micky is never full."

He chuckled at his little joke. Micky scowled afresh and seemed inclined to hand in his notice once more. Then he said that anyhow it was no good stopping off at the Conqueror. They had never had any whisky and now they hadn't even beer; and Kram, who seemed inclined—even oddly inclined—to revenge himself for the notice received by trying to exasperate the Irishman as much as possible, interposed to declare that if Micky didn't stop off at the Conqueror, it was the only exception among all the public houses on his route.

"Because," Kram explained, "the more time he loses at a pub., the more excuse he has for speeding on the road to make up."

Micky received this fresh pleasantry with a fresh scowl. In answer to a question from Bobby, who had listened to this backchat between master and man with a good deal of interest, Micky agreed that he had been the first to think of using the road by the Conqueror Inn, though now others were following his example. He mentioned the names of various drivers, including that of the Loo Leader Bobby had already met.

"If there's been a murder round about there," Micky added, "most like it's Loo."

"Why do you say that?" Bobby asked sharply.

"Loo's a swine," explained Micky and seemed to think that was enough.

"Micky and Loo don't hit it off," Kram explained. "Micky thought he had made a find all to himself, using that road by the Conqueror, but Loo spotted what he was up to and now he uses it too, and told the others as well. Loo's a bit of a speed merchant himself."

"Cut in ahead of me only last week," Micky said, looking virtuous.

"A thing Micky Burke would never do, oh, no," jeered Kram, and Burke scowled once more and suggested that unless Mr. Kram wanted to pay him off on the spot, now his notice had been given in, he had better get started.

Bobby had no more questions to ask and so Burke was allowed to depart on his trip.

CHAPTER XI
PISTOL SHOT

Bobby had, however, one or two more questions to ask of the head of K. and K.M.T.C.—to the disappointment of that gentleman, who had optimistically hoped that the departure of Micky Burke would be followed by the departure of Bobby.

Not so, however, for now Bobby was saying:

"I believe, Mr. Kram, you have visited the Conqueror Inn yourself, haven't you?"

notes. Presumably someone was feeling the loss of that money pretty badly and that someone would be all the more likely to take steps towards recovering it, if he—or she—did not know it was in the hands of the police.

Yet if it belonged to the murderer, possibly he would prefer to run no such risk of discovery as would be involved in any attempt to secure possession. Skin for skin and much more, yea, even £2,000 in untraceable one pound notes, will a man give to protect himself from danger of the gallows.

Or again the money might have belonged to the dead man and dead men make no claims.

Bobby roused himself from thoughts that were running, he felt, too far ahead. No use his trying to evolve a solution from his inner consciousness as the legendary professor is said to have tried to evolve an idea of the elephant. Sitting at his desk he made out a list of the points he thought interesting, and possibly significant, learnt by him that morning. Five of such details at least, he told himself, that it would be as well to keep in mind. Next he set in motion routine inquiries to check as far as possible the different statements of fact that had been made. Burke's statement, for instance, that he had been born in Midwych and that he had a nephew named Larry Connor. Then, too, it would be as well to make sure that Larry had really tried to enlist in the R.A.F., and been turned down for bad eyesight. Again there was the story of the Ingle-side Camp sergeant and the spanner, though an anonymous sergeant would not be easy to trace.

All very small and unimportant details as far as could be seen at present, but more than once, in Bobby's experience, had some small discrepancy, some small and trivial departure from the facts, provided, if not proof of guilt, yet the needed clue to show where that proof was to be found.

It was one of his theories—one of his slogans, Mr. Kram would probably have said—that a lie is often more revealing than the truth. For truth provides its own cause and reason but a lie has a motive to know which is often to know all.

Also he set on foot another inquiry by less usual and official methods to try to hear of any business man, firm, or private individual, showing signs of being in unexpected financial difficulty.

After all, most firms or private persons losing such a sum in ready cash as £2,000, might be expected to show signs of inconvenience. Hints might be dropped to money-lenders, for instance, that any information regarding a request for a loan of that amount would, of course, be considered as most strictly and utterly confidential but would also be gratefully received and gratefully remembered. And some money lenders would be quite glad to feel that the police remembered them with gratitude. Banks, too, grant loans and though more difficult to approach—in fact notoriously sticky—even with them something might be done. Discreetly. There were other channels again that might repay investigation.

Hopefully Bobby told himself that surely a two thousand pound gap could not be filled without some sign showing somewhere of the strain and effort required.

It was lunch time now, so Bobby got something to eat and started off again to pay another visit to the Conqueror Inn and to test that idea which had flashed into his mind when he learnt that Maggie Kram had vanished from the K. and K. premises.

Much to his relief there was at the scene of the murder, or, rather, since the actual spot was not certain, at the scene of the victim's burial, no such crowd of curious spectators as he had feared to find. Presumably in time of war there are fewer people with time—and petrol—to spare. Then, too, the accounts in the papers had not been very explicit as to the exact locality.

In any case the inn showed as solitary, as aloof, as when he had first seen it. Secret, too, it seemed as it brooded there in quietude and stillness, for who could tell what things might not here come to pass, so far from general haunt or knowledge.

At a distance of a mile or so Bobby halted his car and sat there, watching and thinking.

Five points of possible significance he had noted down as having emerged from his conversations of the morning. Equally there were other details he had now learned—such as that of the light in the attic window of the inn followed by the examination by the two men of the Home Guard of the room in which the black-out curtain had collapsed—which might equally well carry their own significance. But as yet for all his thinking he could see no trace of any general pattern into which such details could be fitted.

The two Krams, father and daughter; Micky Burke and his nephew, Larry Connor; Captain Peter Wintle of Ingleside Camp; the members of the Christopherson family; Loo Leader and his pugilistic mate; they all played their part, Bobby felt very certain in the drama that had culminated in that solitary grave it had been so evidently and so dreadfully intended should preserve its secret inviolate for ever.

But what part it was each one of these played, there was as yet little to show and for the present Bobby could see nowhere any suggestion of a connecting link. Nothing in fact but a mass of unrelated and very possibly wholly irrelevant detail.

As he sat there in his car, letting as it were his sub conscious mind absorb all these different impressions and beliefs floating vaguely and disconnectedly in his thoughts, watching, too, the old inn where it stood aloof and solitary and alone as it had done during all the long past centuries, there came within view on the skyline, at a distance, the figures of two men, walking together.

Bobby had brought with him, he hardly knew why, perhaps because the vast bare expanse of the moor had made upon him its own strange impression, a pair of field glasses. He adjusted them and by their aid was able to make out that one of these unexpected pedestrians was Mr. Christopherson, the landlord of the Conqueror Inn. Enjoying a stroll across the moor perhaps; and a trifle curious, Bobby thought, that a man so clearly hardworking, with so much upon his hands, since with only his daughter's help he had to look after both his inn and his little farm, should be able to spare time for pleasant afternoon strolls. His companion seemed a younger man but was so screened by the landlord's tall form that Bobby could not see him clearly till presently he stopped, shook hands and went off in another direction. Then it could be seen that he was in clerical dress, the local vicar or curate perhaps, presumably out on the moor on some parochial errand. Bobby promptly lost all interest. But he was still inclined to wonder how a hardworking smallholder—and that Christopherson was hardworking the condition of his fields and crops showed plainly—could spare time for pleasant walks in the sunshine. Yet again what possible significance could lie in an hour or two's absence from work? All the same, yet another small and unexplained item to be added to the list of the possibly significant.

Bobby drove slowly on and when he came to the inn he was not surprised to find it closed and to receive no answer when he knocked. The licensing laws were strictly observed here, he knew, and very likely not only Christopherson but also his wife and daughter were out. He would wait for their return, he decided, and suddenly he heard ring out in the still, calm air, coming from somewhere at the rear of the building, the short sharp crack of a pistol shot.

CHAPTER XII
LIARS BOTH

THE CONQUEROR INN was a long straggling building, dating from days when time and labour and material were all for more free and lavish use, since immediate monetary profit had not then been recognized as the ultimate test of the good. Had Bobby turned right instead of left as he started to run when that sharp pistol report rang out in the clear calm moorland air, he would have come at once to a side entry that would have led him straight to the back regions. But he turned left and so had to make nearly a complete circuit round the house. It took some moments, swiftly though he ran. Near the house walls, too, the ground was paved with cobble stones. On them as he ran his footsteps sounded loudly. When he came into the inn yard, all he saw was two young women chatting together. One of them was saying loudly:

"Have you any eggs to sell? Any eggs to sell?"

Neither of them took any notice of Bobby's appearance, even though the fact that a young man had just burst upon them at full speed might have been expected to attract their attention. The girl who had made the inquiry—unanswered—about the eggs was Maggie Kram, so Bobby knew his guess had been a good one and when she left K. and K.M.T.C. headquarters it was here she had come. The other was Rachel Christopherson. Instead of answering Maggie's request for eggs she now turned slowly and bestowed on Bobby the tranquil, calm, untroubled gaze he remembered so well. Maggie, instead of repeating her demand for eggs, turned, too, but away, with her back to Bobby. Bobby said:

"What's going on here? What was that shot?"

Rachel replied by the counter question:

"Why? What shot? What do you mean?"

"I heard a shot. Who fired it?" Bobby demanded.

"I heard nothing," Rachel said. "Perhaps someone was shooting rabbits." To Maggie, or rather to Maggie's back, she said: "Did you hear anything, Miss Kram?"

Maggie shook her head and then turned slowly. Her face was deathly white, but in the centre of each pale cheek burned one small spot of flaming red and again those remote withdrawn eyes of hers had grown like two distant points of fire.

"Why, it's that nice big policeman again," she said, and managed, though with visible effort, to produce a somewhat tremulous giggle.

"Don't lie to me," Bobby said angrily. "I heard a shot and so did you. Who fired it?"

"I heard no shot," Rachel said quietly. "Nor did Miss Kram. Did you?" She appealed again to Maggie.

"No, of course not, there wasn't one to hear," Maggie agreed.

"Then why is there a smell of powder in the air?" Bobby asked.

"I can smell nothing," Rachel said. "I think there is nothing to smell. Can you, Miss Kram?"

Maggie shook her head. There were some empty wooden cases lying near. She went over to them and sat down on one. The flaming red spot on either cheek had vanished now and she looked even more pale, shaken, trembling than before.

"I should like a glass of water," she said, not too steadily, and indeed she gave the impression of being very near to fainting.

"I'll get you one," Rachel said and hurried away to the house.

That meant more time for her to compose herself, Bobby thought gloomily. He looked round. The door of a big barn near was standing open. He went across to look inside. It was empty, a huge great empty place, empty except, curiously enough, for a music stand. Nearby was a violin in its case. Nothing to show it had been used recently. Little there to support any one of the numerous theories struggling for supremacy in his mind, eagerly as he sought for even the smallest confirmatory sign to establish one or other as the most hopeful line to follow. He went back into the inn yard. He felt convinced that one of those two girls had fired upon the other, that one of them had only a moment or two before tried to kill.

But which? Which was the intended victim, which the would-be killer?

And for what motive?

Was it Rachel's extreme, indeed unnatural calm that hid the emotion of the baffled murderess? Or was it Maggie's evident terror, her near approach to collapse, that was the more likely reaction from such an attempt?

A forced self-control or an emotional collapse, either of these could hide a realization of escape—either from death or from the guilt of slaying.

All these thoughts passed swiftly through Bobby's mind. He saw Rachel come to the door of the house, a glass in her hand. Bobby swiftly made up his mind to try what the result would be of a direct accusation. He made two quick steps to where Maggie sat half collapsed upon the piled-up wooden cases and said to her sharply:

"You fired at Rachel. You tried to kill her. Why?"

Maggie did not answer, unless it was an answer that she so plainly called up all her strength to shake her head. Rachel, moving with that swift unhurried ease of which she had the secret, was already at their side. She said to Bobby:

"Leave her alone. Can't you see she is nearly fainting?"

Bobby said:

"No wonder. You fired at her. You tried to kill her. Why?"

Rachel took no notice. She was supporting Maggie, holding the glass to her lips. Maggie drank eagerly. The colour came back to her cheeks. She said:

"You've put something in it."

"A little brandy. That's all," Rachel answered.

She was still holding the glass to Maggie's lips. Maggie's head she supported in the crook of her arm. They made a pretty and a touching picture, sitting there, supporting and supported. It made Bobby feel like a brute and a bully. He reflected moodily that somehow women always knew how to put a man in the wrong. Been at it ever since the Garden of Eden, he supposed. Taking a mean advantage of their sex, he called it. He said sulkily to Rachel:

"Have you still got the pistol on you or did you get rid of it when you went for that water? It took you long enough—time to hide a pistol as well as fill a glass of water."

"I had to find the key of the cupboard where father keeps the brandy," Rachel said. "If you think there's a pistol there, you can go and look," but he noticed that as she spoke her right hand fluttered to her breast as though to guard something she had hidden there. So he said:

"I don't think it's in the kitchen. I think you've got it on you."

She did not answer that. She was holding a handkerchief to Maggie's forehead and he could smell eau-de-Cologne. But her right hand was always protectively before her breast and he was certain he knew why. But it was safe from him. He could not search her. He could not use force, strong though the temptation was. She seemed to realize what was passing in his mind, for she gave the eau-de-Cologne-soaked handkerchief to Maggie and got to her feet, facing him. But she held both hands to her breast and her eyes were direct and calm and resolute. He tried to bluff. He said harshly and roughly:

"Well, are you going to give it me or have I got to take it from you?"

"Even if I had it," she said, "you would have to kill me before you took it from me."

Bobby scowled angrily. It was an acknowledgement of defeat. He said just as a sulky schoolboy might have done:

"Women never play fair."

"I don't know what you mean," she said.

That was quite true, probably, but when Maggie giggled, Bobby found it hard to bear. Exasperating to feel that the evidence was there, lying before him, there for the taking, in this girl's possession, and yet as well protected as though it lay behind triple locks of brass. He could have sworn—and did so to himself. He could have torn his hair—but didn't. He reflected moodily that had his wife, Olive, been present, she, with the eternal freemasonry of sex, would have regarded his discomfiture with amused interest. One blessing; she wasn't there and he would take jolly good care she never knew. To hide his anger, regain his self-control, he walked away the length of the yard and then back. He said:

"One of you tried to kill the other. I'm pretty sure of that. Or why are you both lying so hard? Oh, you are good liars, both of you. But it's clear enough all the same. Well, why should either of you want to protect the one who has tried to kill her—and may try again," he added, hopeful that perhaps this new argument might have some effect.

It hadn't.

Rachel said:

"We have nothing to say, nothing to tell you. Have we, Miss Kram?"

Maggie shook her head and produced once more that annoying giggle of hers. Bobby went away and turned his back to them and swore a little more to himself. There are times when the worse the language the greater the relief. Not that the relief Bobby gained this time amounted to much. Oh, if only he dared stand Rachel on her head and shake her well till that pistol dropped from its hiding place in her bosom. He crossed to look at the spot where Rachel and Maggie had been standing when he burst in upon them. But both lines of fire from there carried out over the open moor, and what chance was there of finding one small bullet that might have dropped anywhere almost? Even if he mobilized the whole police force for the search, the bullet would probably never be found. For that matter, even if it were found, not much good without the pistol—the pistol that lay so snugly there within his knowledge and beyond his reach. He was loath to confess ultimate defeat and he made up his mind to try yet once again. He went back and said:

"Miss Kram came here to ask Miss Christopherson something. She came after I had talked to her, after she knew that a dead man—a man whose face had been mutilated, whose clothes had been removed to make identification impossible—had been found buried near here. I think Miss Kram came to ask who it was."

"If she had," Rachel countered, "I could only have told her what I told you—that I did not know."

"Possibly she did not believe you and tried to frighten you into saying," Bobby remarked. "Or perhaps you did not want to say and you tried to frighten her from asking."

Rachel did not answer. Maggie, however, was almost her normal self again. She produced once more that giggle of hers Bobby was beginning to think one of the most abominable sounds he had ever heard. She said:

"Doesn't he ask a lot of questions? That's the worst of these big policemen. Questions. Questions, all the time. But you've got it all wrong, dear Mr. Big Man. I only came out of curiosity. People always do rush to stare at the scene of a crime. Morbid curiosity. That's me. Ghoulish. I'm a ghoul. That's all."

She giggled once more. Bobby stood still, feeling foolish and wondering very hard what to do next. From Rachel he was now well assured he would learn nothing. Whatever the motive of her silence, he was sure no force on earth would make her speak. Not till she chose. Maggie, he thought, was of a more passionate nature, and passion may sometimes exhaust itself to weakness. But not yet. A new idea came to him. Was Maggie herself guilty? Had she come here in the belief that Rachel knew something and determined to make her silence sure for ever?

Not much profit, though, in all this speculation and mere guesswork. And not much likelihood, he supposed, of finding anything out till the fundamental puzzle had been solved—that of the identity of the murdered man on whom an inquest was to be held next day. He might as well go back to Midwych, he supposed, though he did not like the idea of leaving the two young women alone again. That hidden pistol in Rachel's possession might come into play once more. He said to Rachel:

"Will it be long before your father gets back?"

She looked puzzled and a little startled, as if wondering how he knew Mr. Christopherson was out. Seeing this he added:

"I caught sight of him having a walk on the moor with a friend."

To his increased bewilderment, at that she went as pale, looked as shaken and as alarmed as Maggie had done a few minutes before.

"You saw? ... you didn't ... it's not true, is it?" she stammered out.

He took a leaf from her book and did not answer, hoping she would say more. Instead she turned and set off running, running with swift long strides that took her out of the inn yard and on the moor, almost before Bobby knew that she had moved. Bobby watched in bewilderment her vanishing figure. He wondered whether to pursue. Useless probably. So swift she ran, he was not even sure he could overtake her, at any rate not easily. In any case open pursuit would almost certainly defeat its own end. Once again Maggie Kram began to giggle. He turned to give her a glare that made her giggle more.

"She's gone to warn him he's been seen," she said.

"Warn who? What of?" Bobby asked.

"Warn her dad there's a policeman on the prowl," Maggie answered. "What else? I'm going home."

"How did you come?" he asked.

"On my motor bike," she answered. "Did you think I walked or flew?"

"You wouldn't like to tell me what really happened?" he asked, without hope.

"I couldn't if I wanted to," she answered heavily. "It's what I came here to find out and I haven't."

"Is that why Rachel Christopherson tried to kill you?" he asked.

She looked at him and once again set his nerves on edge by that thin giggle of hers.

"The big man's cunning too," she jeered. "Pretty feeble effort to find out whether anyone really did fire a pistol at anyone else; and if it was her at me or me at her. Try again, big man."

She would say no more and he watched her start off. Left alone, he looked longingly at the inn. Empty now, he supposed. He had seen Christopherson on the moor. Rachel had gone to find him. Her mother must be out, too, or surely all this talk and commotion would have made her show herself. Of course, he had no right to go searching people's houses. But was such an opportunity to be neglected? It wouldn't be breaking and entering anyhow, because the kitchen door hung open. But didn't that suggest there was nothing in the house to hide, or would it have been left unguarded like that? The open kitchen door was both an invitation to search and a warning that search would be useless; nor did he know which to accept—the invitation or the warning.

CHAPTER XIII

WHY EGGS?

PROBABLY IT WAS fortunate that Bobby was saved the necessity of making a decision, for now he heard approaching footsteps. It was Mrs. Christopherson, returning from the village on the main road, where she had been, she said, to visit a sick friend. Bobby told her of Rachel's sudden departure that had left the house empty and unguarded. Mrs. Christopherson made no comment. Bobby asked one or two questions, but she only shook her head and said something vague about having spent the whole day with her friend. He had the impression that she had been warned to be careful in what she said. She went into the house and shut the door without taking any further notice of him.

So there he was left standing alone in the inn yard and nothing for him to do but to drive back again to Midwych and his office.

There he found various reports awaiting him. It was true that Micky Burke had been born in Midwych, had served in the army, had a nephew, Larry Connor, born in Ireland at a village near Cork but brought up by Micky, in Midwych, after the death of Larry's parents had left Micky his nearest relative. Micky had looked after and cared for the child like a father. They had always led the quiet, respectable lives of ordinary working people, though Micky never stayed long in one job and in recent years Larry had spent much of his time in Ireland. But he still remained on very friendly terms with his uncle, still came over two or three times a year on visits of varying length. During these visits he took odd jobs when he could get them and it was true that he tried to join the R.A.F., but was rejected on account of defective eyesight.

Nothing in all that of any apparent interest, Bobby decided, and then Sergeant Payne came in to make his report.

"Any luck?" Bobby asked him and Payne hesitated.

"I don't know for sure, sir," he said, "but I think perhaps I'm on something."

"Oh, yes, what?" Bobby asked, interested.

"Eggs," said Payne.

"Oh," said Bobby, and wondered curiously why this odd motive of eggs seemed so constantly to recur. Why eggs? he asked himself and aloud he said: "What eggs, Payne? Do you mean you've found Miss Emma Jones?"

"Oh, no, sir," Payne answered, and Bobby said:

"Well, I'm not sure I haven't."

For it had been running strongly in his mind that the mysterious Miss Emma Jones might very well be identical with Miss Maggie Kram, though at present that idea must remain as a mere guess since there were no means of verifying it. Payne was too much absorbed in his own theories and experiences to pay any attention to Bobby's remark, which indeed had been in the nature of an aside. Payne had been busy getting out a fat notebook and finding his place in it. Now he said:

"In the first place, sir, I made inquiries at Ingleside camp. I couldn't get track of any one in the camp who had heard of Micky Burke or of any sergeant who wanted to get him enlisted. Most of them seemed to think it was a leg pull. Said the tank corps wasn't so hard up as all that for class drivers and anyhow sergeants had plenty to do without going round hunting up recruits."

"I suppose," Bobby remarked, "if a sergeant had been mixed up in a bit of a row and heard police were making inquiries, he mightn't be too anxious to come forward."

"No, sir, there's always that," agreed Payne, "especially if he had pinched a spanner as well."

"Not much confirmation of Micky's story," Bobby remarked, "but that doesn't prove it isn't true. All the rest of it is O.K.?"

"Apparently so," agreed Payne, who was as cautious in accepting statements made to him as a good policeman soon learns to be. "About Captain Peter Wintle. He is second in command of his company. He seems well liked but has the reputation of being reserved and of keeping very much to himself. More respected as a good soldier than liked as a good mixer, if you see what I mean. Got his commission from a Territorial regiment on the outbreak of the war. No one seems to know anything about his family and most officers know all about each other's backgrounds. The batmen know it, too, generally."

"I can believe that of the batmen, anyhow," remarked Bobby.

"He would have no difficulty in leaving the camp at night," Payne went on. "He is strict about guard duty, a fad of his, the men say. The story is that during the Dunkirk retreat his company was badly cut up by a surprise attack. He says a better look-out might have averted it. So he has a trick of prowling round at odd intervals to see that sentries and guards are all on their toes. Sometimes he'll do that two consecutive nights, sometimes he'll let a week pass or more. If anyone saw him out at night it would be taken for granted that's what he was doing—inspecting the guard. If he were missed from his quarters, the same thing. But nothing to stop him slipping off anywhere he wanted so long as he was back in reasonable time."

"Being second in command has its advantages," commented Bobby. "Nobody to check him except the company C.O., and most likely he thinks it's fine to have a Second who keeps the men up to the mark. And if Wintle had a car parked handy or a bike hidden, he could be over half England and back before daybreak, without the Ingleside people either knowing or caring. What about the Saturday night when the Conqueror Inn was broken into and the Monday night of the murder?"

Payne was referring to his notebook again.

"He had leave over Saturday till Sunday six o'clock, when he returned to camp," Payne announced.

"Have to ask him some day where he was," Bobby remarked, "but not yet. He would only tell us to go to hell."

"Yes, sir," agreed Payne. "It was noticed that he had a black eye when he returned and he explained it by the same story—that he had run into a door in the black-out. On Monday he didn't dine in mess. He was busy preparing a report on some tactical exercise or another and told his batman to bring him some sandwiches to his room and see he wasn't disturbed. Nothing to show whether he actually spent the evening writing his report or not."

"And nothing in the shape of an established, comfortable alibi to save us bothering about him any more," Bobby said sadly.

"No, sir. Returning to Miss Emma Jones, no one known of that name at Wayside Cottages or anywhere else in the neighbourhood."

"No egg hunters known? You said something about eggs, didn't you?"

"I've got a very clear impression," Payne answered, "that there is something queer going on about eggs on the moor, but I couldn't put my finger on anything definite. But everyone I asked had heard some sort of vague story or another and someone else had been before me, asking questions."

"Who?" asked Bobby as Payne paused, evidently for dramatic effect.

"That Loo Leader chap," said Payne, and was entirely satisfied when Bobby emitted a loud whistle.

"So Loo Leader comes into it again, does he?" Bobby said. "Have to keep an eye on him and ask him a few more questions presently." Then he paused and rubbed thoughtfully the end of his nose. "I don't get it," he said. "Why eggs? All the big egg producers are known. None of them could let their output go down without it being noticed. No one bothers about the cottages with ten or twenty birds. Anyhow, the hen population out there on the moor doesn't amount to anything much. You might hunt half the day and not get enough eggs to make a man-size omelette."

"Yes, sir, that's rather what I thought," agreed Payne, "so then I began to wonder if when eggs were talked about, perhaps something else was meant."

Bobby sat upright.

"What?" he asked.

"Well, sir," Payne said, a little hesitatingly now, for he was afraid of being accused of possessing too lively an imagination, "you know the French call them pills—'pilloner' a place, they say. The R.A.F. call them eggs—laying eggs, they say. Or used to. Bombs is what I thought of."

Bobby rubbed the end of his nose harder than ever. The idea did not in fact much appeal to him. But he supposed that might be because he had not thought of it himself. Payne was evidently extremely taken by it, as taken as we always are by our own ideas. Nor for that matter is any idea too fantastic for these fantastic days in which we live. Payne went on: "They could be dropped by parachute. They could be landed by boat from a submarine. They could be smuggled in from Ireland for that matter. For use against vulnerable spots in case of invasion—or even for sabotage."

"Have to keep it in mind," Bobby said slowly. "It might be. Only where does Captain Wintle come in?"

"He may have heard something and be doing a bit of watching himself," Payne suggested and Bobby supposed it was possible.

"Only even if it's so," he remarked, "it doesn't throw much light on who is guilty of the murder or why it was committed or on the poor devil's identity. But I think we must watch Loo Leader. And the Conqueror Inn, too."

"The sort of place where anything might happen," Payne said. "All alone up there, not a soul near. First-class place for hiding things. You could store anything you like there and no one know."

Bobby remembered that Mr. Merton Kram had spoken of hiring those vast outbuildings for storage purposes.

"We'll have to keep an eye on K. and K.M.T.C., too," he remarked thoughtfully. "We may pick up some useful facts. At present we've got precious few—only a medley, all unconnected and mostly irrelevant I expect. Anyhow, interest is getting focused in four different directions. The K. and K. lot. Loo Leader and his interest in eggs. The Conqueror Inn, and its great empty outbuildings. Ingleside Camp and Captain Wintle. And if you can tell me, Sergeant Payne, how to set a watch on a captain in the army busy training for a date with Hitler, I'll be glad to hear it."

Sergeant Payne had no suggestion to make on that score. But a man was told off to keep an eye on the K. and K.M.T.C. headquarters and to try as far as possible to get on friendly terms with the drivers. Another man was selected for watching Loo Leader and his pugilistic mate, and yet a third man to be sent to find out what he could about the Conqueror Inn. And Bobby was still in his office, though on the point of leaving for home whence he had just received a plaintive 'phone call from his wife, Olive, to ask whether she was likely to see him before or after midnight, or not till next week, when another 'phone call came.

"Briggs speaking, sir," said the small and distant voice, giving the name of the constable assigned to the K. and K.M.T.C. watch. "I thought I would have a look round on my way home, sir. It's a young lady, sir. She's sitting out at the back of the K. and K. premises, between a lorry and the fence, a-sobbing and a-sobbing, sir, like to break her heart."

CHAPTER XIV

A WOMAN'S TEARS

BOBBY STOOD so long, holding the receiver to his ear but not speaking, for of this piece of information he did not know in the least what to make, that presently a small discreet cough sounded over the line, a kind of timid and respectful: 'Are you there?' So Bobby said something to indicate he was listening and the distant voice said:

"Instructions were to report anything out of the way, sir."

Out of the way certainly, Bobby thought as he listened, and certainly within the terms of the instructions issued—this story of a girl weeping alone in the night, in her father's yard between a lorry and the fence.

Yet after all, was it so out of the way, since this is a world in which many women often have good cause to weep.

"That's all right, Briggs," Bobby said to the 'phone mouthpiece, replying more to the evident hesitation in the man's voice than to his actual words. "I'll come along. Look out for me."

Fortunately, as he had been on the point of leaving for home, his car was at the door and ready. He knew the address, knew his way, and within a very few minutes drew up where Briggs was waiting for him in the dark, but showing his position by an occasional flash of his torch on the ground.

"It sounded sort of rummy, sir," he explained. "Sort of heartbroken it sounded."

"Wait here," Bobby said. "May as well see if anything's wrong or help's needed or anything."

He went down an alley that ran behind the house. On one side was a high wooden fence, the boundary of what once had been a garden, a garden now derelict, for, as the works and factories encroached and wealth and smoke and fumes increased, so defeated nature withdrew, unable to grapple with an atmosphere so different from any nature had ever contemplated.

By this fence, noting that it was in bad repair, Bobby made his way, picking his path with care in the darkness and the shadows. About twenty yards along, the constable said. Bobby counted twenty-five paces and listened. He could hear plainly the sound of sobbing, not loud now as Briggs had described it, but soft and low and intent with the last extremity of misery and despair.

Strange to stand thus in the dark night and listen to these sounds that told of a human soul in agony. For Bobby felt, as Briggs had done before, that this was no ordinary grief here pouring itself out. There was a note in it that told of other feelings as well—a kind of despairing rage, he thought, as of one caught in a trap of circumstance from which there was no escape.

Purposely he stumbled, making a disturbance that in the quiet night would certainly be heard. The sound of sobbing ceased. A voice called:

"Who's that? Who's there?"

Bobby thought he recognized the voice, strangled and changed and hoarse as it was with tears unshed and shed. He risked a guess and called back:

"Oh, is that you, Miss Kram? This is Inspector Owen. Is anything wrong? The constable on the beat reported suspicious sounds."

"That's a lie. He didn't. You're spying, peeping, watching. What for? What for?" came Maggie's voice in return, shrill and hysterical.

"Oh, I assure you, really," Bobby protested. "I say, I can't talk over a fence. May I come through to your side? There are some slats loose."

Without waiting for either consent or refusal, neither of which was given for Maggie did not answer, and widening the gap he had found at hand by pulling out another slat, Bobby squeezed through. He switched on his torch. The night was dark, but he knew the direction whence the voice had come. When he had gone a few steps he was able to make out a dim form standing upright. He flashed the torch again and made sure it was really Maggie Kram. She said in the same hoarse half-strangled tones, as though her tears had nearly drowned her voice:

"What do you want? Why are you watching, peeping, listening?"

"If we are, why should that make you afraid?" he countered.

When she made no answer he went on:

"My constable reported hearing sounds he did not understand. So I came along. I could hear you. You were crying, in great distress I thought."

He paused but she was still silent. He continued:

"I wondered why you had come out there from the house, to sit alone in the dark."

"You've no right ..." she muttered.

"No right to wonder?" he asked gently. "But there's a lot that has set me wondering. I am wondering for instance whether you did not wish your father to hear you, or whether there was some other reason—a quarrel or a misunderstanding of some sort perhaps?"

"It's nothing to do with you," she told him, but without spirit, as though her recent passion of emotion had left her oddly weak.

"I'm wondering another thing," he went on. "A man has died alone at night out there on the moor. A woman is heard crying to herself alone here in the city. That makes me wonder, too; wonder if the one thing is because of the other."

Again she did not answer and he felt rather than saw how she shrank away. He had the impression that she would have slipped off, had she not been blocked by the fence behind, by a tool house or some such shed on her left, by himself in front. He said again:

"Is it because of that dead man … ? If it is, won't you tell me?"

"I can't, I won't, leave me alone," she answered, and he could hear how her breath came in quick sudden gasps. "You don't understand, you don't, you can't."

"I think you know who is that dead man someone tried so hard to be sure should never be recognized," Bobby went on. "If you do, why won't you tell me? Was it someone you knew?" He paused a little. He said: "If it was someone you were fond of, remember he was brutally murdered." Bobby's voice that had been gentle grew suddenly stern. "Brutally murdered out there on the moor. His face battered—"

"Oh, don't, don't, don't," she cried, shuddering violently.

"Why won't you tell?" Bobby repeated. "I think it was someone you cared for. I ask you for a dead man's sake—"

"You don't know what you ask," she interrupted, and her voice was so heavy and so strange that Bobby fell silent, wondering what she meant.

Presently he said:

"Is the dead man Larry Connor?"

She began to laugh. It was rather horrible. She stood and laughed, and he listened to it in the darkness and knew that it was false.

Abruptly she said:

"Here is a letter from Larry I got this evening."

She held out something towards him. He could see the paper in her hand, faintly white in the darkness. He took it and he said:

"Well, that proves Larry isn't the dead man, doesn't it?"

"Yes, so it does," she agreed, still laughing and her laughter was still rather horrible, the laughter of a lost soul welcoming another. Then she stopped laughing, abruptly, as if it had been cut off as one cuts off an electric current. She said: "Well, I'll tell you. The dead man was Rachel Christopherson's lover and I think she killed him, but it may have been her father, and I don't know why."

Before he could say anything she slipped by him and was running towards the house.

He could not follow. He heard her steps die away. He heard a door open and shut. Everything was silent then. He went back through the gap in the fence and along the alley to where Briggs still stood guard over his car.

"I tried to speak to the girl," Bobby said, "but she ran off to the house. Nothing we can do."

"No, sir," agreed Briggs, still uneasy, "only it seemed a bit queer like and being told to report anything out of the way—no matter what it was ..."

"That's all right," Bobby interrupted. "You were quite right to ring up. Cut along home now and in the morning try to see if you can pick anything up. Don't much expect you will, though. Deep business this and more to it even than murder, I think."

"Yes, sir," said Briggs and saluted and retired, and Bobby drove off home to the supper there awaiting him.

Over it he told Olive of the events of the day and examined very carefully the letter Maggie had thrust at him before rushing away back to the house. It was a stiff little letter, written in a stiff angular hand, dated from London, giving no address, and it said in effect that the writer had thought it best to leave Midwych for a time, was not sure of his future movements, but would write again and would Miss Maggie please be patient till then.

"What do you think of it?" Bobby asked.

"Fake," said Olive promptly. "And Miss Kram knows it."

"I thought it might be a fake," Bobby agreed, "but why do you think she thinks so?"

"My good lad," said Olive, "do you suppose for one moment she would have handed it over to you like that if she hadn't known it was a fraud?"

"Um-m," said Bobby, considering.

"No um-m about it," retorted Olive.

"If it's like that," said Bobby, "it means the dead man most likely is Larry Connor, but how are we to prove it?"

"Fingerprints?" said Olive hopefully.

"Where are we to get them?" Bobby asked. "So as to be sure they are his? The people who did what they did to hide his identity will have looked after that."

"The Micky Burke man?" suggested Olive. "He might help. You say he is said to have been fond of his nephew?"

"Like father and son, they say," Bobby agreed. "But Micky is in it up to the neck, whatever it is."

"Can he be the murderer?" Olive asked.

"Why should he? There seems plenty of confirmation for the like father and son story. It's certain he brought Larry up from a child. Why should he murder him now?"

"Why should anyone?" asked Olive.

"Yes, I know," agreed Bobby. "We may have got the identity part of the puzzle solved, but there seems no hint of any motive as yet except—"

"Jealousy," Olive completed the sentence. "Miss Kram says it was Miss Christopherson. When a woman murders, jealousy is a likely motive. But then Maggie Kram may have said what she did out of jealousy, too. At any rate, I think the solution lies in the Conqueror Inn."

"Likely to stay there, too, for all I can see," Bobby said, looking dispirited. "There was certainly a shot fired this afternoon by one of those two at the other. But no way of knowing which. Unless one of them tells—and then most likely it wouldn't be true."

"Put down what you really know," Olive suggested, "and see what it looks like on paper. If you get all the actual facts together, you may be able to see where they lead."

So Bobby got a piece of paper and started to write but found there was no ink in his fountain pen. So he got a pencil instead and wrote:

"Fact 1. A man killed and great pains taken to hide his identity.

Deduction: Hiding his identity was as important as hiding the murder itself.

Fact 2. Larry Connor vanished and a letter arrives signed by him, but possibly a forgery.

Deduction. Attempt by the murderer to prevent Miss Kram from making inquiries.

Fact 3. Miss Kram was in a state of great distress to-night.

Deductions. Various and uncertain. She may think Larry is dead. She may be afraid someone else is dead and Larry is the murderer. She may be the murderer herself, there was fear as well as grief to-night. Or—"

"I don't," interposed Olive, "call that deduction. I call it guessing."

"Objection upheld," said Bobby, "but what else can a detective do but guess and guess till he makes one that holds?" Then he struck out all he had written from the word 'Various' and substituted 'Many and doubtful.'

"That's better," said Olive.

Bobby went on writing.

"Fact 4. An attempt was made to break into the Conqueror Inn last Saturday night, but nothing was taken, or so the Christophersons say.

Deduction. There's something there somebody wants to know about.

Fact 5. Captain Wintle won a black eye about the time the dead man had a thrashing which seems to have been about the time of the attempt to break and enter.

Deduction. Captain Wintle and the intruder came into contact; the black eye and the thrashing mutually resulting.

Further deduction. Captain Wintle knows why the breaking and entering attempt was made and was there to stop it." Here Bobby paused and considered the last sentence.

"Is that sound reasoning?" he asked.

"No, it's guessing," Olive answered. She took the pencil out of Bobby's hand and wrote instead:

"Further deduction. Captain Wintle was on the spot for an unknown reason."

"Unknown reason," said Bobby bitterly, reading this. "Why, it's all one unknown reason."

Then he took his pencil back and wrote:

"Fact 6. A fiddle and music stand were in the Conqueror Inn barn.

Deduction. Someone at the Conqueror Inn plays the fiddle."

"Well, why shouldn't they?" asked Olive. "Didn't you say the son who was killed at Dunkirk was a violinist?"

"Yes," said Bobby, "but as another guess—suppose he wasn't killed there and suppose he's the murdered man. That would suggest Larry Connor not as victim but as murderer—explain why he's bolted—explain the mutilation—most of the people about there would know Christopherson's son."

"Oh," said Olive, very surprised, "oh, I never thought of that. Oh, but why?"

"We haven't got as far as 'why,'" Bobby told her. "Not by a long way. You see, there's that story of the light in the attic window at the inn and the inspection by the Home Guard to prove the black-out curtain had been blown in and so it was an accident. Christopherson said he had been sleeping in the room, but if so he and his wife occupy separate rooms, which I don't think likely, and anyhow, why an attic?"

"I see," said Olive thoughtfully and added with all the reluctance of a wife praising a husband and risking giving the creature a swelled head: "You know, it was rather clever of you to think that out."

Bobby beamed; for praise from a wife is praise indeed—so seldom does the poor mutt deserve it. Then he continued with his writing:

"Fact 7. Miss Kram went to the Conqueror Inn, saw Miss Rachel there and a shot was fired.

Deduction. One of them tried to kill the other.

Only which and why?"

"Not a very useful deduction," observed Olive. "Put it: Deduction. One of them was jealous of the other. Because, I've told you before, if a woman shoots at someone, it's always jealousy."

So Bobby wrote that down too and yawned and looked at the clock.

"I expect I've forgotten all the most significant facts," he said.

"You've forgotten Loo Leader for one thing," Olive said.

"Not me," protested Bobby with energy. "I'm putting a man on to see if he can find out anything. You remember what I told you about Leader that morning when we were digging up the dead man's body?"

Olive shuddered slightly, for that grisly story had always seemed to her one of unusual horror, and Bobby went on:

"Well, there are the main facts so far as we know them at present, and it does seem as if, if you put them together, some sort of pattern does show some sign of beginning to emerge."

"Does it?" asked Olive, not without irony.

"Only I've not an idea in the world," added Bobby with a sigh, "how we are going to get the evidence to act on. Oh, by the way, I wanted to ask you—what are tinned eggs?"

"Tinned eggs?" repeated Olive. "There aren't any, not that I ever heard of. Dried eggs you mean, don't you?"

"Leader said 'tinned eggs,'" Bobby replied. "I wondered what he meant."

Olive shook her head, said she had never heard of 'tinned' eggs, perhaps it was some sort of joke. Bobby thought that very likely, and leaving the subject of eggs, Olive said:

"There's one thing you've never said a word about and very likely the most important of all. All that money—£2,000, wasn't it?—left lying in the road."

"I've not forgotten it, not by a long way," Bobby assured her. "I only left it out because I can't even guess where it comes in. If it was the motive for the murder, why was it left lying behind in the road?"

CHAPTER XV

VOLUNTARY STATEMENTS

No great surprise to Bobby when he reached his office next morning to find that Mr. Kram was already there, anxious for an interview.

A trifle embarrassed he seemed how to start the conversation, nor did Bobby give him much help but waited patiently for him to begin.

"All cards on the table," Mr. Kram explained, "that's my slogan. And I live up to it."

He paused. Bobby waited. Mr. Kram continued:

"Of course I should like you to understand that what I want to say is private—private and personal. Very private."

He paused again and Bobby said:

"Mr. Kram, this is a public matter and I am in the public service."

"Oh, it's not that at all," protested Mr. Kram. "Only Maggie's my girl, and a girl's got her pride, and the truth is, she's badly in love with Larry Connor."

"Oh, yes," said Bobby. "Micky Burke's nephew. Yes?"

"Breaking her heart about him," said Mr. Kram gloomily. "You can guess how I feel. I don't know if she told you last night?"

"No," said Bobby.

"She said you had been asking her questions," Mr. Kram continued. "She's only a girl. Don't you think it might have been fairer to wait till she had her father with her?"

"No," said Bobby.

"I thought she was in her room," Mr. Kram went on, accepting this negative quite meekly. "Then I heard her come in. All upset she was. Crying her eyes out. I knew she had had a letter from Larry because I saw the envelope and I knew the writing."

"Oh, yes," said Bobby, interested.

"I didn't say anything. Let well alone. Let bad alone. That's my slogan. Not easy to live up to, either. You see, it's this way, Inspector. Larry wasn't in love with her."

"It would have been a good match for him though, wouldn't it?" Bobby remarked.

"I'll say this for him," Mr. Kram said. "I don't think that counted. It was just that he didn't feel like that. Not very nice for Maggie, not very nice for me in a way. Very unpleasant situation all around. The thing is, Larry had a girl already."

"Did Miss Kram know that?"

"Infatuated she was," Kram said. "Larry had a way with him— the Irish way. Share his last penny with you. Go to any amount of trouble to do anything for you. But two minutes after he had left you he had forgotten that you even existed. The Irish way. I may as well tell you the whole story. I gave him £10 to go back to Ireland. I don't want Maggie to know. She would never forgive me. You won't mention it?"

"Not unless it becomes a relevant fact," Bobby answered. "Nothing relevant can be hidden in a case of murder."

"That's what made me notice the letter when it came," Mr. Kram continued. "I thought he hadn't lost much time writing and then I saw the postmark was London. That worried me because what he said was, he would go back home and write and say good-bye. Made me a bit uneasy when I saw it came from London. To tell you the truth, I was more than worried. I thought perhaps it was to ask her to join him."

"Do you know what was really in the letter?"

"No, she didn't tell me. But I knew it wasn't that because the poor kid looked as if she were going to faint. And she started to cry. Well, I pretended not to notice. Well, at last I felt I couldn't stand it any longer. So I asked her. I said her letter was from Larry Connor, wasn't it? She didn't answer. She just ran out of the house and I can tell you I felt about as bad as she did. I suppose if her mother had lived—I lost her when Maggie was a kid, she hardly remembers her—well, I suppose it would have been different. But I didn't know what to do. I just sat there feeling bad and telling myself she would get over it in time. Then she came back, looking all washed up, and said you had been asking her questions. I don't know what right, Inspector, the police have to do a thing like that."

"Surely," Bobby said, "anyone has a right to ask questions. Why not? I would like to ask you one if I may. Do you know who the other girl is, the one Larry Connor is in love with?"

"Well, yes," Kram answered slowly. "Yes. At least I think so. If I'm right—Rachel Christopherson, the girl at the Conqueror Inn."

"Can you tell me what makes you think so?"

"Something he said once put in my mind that was why, why he wasn't taking any interest in Maggie," Kram answered. "I asked Micky Burke. Micky Burke didn't know for certain. But he said it might be that way. He said Larry had seemed different since they began stopping at the Conqueror Inn. Micky didn't like it. Words they had. You see, Micky and Larry, they are both Roman Catholics. Put quite a lot of store on their religion. But Christopherson's a freethinker. Doesn't hold with religion. Reads books about philosophy, Micky says. Like father, like daughter, that's Micky's slogan, and he hated to think Larry might marry an atheist and perhaps become an atheist, too."

"But why atheist?" Bobby asked. "A Roman Catholic can be a philosopher, can't he?"

Mr. Kram seemed to think this was more than doubtful and Bobby decided he wouldn't refer to St. Thomas Aquinas or the

'Summa Theologiae,' especially as he knew very little about either. Mr. Kram went on:

"Micky was upset, too, because he had a sort of idea that Larry might have been out there on the quiet at night, visiting the girl. He didn't know, but that's what he thought, and he didn't like it."

Bobby considered this. He was not inclined to put too much trust in Mr. Kram, but the story was plausible, it hung together, it explained much of his daughter's conduct. Jealousy, Olive had said, was the only reason that ever drove a woman to the use of a revolver. Here was the jealousy motive. Again here was a possible explanation of that breaking and entering at the Conqueror Inn. Possibly Larry, locked out, had nevertheless effected an entry, and Rachel, whether she had yielded to him or not, had been unwilling to raise an alarm.

"When did you see Larry last?" he asked.

"Monday morning, when he went off with Micky. He often went with Micky to lend him a hand."

"When did Micky see him last?"

"That would be the same evening, after they got back. Larry said he had been promised a lift on a Holyhead lorry. Apparently he went to London instead. Micky was as surprised as I was when I told him Larry's letter came from London."

"Have you any examples of Larry's writing?" Bobby asked.

Kram looked a little startled at the question but shook his head.

"His signature to a pay sheet, for instance?"

Again Kram shook his head.

"Larry wasn't working for me," he explained. "I never paid him anything—at least not directly. Once or twice I gave Micky something extra if he said Larry had been helping and I suppose he passed it on. But that's all."

"Where is he? Micky, I mean."

"Loading up. You might catch him before he gets off if you like to give my office a ring."

Bobby said he would try, and over the 'phone learned that neither did Micky possess any specimen of Larry's writing. Larry seldom wrote anything more than a postcard and Micky had never kept any of them. Had Larry a bank book? Bobby asked next. Micky didn't know but he didn't think it likely. A free lad with his money, and if Larry had a bank book, he would have it with him.

"Not the saving sort," said Micky over the line.

So Bobby thanked him, asked him to come round for a minute or two's talk before he started, and rang off.

"Not that I expect he'll be able to tell me anything," Bobby remarked to Kram, "but you can never tell. Some small detail or another. By the way, I don't think you've ever happened to mention where you were that Monday night?"

"Monday night?" repeated Mr. Kram. "No. Why?" He looked startled. "Good God," he exclaimed, "why do you want to know? You can't imagine that I—I—"

He left the sentence unfinished, staring at Bobby, his mouth open, in evident dismay. Bobby said:

"I'm not imagining anything. Why should I? Just a routine question. We have to check up on everybody, you know."

"Oh, well, yes, of course," Mr. Kram muttered, though still not looking too comfortable. "All the same, you know. A bit disturbing. Monday night? I was at home all evening. As a matter of fact, I generally am. Have to be up early in my line. Busy days, and I'm generally glad enough by evening for a pipe and a book and a chance to listen to the wireless."

"What is your private address?" Bobby asked.

"Oh, it's the same as the business. I had the upper part of the house fixed up for Maggie and me. Quite comfortable. And I'm always on the spot."

"Good idea," Bobby approved. "Very convenient, I'm sure. Did Miss Kram spend Monday evening at home, too?"

"Oh, yes. You can ask her if you like. Want confirmation, I suppose? Is that it?"

"Well, in a way," Bobby agreed. "Any other confirmation? Any friend happen to drop in? Any 'phone calls? Anything like that?"

Mr. Kram shook his head and looked depressed.

"No," he said. "No. Maggie and I just spent a quiet evening together as we often do and glad of it. We are both pretty well tired out by the end of the day. You don't expect to be asked to produce proof you've done what you do nine evenings out of ten."

"No, of course not," agreed Bobby. "What about servants?"

"That's no good," Kram answered, shaking his head again. "We have a daily woman, that's all—the wife of one of our loaders. She leaves supper ready. Sometimes Maggie cooks a little something extra. Then she clears the things away and Mrs. Hornby washes up when she comes. That's all."

"Oh, well," Bobby said cheerfully. "Quite natural, of course. Sometimes it's more suspicious to have an alibi than not to have one. Most people would say much the same as you've done. Another point. I was looking through the Firearms Register. You have a licence for a point three two revolver, I think?"

"Yes. For protection. When I was making some long trips with rather valuable loads. But it was a point forty-five that was used on Monday, wasn't it?"

"Oh, yes," agreed Bobby. "That's so. But I have reason to believe a shot was fired while Miss Kram was at the Conqueror Inn yesterday. She denied it. So did Miss Christopherson. Frankly, I wasn't satisfied. Could you let me see your revolver?"

"Certainly. I'll go and get it at once," declared Mr. Kram, and went off home; but Bobby was not much surprised when presently Kram rang up to say it had been mislaid, but every effort would be made to find it, and as soon as it was found it would be sent round.

"Means," Bobby told himself when he hung up after receiving this message, "that it is the pistol that was used at the Conqueror Inn and Miss Rachel has got it, but Kram hopes to get it back for my benefit."

In the meantime Micky had put in an appearance. He looked pale and worn, Bobby thought, as if he had not slept well of late, and he seemed nervous, too, and ill at ease. But he confirmed in every detail everything that Kram had said, and he admitted that his nephew had been much upset by Maggie's open display of her feelings.

"He did know about it, then?" Bobby said.

"He couldn't help," Micky asserted. "How could he, and she making it as plain as a lighted-up window in the blackout?"

"He didn't return her feelings at all?"

"He did not. It was scared of her he was. Scared."

"What about Miss Rachel Christopherson of the Conqueror Inn?"

Micky bestowed an angry scowl on Bobby.

"I suppose it was the boss put you on that?" he growled. "He had no call to."

"Do you think it's a fact?"

"If I do, it's not along of anything Larry ever said, and me telling him that to wed a heretic or worse was a sure road to trouble nor a thing any of our kin had ever done. But I had seen the way he looked at her, and her pretending not to notice; that's the best card a girl can play and well they know it. Then what was he out for at night and not sleeping in his own bed but maybe in a bed where it was mortal sin to be? But he denied it to my face, and it's as wise as Solomon you have to be to know where the truth ends and lies begin."

"So you have," agreed Bobby with some feeling.

He asked one or two more questions, trying to find out what Micky knew or thought of Mr. Kram's attitude towards his daughter's infatuation. He tried to discover, too, what was Micky's own feeling about it all and more especially his opinion of his employer.

There emerged a curious contradiction. Everything that Micky said was in Mr. Kram's favour. A considerate, a generous employer. Everything, too, he said confirmed in every detail the story Kram told. Yet Bobby seemed to feel a most curious undercurrent of strong emotion that, unless he was letting his imagination deceive him, was something resembling a passionate, deeply felt enmity.

But why should Micky, who spoke so well of his employer, who backed him up in every detail, entertain for him the deep, fierce anger that Bobby believed he saw smouldering, and sometimes aflame, in the depths of the Irishman's small, bleak eyes?

Bobby said:

"Mr. Burke, I want you to listen to this very carefully. Your nephew, Larry Connor, is the only man we know of with whom we can't get in touch. He is the only man we can hear of who has, so to say, vanished from his usual surroundings. So, you see, we have to ask ourselves—is it possible it is Larry Connor whose body we found out there on the moor?"

"And how could it be possible," Micky answered steadily, "when I was with him till near midnight on Monday and now the boss tells me there's a letter come he wrote from London to Miss Maggie?"

"Yes, that seems conclusive, doesn't it?" Bobby agreed. "Larry was like a son to you, they tell me."

"He was that and more than a son is to some fathers," Micky answered simply. "Not much more than a babe only beginning to take notice when I had him first after my sister died, God rest her soul. He was all I had and a good lad as ever lived."

"You said 'was.' Why do you say 'was'?" Bobby asked.

"For that now he's grown, he's left me," Micky answered. "Comes once or twice a year maybe to see the old uncle and then off again. Not like it—was," he said with a faint emphasis on the last word.

"You understand our difficulty," Bobby said. "We can't identify the body. Someone smashed in the dead man's face—deliberately. Pretty beastly. Devilish."

"Devilish it was," Micky said; and now there was no doubt of the strong emotion in his voice, the deep, bitter hatred in his eyes. "Let be the man who did it to roast a thousand year in hell. And soon."

He flung out the last word with an emotion, an emphasis that startled Bobby. He seemed to feel how questioningly Bobby was looking at him. More quietly but still with feeling, he said:

"Who but a beast that was worse than the beasts in the field would be doing a thing like that to the image of God that is man?"

The remark puzzled Bobby. It seemed to show an aspect of Micky's character that hitherto he had not suspected. There was no more he had to ask, but it was with an uneasy feeling that he saw the Irishman depart, for he had seemed to feel in Micky's last words a threat implicit that might be a hint of still worse things to come.

Yet if he believed the dead man to be his nephew, why should he so strongly deny it? Why should he seek to protect the murderer of the boy he had brought up from a baby, for whom it was quite certain he felt a strong affection?

Incredible, Bobby felt, that he should do what, if the dead man were really Larry, he was certainly doing.

Yet if the murdered man were a stranger, why should he show so much emotion at the thought of the mutilation the dead features had undergone?

A contradiction there, and one that Bobby saw no way at present to resolve.

He was still brooding over these two strange interviews, neither of which did he feel he had succeeded in understanding, when word was brought to him that Captain Peter Wintle was there and would like to see the inspector in charge of the moor murder, as the papers had begun to call it.

"Well, that's all to the good," Bobby commented to Sergeant Payne, who had brought him the information, "it's when witnesses begin to make voluntary statements that you begin to get at the truth."

CHAPTER XVI
CAPTAIN WINTLE'S INDIGNATION

PLAIN ENOUGH THAT Captain Peter Wintle was in truculent mood, and indeed he took no notice either of Bobby's greeting when he entered the room or of the offer of a chair pushed forward. Abruptly he said:

"I want to know what you are up to?"

"Meaning?" asked Bobby gently.

"Oh, you know," snapped Wintle. "My C.O. asked me about it. I hadn't heard. He had. I said I would come straight along and ask you what it meant. Then I shall consult a solicitor. Do you think I have any intention of putting up with police snooping round, asking my men questions about me? Jolly for discipline."

Bobby in his mind put a big black mark against the name of Sergeant Payne. Payne had been carefully and emphatically warned to be most discreet in his inquiries, to use his utmost endeavour not to start any gossip. And here was the result.

"The whole camp's buzzing," said Wintle bitterly.

Bobby, in his mind, increased the bigness and the blackness of the mark against Payne. Never again could he trust Payne with any investigation that went beyond the most elementary routine work. He contemplated moodily sending Payne back to the uniform branch—minus his stripes.

"It'll have to go before the brigadier," said Wintle. "If I could have found him I would have tackled this Leader fellow at once myself, but he had cleared out."

"Eh?" said Bobby sitting up sharply. "What's that?"

"I said I would have tackled this Loo Leader man of yours then and there if I could have found him," Wintle repeated. "Just as well I didn't perhaps or I might have been tempted to give him a good thrashing."

"Rather fond of giving people good thrashings, aren't you?" Bobby murmured, and as Wintle flushed and glared, Bobby went on: "Let's get this straight. I do wish you would sit down, though. You know, extraordinary how difficult it is to get people to tell a straight story. Even captains in the army apparently. Now, will you explain exactly what all this is—about someone called Leader, is it?"

"Isn't he the man you've sent to 'make inquiries' as you call it? About me? I want to know why. Then I'm going to see a solicitor."

"Well, that's often very wise," Bobby agreed, "but it's even more wise to be sure of your facts first. I gather from what you say that a man named Leader has been asking questions about you. And that he said he came from us?"

"Didn't he?"

"I can assure you," Bobby answered with perfect truth, "that we have sent no one of that name to make any inquiries about you or anyone else—there's no one of that name in the force for one thing. Can you describe him?"

Wintle shook his head. He looked puzzled. And relieved. Very relieved. When Bobby again suggested that he should sit down, he complied. He said:

"No, I didn't see him myself. I knew nothing about it at the time."

"If it's the man I think ..." Bobby said and left the sentence unfinished.

He was feeling a little excited, a little puzzled, too. More than interesting, he thought, this sudden return of Loo Leader into the orbit of the case. Also he hurriedly rubbed out in his mind that big, black mark he had placed against the name of Sergeant Payne.

"Captain Wintle," he said, "if a man named Leader has been making any inquiries about you—or about anyone else—he has been doing it on his own account and for his own reasons. He has no authority from us, no connection with us whatever."

"Not one of your men at all?" Wintle asked, still looking both astonished and relieved and yet doubtful as well.

"Most certainly not," answered Bobby, "and if he is the man I think, I'll have a talk with him as soon as possible. Have you definite evidence he claimed to be a policeman?"

"I don't know," Wintle answered. "I don't know much about it. All I know is the C.O. sent for me and said that was what he had heard and what was it all about? Naturally he was upset. You can't expect a C.O. to take no notice if he hears police are asking questions about one of his officers. I'll have the skin off the chap if I can catch him," added Wintle grimly. "It's a bit of a relief to hear he is not a policeman. I was half afraid you suspected I might have something to do with this murder."

"Oh, we do," said Bobby.

Wintle, who had been getting to his feet to depart on the assumption that the interview was over, sat down again abruptly.

"What do you mean by that?" he asked, calmly enough but with a catch in his breath, too.

"What I said," Bobby answered. "We suspect you are in some way or another mixed up in the murder of the unknown man found buried near the Conqueror Inn, and it looks to me as if this Mr. Leader you tell me about thought so, too. He may know something. In fact, it is fairly certain he either does or thinks he does. Or why is he asking these questions? So the first thing now for us to do is to get hold of him and ask him what he knows—or thinks he knows."

Wintle was looking more and more uncomfortable. Even the bravest man, guilty or innocent, can hardly face with composure the knowledge that he is under suspicion of the crime of murder, even though as yet that suspicion is but faint and distant.

"Don't you think you had better tell me yourself?" Bobby asked gently. "Much wiser always to tell the police anything there is to tell. I mean, if you're innocent. Of course, if you're guilty—"

"Guilty?" repeated Wintle in a voice that began on a high note and ended on a low one, and whereas at first he had been very red now he had become very pale. "Come to that, has it?" he said with a harsh, unnatural laugh.

"I said 'if,'" Bobby reminded him. "Clearly this man suspects something. Or why is he asking questions? I don't know what his motive is. It may be a pure thirst for justice. Not very likely perhaps. But possible. A pure thirst for justice generally brings people to us.

Only sometimes they are a bit shy or nervous and want to be sure. Afraid of being laughed at. Or it may be blackmail. Can't tell. Or it may be something quite different, I am only suggesting that if there is anything you can think of that Leader may know of, then it would be wise for you—and might be useful to us—if you told us. You will notice I assume that you are innocent."

"Not you," said Wintle harshly. "What you mean is, you assume I'm guilty and hadn't I better out with a confession? Sorry to disappoint you. Naturally I shall consult a solicitor at once."

"Your wisest course, no doubt," agreed Bobby. "We shall be pleased to see any solicitor you ask to represent you any time he wishes. We shall point out to him the coincidence in time of the injury to your eye with the injuries found on the dead man's body. We shall have to admit that we don't find your story of the door-post in the black-out very convincing. I notice, too, that you are rather prone to think in terms of giving people thrashings. It is what you thought of at once in connection with this Leader person. Then there is the fact that the murder took place near the Conqueror Inn and that you have been a visitor there several times lately—in fact, the only guest they seem to have had for some time. You explain you stayed there out of sympathy for the family of a man to whom you owed your life at Dunkirk and who lost his own life there. Was that the only reason?"

"Isn't it enough?"

"Well, that's what I asked, isn't it? Can you tell me where you were on the Monday night—the night of the murder?"

Captain Wintle was looking paler than ever. He said:

"I was at the camp. I think that Monday night I had a look round to make sure the sentries were on their toes. On active service a careless sentry may mean disaster—defeat. I try to make sure they understand that. So I do a prowl round at night sometimes. I daresay some of them would remember my going the rounds that night."

"You see, what I have to remember is this," Bobby said. "I have to ask myself even if your sentries saw you, if there was also time, in between whiles so to say, to use a car or a cycle you might have had waiting in order to pay a visit to—the Conqueror Inn."

Captain Wintle said:

"I see you'll have me hanged yet."

"Well, of course, if you're guilty," murmured Bobby deprecatingly. "Not that hanging anyone is any business or interest of ours. Our job is to say to the law of England, 'We think such and such a man committed such and such an action, and this is why we think so.' Then it is for the law of England to say if it thinks so too, and, if it does, what ought to be done. A policeman may call himself a soldier of the truth."

"Why am I supposed to have committed this murder?" Wintle asked.

"Now, please," Bobby protested, "we haven't got anywhere near supposing that as yet. Not by a long way. We have only got as far as asking questions and noting the replies we get—or don't get. Also noticing such facts as we are sure of—curious facts, some of them. For example, the fact that two nights before the murder someone broke into the Conqueror Inn by removing a pane of glass from the window of the bar."

He paused. Wintle made no comment. But his bright quick eyes were steady upon Bobby's face, and Bobby said:

"Sorry. A slip. I should have said the kitchen window—not the window of the bar."

"A trap, I suppose," Wintle commented, "to see if I knew?"

"And did you?" Bobby asked. "Anyhow, you knew there might be a trap, I think. Even that is not without interest. Also there does seem to emerge a possible theory of what happened, a possible explanation of both black eye and thrashing. Suppose—I'll do a little supposing now if I may. But only supposing, you understand. Suppose a Mr. X. happened to run into a man—an unknown man— trying to break into the Conqueror Inn. Or even leaving it. Well, that might have led to questions by Mr. X, resentment by the other fellow, and finally to a thrashing for him and a black eye for Mr. X."

Wintle made no reply, but he passed an uneasy finger round his neck under his collar, as if he felt a growing tightness there that made breathing difficult. It was an unconscious gesture Bobby had seen before, when the net of circumstantial evidence seemed to be drawing closer and tighter. Bobby went on:

"Suppose again that on the Monday night you thought you would take an hour or two when you would not be missed because it would be thought you were inspecting someone somewhere, to run over by car or cycle perhaps—or even on foot. About fifteen or sixteen miles, isn't it, or more? Well, a man in good hard army training might manage that in two hours on foot, going straight across the moor. Stiff going, but possible. Well, suppose that happened, whether on foot or by car or cycle, and suppose he took with him a service revolver—oh, not his own, of course, he would hardly be so simple as that—and suppose—"

"Suppose," interrupted Wintle, "suppose he found the same fellow again entering or leaving the Conqueror Inn and suppose this time he shot him. You are good at supposing, Inspector. How many men have you supposed to the gallows?"

"Why, none, I think," Bobby answered quietly, "but there are some I have supposed to answer before the law for their acts and so others have been able to go in peace and quiet about their daily business. Does that strike you as an unworthy activity? Undesirable, no doubt, from the point of view of an—assassin. Well, let's leave supposing. Here's another fact. Miss Rachel Christopherson."

Wintle's self-control, already strained, snapped.

"Leave her name out of it," he said in a low, intense voice.

"Captain Wintle," Bobby answered sternly, "in a case of murder, no name, either yours or mine or any man's, can be left out. Miss Christopherson is very clearly 'in' already. You'll find mention in every newspaper account of the landlord of the Conqueror Inn and his wife and daughter. Reporters already know that entry was made one night but that nothing was missed and that no complaint was made. Reporters know, too, of the presence of Miss Rachel in the inn, and I am afraid they are cynical enough, or experienced enough, whichever way you look at it, to start guessing. They daren't say anything yet, because they aren't sure, and they have a healthy respect for libel actions and contempt of court and so on. But I have already had them coming to see me and dropping hints about crimes of passion and father avenging his daughter's honour and all that sort of thing."

"Dirty-minded brutes," growled Wintle, his cheeks that had been so pale before now flushing red again.

"Oh, I don't know," Bobby said tolerantly. "Such things do happen. Of course, I told them to do their own guessing—and on their own responsibility. That shut them up for the time. But I shall be very surprised if some of them pretty soon don't find out that a certain young man has vanished from his usual surroundings. Do you know anything about a young man named Larry Connor?"

"No," said Wintle.

But then he got up and went to the window and stood there, his back to Bobby. Bobby said:

"Do you know—I think perhaps you do."

Wintle did not move for a minute or two. Then he came back and sat down and again those quick yet steady eyes of his looked straight at Bobby.

"I know nothing of him," he said. "To my knowledge I have never seen or spoken to him. But I do remember hearing Rachel— Miss Christopherson—say to her father that Larry Connor was there and would he attend to him because she was going to keep out of the way till he had gone. I believe he was driving a lorry and stopped at the Conqueror Inn in passing for a drink or something. I never saw him."

"You see," Bobby explained, "we think it just possible Larry Connor may be the dead man. But there's no proof. Identification made difficult by the rather horrible mutilation that was carried out. Perhaps proof will turn up somewhere. Perhaps this Leader you've told us about may know. He'll be asked. Oh, there's another point. Miss Christopherson seems to be in possession of a revolver."

"I'm sure she isn't," Wintle said quickly. "I told her to make sure—I mean, I asked them if they had any firearms. They haven't, not even a shotgun for rabbits. Nothing."

"Why did you ask that?"

"It's a lonely spot," Wintle answered.

"A curious question all the same," Bobby remarked. "I wonder— well, never mind. But I think it is a fact that Miss Rachel is in possession of a pistol. I heard a shot fired at the inn, and when I ran round to see what was happening, Miss Rachel and Miss Kram were together and I could smell powder in the air."

"Miss Kram," Wintle repeated. "What was she there for?"

"They both denied a shot had been fired," Bobby went on. "I think they lied. I think somehow only a strong motive would make Miss Rachel lie. A difficult case. Difficult to see a way clear through such a tangle of emotional relationships. Two girls talking and a shot fired. Why? Was it one of the girls fired? Or someone else? No one else visible but plenty of hiding places in those vast old barns and stables. If one of the girls fired, why? When women take to shooting, generally the cause is jealousy. Was it this time? If so, who was jealous and of whom? I will ask you to regard it as confidential, but a suggestion has been made to us that Miss Kram was interested in Larry Connor."

"You seem to have got it all taped out," Wintle muttered.

"Not by a long way," Bobby retorted. "Nothing like it. There is only a confusion of possibilities, no one of which may be correct, and a wooden box stuffed with bank-notes that fits into none of them."

"If a shot was fired," Wintle asked, "why should you think it was Miss Christopherson rather than Miss Kram?"

"I don't," Bobby said. "What I said was that Miss Rachel had a pistol in her possession. At least, I thought so. But I was helpless. I had no grounds for arresting her. I couldn't search her. A man can't search a woman. She ran a bluff on me and brought it off. All the same she had that pistol on her, and I am wondering if it is the one that fired the shot that killed the man whose name I do not know."

CHAPTER XVII

ON WATCH

Captain Peter Wintle had gone, looking an older man by far than when he had come, and Bobby still sat and stared at the blank wall opposite. He roused himself presently to set in motion various routine inquiries. Obviously important to get in touch with the man, Leader, as soon as possible. Already instructions had been given for unostentatious watch to be kept on him. Soon information came that both Leader's lorries were out, and he with one of them. Nothing unexpected in that, for it was known Leader was working on a contract with a Fleetwood firm. But the lorries required only one driver each, and the lorry driven by Leader had carried Alf Hall also, as a passenger apparently. Nothing therefore to prevent Leader from alighting at some spot or another and being picked up again on the return trip.

A small independent road transport business had its advantages, Bobby reflected, for those who wished to play hide and seek with the law. He remembered, too, that examination of the box of bank-notes found on the scene of the murder had revealed the presence of fish scales as well as of coal dust. Fleetwood suggested fish, but then both fish and coal were common loads. K. and K.M.T.C., for instance, carried both often enough, as he had taken pains to find out.

Not much help there, Bobby felt, and as he could not expect to hear the result of other inquiries just yet, he turned his attention to work waiting on his desk. That dealt with, he got out his own small two-seater he was using now for official work since it needed less petrol than the ordinary police car, and started off once more on the now familiar moorland road that led to the Conqueror Inn.

Once more as he drew near he was struck by its aloof and secret air. Solitary it stood on the ridge of the great bare moor that fell away in a gentle slope on either side and none could approach without being seen and noted. Then came a rush of great lorries, four of them racing past the inn towards Bobby. The road was narrow and he drew aside to let them pass. As he did so, the thought came to him to wonder whether this renewal of traffic on the road that, until the K. and K. people found it, had been so little used, was welcome to the inmates of the inn. It certainly did not seem, he thought, that much effort had been made to attract the patronage of travellers.

He had halted to let those lorries pass. There was a pair of binoculars in the car. He adjusted them on the inn. No movement was visible, no sign of life. Was it only his fancy, he wondered, that gave the place its curious air of silent watchfulness, of being, as it were, eternally upon its guard? All England, for that matter, was to-day silently watchful on guard. But against a known and open enemy, and what strange fear or danger was it that forced the Conqueror Inn to wear this aspect of attention? As he watched he saw a movement at the attic window, the window he supposed from which light shining by reason of a displaced curtain had attracted the attention of a Home Guard patrol.

The distance was too great for him to be able to see who it was, but certainly some human being had stood for a moment at that upper window and then had closed it and gone away. Almost at once he saw a woman come out from the inn door and stand there looking in his direction. Rachel, he thought, for though he could not be sure at that distance, he seemed to recognize the rhythmic grace, as of some free creature of the open lands, one who knew nothing of the cramping life of cities, that he remembered as instinct in every movement she made.

"A watch kept up there in the upper windows," Bobby muttered to himself, "and a warning called down that someone was coming. So the girl comes out to see who it is. And now everything will be all nicely ready for me by the time I get there."

He started his car again. When he drew up before the inn Rachel was standing in the road before the door. She had a little the air of being on guard and he wondered if she hoped to prevent him from entering. He greeted her and asked if Mr. Christopherson was in. It appeared not. He had gone to Midwych on business and Rachel did not know when he would be back. So Bobby said he was sorry to have missed him and added carelessly that he had thought he saw him at the attic window as he drove up.

"Someone else perhaps?" he asked and Rachel said:

"There is no one in the house but myself and my mother."

"Perhaps it was her, then?" Bobby remarked.

"It may have been, why not?" Rachel said. "Why do you ask?"

Bobby did not explain that the impression made upon him had been of someone constantly on watch or how that thought had instantly linked itself in his mind with his recollection of Mr. Christopherson out on the moor as if searching. Watch at home, search on the moor. Watch and search. But why? For whom or for what? He said:

"Will you let me go over the house and see for myself there is no one else here?"

She looked at him steadily and delayed answering for a time. Then she said:

"No. I think not. No. Why should I? You can come again when my father's here and ask him if you like."

"May I come in and wait till he gets back?" Bobby asked.

As before she looked at him steadily and in silence for some moments before replying. He felt she was asking herself what reason lay behind his request, and that it troubled her. She said finally:

"Why do you ask that? You know this is a public house and licensed, and everyone has a right to accommodation."

She went back into the building. He followed her; and she made no comment when he followed her, too, into the kitchen, where Mrs. Christopherson was sitting with some sewing before her, but not as though she were much occupied with it. She took no notice when Bobby entered, she might not even have been aware of his presence, but he noticed that she was fidgeting with her feet and that her toes seemed restless inside her shoes. People exercising self-control so often forget that agitation may show in movements of the feet as easily and as plainly as in the features or as in restless hands.

"If you don't mind, I'll wait here," Bobby said.

Rachel sat down by the window, her hands in her lap. She sat upright and still and yet even so managed to convey an impression of a lithe and active grace. Bobby, who had a natural eye for form, told himself she would make an ideal model for a painter, that is, for one with genius enough to reproduce that effect of, as it were, a still and motionless rhythm. Mrs. Christopherson gathered up her sewing materials and without looking at Bobby went out of the room. Bobby said:

"I am sorry if I have disturbed your mother."

But the thought in his mind was that Mrs. Christopherson had gone to make sure all was in order and everything as it should be— and not solely from the careful housewife's point of view either. He told himself sadly that police work must be a lot easier when you could use Gestapo methods and just bang about anywhere and anyhow, without bothering at all about people's rights and privacies. Or would it? Perhaps after all Gestapo methods were not the best fitted for arriving at the truth.

Rachel, still motionless, her hands folded in her lap, said:

"Why do you torment us so?"

"Because a man was done to death near here not yet a week ago," Bobby answered.

"Yes, I know," she said, and gave somehow the impression of admitting his reply.

"Because also," he went on, "I think you know more than you have told me yet."

"I have told you all I can," she said.

"But not perhaps all you know," he replied. "'Can' is a word that may have its own meaning."

Again she looked at him long and steadily before replying. Then she said:

"You are very clever, aren't you? Very quick."

"Very persistent might be nearer the truth perhaps," he answered. "I've just had a talk with Captain Wintle," he added, after a pause.

She made no comment, but her attitude stiffened suddenly. If before she had seemed like deep water flowing so quietly it appeared still, now she gave the impression of water frozen suddenly into immobility. When she continued silent, Bobby went on:

"You see, he is uneasy because he thinks he is suspected of complicity in the murder." Still she made no comment, but he felt that she was listening with almost anguished intensity, listening as a condemned man might listen to the reading of his death sentence. "Of course, he is quite right about that," Bobby added.

At that she turned on him sharply and angrily.

"Why?" she asked. She got to her feet, erect and fierce and graceful still in her attitude of strong resentment and indignation. Like an offended deity she stood, tall and upright, one hand held out. "Why?" she repeated. "Why not my father as well? Or do you?"

"Yes," said Bobby.

At that she stared, losing her aspect of offended goddess to turn into a bewildered and very astonished young girl.

"Oh, that's silly," she protested. "Perhaps you suspect me, too?"

"Yes," he said once more.

She stared again and then she laughed outright, a rich, bubbling laugh. She sat down once more and Bobby thought somehow that mingling with her first surprise and indignation and her later amusement, there was also a feeling of a great relief.

"Oh, well," she said. "We can't all be guilty—all three of us, can we?" she asked with once more that low bubbling laugh of hers.

"Why not?" said Bobby.

"Oh, well, now then," she said, looking at him.

"Not all of you could have fired the shot that killed," Bobby agreed, "but you could all three have been concerned in what happened."

"I suppose we could, I suppose you are right," she admitted with an air of considering an entirely new and not very welcome proposition. "I see what you mean. Yes. Well, we weren't. Why should we?"

"If I knew why the murder was done, I should know it all, I expect," Bobby said. "I have to remember that there is at least identity of time and place both for you and for your father. I have reason to think Captain Wintle was near here on Saturday night and if that's so, it does suggest that possibly he was here also on the night of the murder. Difficult to think there is no connection between the fact that he got a bruised eye that Saturday night and the other fact that the dead man's body also showed bruises probably received on the same night. And I'm not satisfied about the attempt, whether it succeeded or not, to force an entry here. I think you must know more about that than you have told me."

"All the same, we don't," she retorted with energy. "We found the glass out on Sunday morning and father put it back and that's all we know."

"Or need to know?" Bobby asked. "There is a young man named Larry Connor. I think you know him, don't you?"

He could see the question troubled her profoundly and again she took time to answer. But this time her gaze was on the floor, not on him.

"You mean the young man who helps with a K. and K. lorry?" she asked. "You don't think he is the man who was killed, do you? Father heard that he had gone away."

"I must ask you this," Bobby said. "It is suggested he was in love with you. Is that true?"

At that she stared again, her eyes wide, her mouth a little open, apparently very much surprised.

"Good gracious, no," she said. "Whatever made you think that? Why, we had hardly spoken."

Bobby thought to himself that sometimes lovers are oddly tongue-tied and that there have been cases when men have loved—and women too perhaps—with no word spoken on either side.

Rachel was still looking at him in what seemed genuine astonishment. But how could he be sure that it was genuine? Deep waters he had always felt from the beginning of this case and in them strange eddies. Neither had spoken again when they heard a step approaching down the long flagged passage that led to the kitchen. The door opened and Mr. Christopherson came in and stood there, looking gloomily at Bobby.

"I thought that was your car outside," he said. "Why have you come to trouble us again?"

CHAPTER XVIII
GUESSES

To Bobby's surprise, before he could speak, Rachel answered the question. She said:

"There must be trouble for all when a man has been killed."

Bobby noticed that she did not use the word 'murdered.' Mr. Christopherson came across the room to the fireplace and stood there. He said, almost as if speaking to himself:

"Death's so common now with men dying all round the world by the hundred and the thousand."

"Is that what your philosophy teaches?" Bobby asked, watching the big man curiously, "that death's so common it has no significance?"

"The insignificance of death, perhaps," Christopherson answered musingly, "but still more the significance of life. That matters. Well, why have you come again?"

"I was telling Miss Christopherson," Bobby explained. "There is a young man named Connor, Larry Connor. He used to help with one of the K. and K. lorries, one that stopped here sometimes. I expect you remember him. We are trying to get in touch with him. So far we have failed. We think it possible he may be the dead man. We don't know. It is only a possibility. We have to consider it. We have received information that he was greatly attracted by Miss Christopherson. I thought it best to come and ask her about it."

"A silly tale," Christopherson answered. "I remember the young man you mean. I doubt if he and Rachel ever spoke to each other. They did once. I remember that. He tried to be familiar with Rachel, asked questions she thought rather impudent. Next time when she was serving and he came in, she called me and asked me to attend to him. I don't think he came again. Silly gossip some fool invented for the sake of talking. Larry Connor may have talked loosely, young men do sometimes, boast about every girl they see. I don't know why you paid it any attention."

"The suggestion is," Bobby said, "that that is why an attempt was made to break in here the Saturday night before the murder. Please understand the suggestion is not ours. I don't want any mistake about that. But it has been made to us. A newspaper man told us there was talk going on on those lines. Possibly he invented the talk himself to try to fish for information from us. I told him we had nothing to say and he had better remember the libel and slander laws and he said newspaper men were brought up on them from birth. The point is, you realize that if it were true, it would provide a motive at once—the father protecting his daughter. A classical motive."

"It seems the most utter nonsense to me," Christopherson said harshly, and yet, or so Bobby thought, with relief in his voice and manner. "If I caught any young man making a nuisance of himself to Rachel, I might give him a good thrashing—"

"Father," Rachel interrupted warningly.

"Well, I might, but I shouldn't shoot him," Christopherson retorted and then added: "Oh, you mean the dead man had had a thrashing and the police may think what I said means it was me. Well, if they do, they must. But it wasn't and I don't know who it was."

"Well, at present," Bobby said, "I am more inclined to think it was Captain Wintle."

"Captain Wintle?" Christopherson repeated. "That's nonsense too. He's not been here for two or three weeks. Has he?"

This last question was addressed to Rachel. She shook her head in reply, but Bobby noticed that her cheeks grew suddenly red.

Christopherson looked back at Bobby. He said:

"You can't mean you are beginning to suspect him. What on earth do you think he has to do with it?"

"Well, you see, he has stayed here several times," Bobby pointed out. "Your only visitor. One wonders why. Perhaps there is an attraction here. No one who has seen Miss Christopherson could be surprised." He stopped to make a little bow to her whose cheeks now were flaming. "So there's an obvious possibility. Suppose he happened to come across the dead man—Larry Connor or another—trying to break in here. That would account for the injuries both the dead man—whoever he was—and Captain Wintle received, the same night. I mean, if a fight of some sort developed. And if the same thing happened again, on the following Monday, there might have been more serious consequences."

Christopherson was smiling now and Bobby had once more the impression that what he said was giving the father, as it had done before the daughter, considerable relief. He wondered if they had feared his suspicions might take another road, and that was why they had both in turn given him this feeling of a relaxed tension. There was even a touch of good-natured contempt in Christopherson's voice as he said:

"That all seems rather wild guessing—rather silly, too, if you don't mind my saying so. Far fetched. You can sit and guess and guess for ever and be wrong for ever."

"When we know so little and when those who know so much tell us nothing, what else can we do but guess?" Bobby retorted.

"I am afraid you mean that for us," Christopherson said, smiling again. "I can only repeat that we know no more than you do who was killed or why. If you won't believe us, we can't help it. It's the truth all the same. Isn't it, Rachel?"

"Yes, father," she said.

She left her seat by the window to come and stand, at his side before the great old fashioned fireplace. Tall man and tall daughter they stood there side by side, and together they gave out an aura, so to say, of implacable unswerving force. Whatsoever they made up their minds to, they would carry through, Bobby felt. Nothing mean, petty or malicious, he thought, would they ever be guilty of. But he was by no means so sure that when their wills or their consciences approved, they would draw back before any convention or consideration of law, of custom, of ordinary every day respectability. Nor did he feel sure that there was anything, even to the shedding of blood, from which they would shrink if, for any reason at all, they felt justified. In them he seemed to see alive again the old grim Puritan spirit. He realized abruptly that he had been sitting there silent for some minutes and that they were waiting for him to speak.

"Captain Wintle told me," he said, "that his life was saved at Dunkirk by your son. He told me, too, that afterwards your son himself was killed there."

Immediately Bobby was aware of a sudden change in the attitude of both father and daughter. Gone now was that air of invincibility which before had lain about them like a living thing. He saw Rachel start, heard her catch her breath. Even more revealing was the abrupt stiffening of her father's attitude, as though holding himself erect against a swift and sudden blow. It was like a summoning of all his forces to receive and to repel attack.

Rather to his surprise, Bobby found that he, too, was standing up. He said:

"I have my duty to do. I am sorry." He repeated. "I am sorry. I must do my duty."

"I know," Christopherson answered quietly, and with an infinite gentleness he laid his hand on Rachel's shoulder. It was a gesture that said as plainly as words: "Be strong." To Bobby he said, still very quietly: "Go on."

"Is it true that your son was killed?"

Christopherson, instead of answering, turned and went out of the room. Rachel turned, too, and stood with her back to Bobby, looking down at the embers smouldering in the great fireplace so that he could not see her face. Christopherson came back. He handed Bobby some papers. One was the usual War Office official announcement that Private Derek Christopherson was missing, believed killed. Another was a letter from the officer commanding the company in which the young man had served. It spoke of him in terms of high praise. It referred, too, to the pleasure his violin playing had given all ranks, and how it had helped to pass the tedious hours of what had come to be known at the time as the 'phoney' war. In restrained language it gave the story of a fellow soldier who had seen a bomb from a German aeroplane burst where young Christopherson and two or three others had been standing, and then, when the smoke and dust cleared away, nothing—nothing but that horror of shattered, scattered human bodies which modern war has made a commonplace. There were two other letters to the same effect from comrades, one of them another musician who had helped young Christopherson in giving concerts.

Bobby read the papers through and handed them back.

"Your son was evidently a very clever musician," he said. "I have been told so before. I think he played with the Midwych

Philharmonic Orchestra, didn't he? Perhaps he inherited his talent from you, Mr. Christopherson?"

"I am no musician," Christopherson said heavily. "Why do you ask that?"

"Miss Christopherson," Bobby continued, "is a violinist, too, perhaps?"

She did not turn or give any sign of answering and her father said:

"I don't know why you should ask. I don't know why we should answer. But I suppose you could find out. You could ask the neighbours. Perhaps you have already. I think you are thorough in your methods. I think very likely you know already that Rachel does not play."

"Derek was the only musician among us," Rachel said then, still without looking round. "Every one about here knows that."

"If he inherited his talent from anyone, he got it from my father, his grandfather," Christopherson said. "There is a story that my grandfather used to play the fiddle. I don't know if it's true. Very likely it is. Why should it interest you?"

"I suppose I am guessing again," Bobby said. "I have an uncomfortable feeling that even if you don't know what you say you don't know, yet all the same there is a good deal you could tell me if you would. Well, I've given you every opportunity, but I think you have made up your mind you won't. So what can I do but guess?"

"A guess is still only a guess," Christopherson said.

"Even a guess needs some facts to build on," Bobby said. "When I was here, before, that time when I thought I heard a shot fired, though both Miss Kram and Miss Rachel denied it, I noticed in the big barn a music stand and a violin as if someone had been practising."

Very quickly Rachel said:

"I have been trying to learn, to teach myself. That's all."

"I don't think I much believe you," Bobby said. "I'm sorry, but there it is."

She was silent. Mr. Christopherson was looking down darkly at Bobby. He gave the impression of one standing at bay. Bobby knew well how they were suffering. But he had to do what he had to do. He went on:

"I have to get to the bottom of all this. You are not giving me much help. It would save us all a great deal if you would tell me the truth. I mean the whole truth. You see, in the end, the truth has got to come out."

"It would be kinder," Rachel said, "if you would tell us what you have in your mind."

"Very well I will," Bobby answered, "it's only that I thought it might be easier if you would speak of your own accord. There are little things I've noticed and even small things have a meaning. Odd things, too. Odd, for example, that an innkeeper should show so little desire for custom. Odd, again, that Mr. Christopherson should choose to sleep alone in one of the attics. Odd again that Miss Rachel should practise playing the violin in one of the barns instead of in the house. Odd that as I got near the house I thought I saw someone at the attic window. Possibly not odd at all that Miss Rachel would not give me permission to go over the house. Nor had I a search warrant."

"You can go over the house as much as you like," Rachel interrupted, "now my father is here."

"At another guess," Bobby retorted, "Mrs. Christopherson has been busy since I got here."

"That's enough of guessing games," Christopherson interrupted harshly. "In plain words, please."

"A plain question then," Bobby said. "Was your son in fact killed at Dunkirk or did he get back? If he did—did he, instead of reporting to his battalion, come here back to you, and have you kept him hidden here, a deserter, liable to arrest and punishment?"

Christopherson flung back his head. Loudly and clearly he answered.

"No," he said. "All guesses. Guesses. Guesses are worth nothing."

"Then who," Bobby asked sharply, "is it in the big barn there across the yard? Two or three times I've seen someone looking out—a man, I think."

"There's no one, no one, no one," Rachel shrilled, but Bobby answered:

"Look, look there."

He pointed from the window. A figure had shown for a moment at the door of the great barn and had then withdrawn again. Bobby ran out of the kitchen out of the building across the yard. He heard Christopherson start to follow him and then stand still. He heard Rachel cry out, though what she called he did not know. He tore open the barn door and found himself face to face with Loo Leader.

CHAPTER XIX
MARRIAGE CERTIFICATE

IT WAS LOO LEADER who spoke first, Bobby's surprise—and in a sense his disappointment—holding him silent for the moment.

"Afternoon, Inspector," Leader said cheerfully, his small eyes bright and alert on either side of his enormous nose. "You having a look round, too, same as me?"

"What are you doing here?" Bobby asked.

"Just like I said, Inspector," Leader answered, "just having a look round." He produced a cigarette and lighted it with elaborate care, an old trick for securing time to think what to say next. For all his off-hand manner, Bobby felt Leader was as taken aback by their sudden encounter as he had to confess he had been himself. "Things going on," said Leader vaguely, "and so I thought as I would have a look round, too. Can't leave it all to the busies, you know."

Bobby looked at him doubtfully, more than a little puzzled. Christopherson and Rachel had come across from the inn to join them. Neither of them spoke. Christopherson's features were impassive but Rachel still looked anxious. To Christopherson, Bobby said:

"Did you know this man was here?"

"No," Christopherson answered. To Rachel, he said: "Did you?" Rachel shook her head. To Leader, Christopherson said: "What are you doing here?"

"Just having a look round, same as I told the inspector," Leader repeated.

"What for?" demanded Christopherson.

Leader's small bright eyes by the side of that great nose of his were still alert and bright, but about his loose, wide mouth a suspicion of a grin was beginning to appear. To Bobby it seemed that both Rachel and her father were waiting his reply with a certain apprehension, and he also thought that when his reply came it merely puzzled them.

"An idea of mine," Leader was saying. "I'm in road transport. So I thought it might be a paying notion to fix up a depot somewhere—storage, you see. Save cross hauls. Cross hauls play hell with road transport. Send up costs, eat up profits. See? So I said to myself as the Conqueror Inn was the very place. Lots of big empty old buildings. See? Near cross roads, too. So I came along to have a look and then I saw the inspector's car and I thought it would be more tactful like to wait till he had gone before starting in to talk business with Mr. Christopherson."

His grin widened. He waited for comments. His air of cheeky defiance was very much that of the man who has just said 'Put that in your pipe and smoke it.' Bobby wondered how much of it to believe and decided very little. Rachel turned and began to walk back towards the inn, and to Bobby it seemed that her step had become less firm, that that graceful upright bearing so characteristic of her had now begun to sag a little. He wondered if Leader's scarcely concealed confidence and impudence had begun to convey some message to her. He glanced at Christopherson and remembered how once he had thought of him as of an ageless man in an ageless land. Was it only fancy, he asked himself, that made him think that traces of the burden of the years had now become apparent? Christopherson was saying:

"Do you mean you come from Mr. Kram?"

"Not me, I'm on my own, I am," Leader retorted. "All my own idea. Has Kram had it, too? Well, now, ain't that the queerest thing going—both of us with the same notion."

"It doesn't seem a very sensible notion to me," Christopherson said. "Mr. Kram dropped it almost at once, I think. I have heard nothing more. And if you have anything to say to me, why didn't you come to the house? I don't like strangers in my barns. These outbuildings are not part of the licensed premises. You are trespassing here."

"Doing no harm," retorted Leader. "Just looking round. No harm in that. Business reasons."

Bobby interposed. He had no wish to see accepted the hint Christopherson had dropped, or for Christopherson and Leader to get together privately before he himself had found opportunity to question Leader further. That there was something behind Leader's unexpected appearance here, he felt very sure. Difficult, though, to say what. He said aloud:

"I think I should like a chat with Mr. Leader myself. How did you get here?" he asked Leader. "That your bicycle?" He had noticed one just inside the barn, leaning against the wall. "Can I give you a lift back to Midwych in my car? We can stow your bicycle at the back."

Rather to Bobby's surprise Leader accepted this suggestion at once, accepted it even with a certain alacrity. In a very few minutes they were on their way, and as Leader settled himself comfortably in his seat next to Bobby, he said:

"Don't much like that Christopherson chap. There's a look about him makes you think he would put you out of the way same as he would a rat, if he thought he had to."

"Yes," agreed Bobby thoughtfully. "I think perhaps he might— that is, as soon as he felt sure you were a rat."

Leader looked as if he didn't much like this remark. Bobby had laid a certain emphasis on the "you." Leader had the air of turning it over in his mind and finding it less and less agreeable the more he thought about it. Bobby went on:

"Well, now perhaps you'll tell me the truth. What did actually take you to the Conqueror Inn? What were you after in that barn?"

"What I said was the truth, same as I'm sitting here," protested Leader. "Looking round I was. Because there's things going on."

"What's it to do with you if there are?" Bobby asked.

Leader looked sideways at Bobby and hesitated for a moment before replying. Then he said:

"Listen. There's a man been killed. That's straight, isn't it? Listen. If there's one been done in, why not another? And how do I know who mayn't be next? Suppose it's me?"

Somewhat startled, Bobby took his attention for one brief moment from his driving to bestow it on his companion.

"Why should it be?" he asked.

"There's more going on than you know nor me either," Leader answered moodily.

Bobby made no comment, hoping more would come if he remained silent.

"You've put one of your blokes on trailing me," Leader resumed. "I reckon that's why you came along, though I did think as I had given him the slip. Seeing as I hadn't told even Alf Hall what was driving where I meant to drop off the lorry. Followed us on a motor bike, I reckon, though I watched and never saw, and then went and rung up when he spotted me pedalling off this way on my own."

"Never mind that," Bobby answered; having no intention of explaining how unexpected to him had been Leader's appearance, since the more that worthy believed in the omniscience of the Wychshire County Police, the better.

Nor was he either surprised or disappointed to know that Leader was aware he was being watched. The officer told off for that duty had been informed he need not be too careful to remain unobserved. A man who knows he is being watched by the police often grows nervous and inclined to come forward with information he would otherwise have kept hidden. Or again, a man who knows he is both guilty and under observation will occasionally try to avert suspicion by offering explanations that help in the end to prove the very guilt he was trying to conceal.

"Not as I mind," Leader went on. "Gives you a comfortable sort of feeling to know there's always a busy within call if so be as you should want him." He spoke jeeringly enough and his grin was pure impudence, and yet Bobby had the oddest feeling that behind the jeer and the impudence there hid a substratum of fact. Hardly possible, Bobby told himself, that a man like Leader should really feel 'comfortable' at the thought that a policeman was always near at hand. Yet that was the impression he received and he wondered if it were connected with—or perhaps merely a result of—Leader's strange remark that since one man had recently been killed, so might be another soon and perhaps himself. Leader was saying now, without either jeer or grin this time: "At least, if it doesn't mean as you've got it in your head it might be me as done in that poor bloke me and Alf Hall saw you digging up?"

"It means at any rate," Bobby answered, "that I am wondering if it was only a coincidence that you came by that morning?"

"Well, it was, just chancy like," Leader asserted. "You can take it from me, I'm no murderer. And if I was I wouldn't do a thing like bash a dead man's face in, so I wouldn't. That's a thing will bring no luck to who done it."

It came back to Bobby's mind that Alf Hall, Leader's companion that Tuesday morning, had said the same thing and with much the same emphasis of genuine feeling that Leader himself was showing now. Abruptly he said:

"Why have you been asking questions at Ingleside Camp about Captain Wintle?"

"Know about that, do you?" Leader said, looking a little disconcerted. "Not much you miss, is there?"

"No, there isn't," agreed Bobby, sadly aware nevertheless how much nearer the truth it would have been if he had answered 'Yes, a lot.' He repeated: "Well. Why?"

"Along of what I said before," Leader answered. "There's more going on than you or me knows about."

"Why should you think Captain Wintle has anything to do with it?"

"Hanging about that there Conqueror Inn, isn't he? And for what?" Leader retorted. "Another thing, he was seen prowling round there that Monday night when the killing happened."

"Oh, yes," said Bobby, doubtful but interested, for if this could be established, the implication was plain. Almost good enough for an arrest, he supposed. "Who saw him?" he asked. "Did you?"

"No," Leader answered with haste and emphasis. "No, me and Alf Hall were far enough off by then, same as I told you. Alibi all right we've got, Alf and me."

Bobby let this pass without comment, though thinking to himself that it was not a wholly satisfactory alibi, since it rested on statements made by Hall and Leader themselves, without any other confirmation. Leader had paused, evidently hoping for an agreement with his alibi claim that did not come. All Bobby said was:

"Well, who did see him if you didn't?"

"Now that," Leader answered, "I can't tell you and I only wish I could. It was a chap I don't know, only by passing him sometimes on the road, as said to me when we was stopped somewhere for a bite to eat as how a pal of his had seen an officer he served under in France walking along the road near the Conqueror Inn about eight o'clock that Monday night. So I said just by way of talking like, what was he doing, and was it a spot of necking, and who was the officer, and the other fellow said he didn't see no girl and it was

Captain Wintle. Never gave it another thought till after me and Alf had unloaded Tuesday, along of what we saw what you had gone and dug up giving us such a turn everything else was drove clean out of our heads."

"Pity you didn't come forward with your story before," Bobby said drily.

"Now, Inspector," Leader protested earnestly, "what would you busies have said to a tale like that and us not knowing who it was told us or where to find him, and him only repeating what another bloke had been and told him? Thrown us out on our ears if we had come pitching a yarn like that."

Bobby had to admit that this was true enough. Certainly the tale was one to which not too much credence could be attached.

"If you can find that man," he said, "we shan't forget it. It would be a great help."

"You can depend on me," Leader said earnestly; and Bobby resisted an impulse to retort that he was very much afraid he couldn't. "I suppose," Leader added, "you'll keep that bloke of yours hanging round my place so as I can always tip him off if I do get to know anything?"

"All depends," Bobby answered. "There's always the 'phone anyway, isn't there?"

Leader grunted in a dissatisfied sort of way, as if to indicate he did not think much of 'phones, and Bobby found himself wondering if Leader really did like the idea of having a member of the police force always at hand? Unique, Bobby reflected, in the full sense of that much misused word, to find a suspect relieved to know himself under observation. It added one more to that huddle of irreconcilable, inexplicable details of circumstances and aspects of character that in their totality were making this case the most perplexing of all those so far he had had to deal with.

A captain in the army with a good fighting record behind him; a business man, head of a flourishing concern like K. and K.M.T.C.; a straight-living, straight-thinking countryman like Christopherson, without a hint of a black mark against his character or he would never have held a licence; a suspect like Leader who seemed actually to like the idea of being kept under observation; finally, two young girls like Maggie Kram and Rachel Christopherson. How could one hope to pick a likely murderer among such people?

There was Micky Burke, too, of course, and Bobby had never much liked the look of that dour and silent Irishman, or of his cold, still eyes of the fanatic, but everything Bobby had learnt went to show that Micky's affection for his nephew had been genuine and deep. He said to Leader:

"Why were you asking questions at farms and cottages on the moor? About eggs, wasn't it?"

"Know about that, too," Leader grumbled. "Know it all, don't you?" He paused, and this time Bobby was not sure that there was not a touch of mockery in the question. Leader went on: "No harm in asking questions, is there? And eggs is eggs, as they say, and sometimes something else as well."

"Bombs, you mean?" Bobby asked, remembering the theory so hesitatingly advanced by Sergeant Payne.

"Oh, well," Leader muttered, evidently slightly taken aback by the prompt response. "On that, too, are you?"

Interesting, at any rate, Bobby told himself, to meet thus again Payne's suggestion. Could there be anything in it, he wondered? Half a hundred or more such stories had come before him already—mysterious lights like signals soon shown to have been caused by the careless opening and shutting of outhouse doors, suspicious strangers who turned out to be harmless evacuees, parachutists seen descending on the moors and proving to be stray sheep on high ground, and so on and so on, all of the stories needing careful investigation and taking up long hours of work before the innocent truth became clear. And all of it no guarantee of course that the fifty and first story would not prove to be extremely well founded.

"I suppose you know," Bobby remarked, "that if you know or even suspect anything of the sort, the penalty for keeping it to yourself would be pretty serious. Death perhaps."

"So it ought to be," agreed Leader with emphasis. "But I hadn't anything to go on except a bloke talking in a pub, about why wouldn't it be possible to drop spies out on the moor there, with bombs in their pockets all ready to blow up factories and such-like. So I thought it might be a good idea to ask a few people round about, but none of them had ever heard of anything of the sort."

"The next time," Bobby warned him, "you had better leave a job of that sort to the police or the Home Guard. Give us any information you get hold of and leave it at that. Or you may be getting yourself into trouble."

"Very well, Inspector," Leader answered meekly. "I'll remember."

They had by now reached the outskirts of Midwych and Leader asked to be set down. Nor did Bobby feel that any further questioning of Leader was likely to be useful just at present or till more was known.

So Leader was allowed to alight with his bicycle and Bobby drove on to his office. There on his desk he found waiting for him a result of one of the lines of investigation he had started. It was a copy of the marriage certificate of Margaret Jane Kram and Laurence Connor, performed some four months previously at a Midwych registry office.

CHAPTER XX
DAUGHTER AND FATHER

BOBBY, SITTING THERE with this unexpected document before him, thought how strange it was that so continually there came into prominence first one and then another of the actors in this drama of which it was as difficult to understand the beginning as to foresee the development. It was as though some power, unseen and unknown, shifted the limelight hither and thither at will, either by caprice or design.

Now apparently it was the turn of the Krams, father and daughter, to take the centre of the stage.

What light all this threw upon the two problems he had to solve— the identity of the dead man, the identity of his slayer—Bobby was not sure. The only thing quite clear was that now there opened up a whole new range of possibilities, a hint of many fresh and different motives that each one must be taken into consideration.

On his desk lay, too, other reports, and of these the one that seemed most interesting, even suggestive, was that on the career of Merton Kram, of the K. and K.M.T.C.

A varied career apparently and one of many ups and downs. He had been the prime mover in at least half a dozen enterprises of one sort or another, and in every case these had begun well, flourished exceedingly for a time, and then fallen by the way, overcome apparently by the burden of their own success. Merton Kram, it seemed, was in business like the runner in a race who holds the lead for three-quarters of the course but has so exhausted himself by his efforts that he collapses before the winning post is reached.

Not uncommon perhaps. Success is intoxicating, and it is difficult to believe when things go well that presently they may go badly instead. Also the temptation to launch out too far for available resources is never easy to resist. One or two of the concerns Kram had originated were still in existence and sufficiently prosperous but in different hands. Others had disappeared. K. and K. Suppliers, an attempt to out-Woolworth Woolworth with no price above threepence, had 'vanished without trace,' K. and K. Caterers, founded to rival Lyons, was still doing well, reorganized as Kook and Kitchen Limited and aiming at a different class of trade. K. and K. White Kitten Cigarettes, intended to shake the tobacco trade to its depths, had apparently found an unknown grave, and K. and K. 'Homes for You,' meant to eclipse the Halifax and all other building societies, had collapsed into a slightly discreditable bankruptcy soon after the outbreak of the war. And Merton Kram had been granted an exceedingly benevolent discharge on the indulgent theory that it was the war that was responsible for the breakdown.

In all this there were two or three points that seemed to Bobby to be of interest. There was suggested a restless energy always prepared to launch out into fresh ventures. There appeared, too, an odd lack of originality leading every time to imitation of already established successes. Apparently a constant search for success in directions in which the success of others seemed to show success was easy. Again the constant use of the initials 'K. and K.' hinted at a vanity perpetually anxious to assert itself; and Bobby knew well, for he had often seen it, that vanity, which so often seems pardonable weakness, can corrode and twist a character into strange shapes, can make the statesman a traitor, the general a coward, persuade the upright business man to fraud. The double initial, too, hinted at a sort of, again, vainglorious affection on the part of Kram for his daughter, since it was always two 'K's'—K. and K.—and the second K was there from the very beginning, long before Maggie could have been an active associate with her father in any business, and yet after the death of her mother, to whom therefore the second K could never have referred.

Bobby thought that Kram must be one of those parents whose conviction that their children are most wonderful comes from the possibly unconscious conviction that they themselves are wonderful and must therefore have brought forth the wonderful.

Not much in all that record though to suggest the potential murderer, though again Bobby found himself reflecting that an unbalanced vanity has been known to issue in murder.

Suppose, for example, Kram had known of his daughter's marriage to Larry, who was after all little more than a hanger-on of one of his own workpeople? Might not results have ensued? Reproaches, defiance, a quarrel, a struggle, death? Or again, suppose Micky Burke knew of the marriage, and disapproved, as apparently he would have done, and there again a quarrel had resulted, this time between two hot-tempered Irishmen.

Possibilities, either of them, Bobby felt, but possibilities only.

And could Micky Burke be described with any accuracy as a hot-blooded Irishman? Irish certainly, but hot-blooded? Remembering those cold, still eyes of his of greyish blue, Bobby doubted it. Nor was there any record of any sort of violence or rowdiness in his life; except, of course, for the story of the recent dispute with the zealous, recruit-seeking, unidentified sergeant from Ingleside Camp, threatened by Micky with the heavy spanner that the sergeant was said to have confiscated.

From these reflections Bobby turned again to the account of Kram's business activities. Another point now struck him. In every other case, when Kram had made a new start, there was something to show where and when and how he had obtained the fresh funds necessary. Something had been saved. He had sold out at a price sufficient to allow a fresh start in another venture. He had been able to secure the help of associates with money. But after his last and worst failure—a bankruptcy, not merely a reconstruction, and a bankruptcy in which the creditors had fared badly—Kram had been forced to take a humble, poorly-paid position as night watchman. That indicated very clearly not only no money but also a loss of business friends and of reputation as well, as if this time it was generally felt he had gone too far. Yet before very long he had made a re-entry in the business world as owner of a road transport concern of quite respectable size, with his own premises and his own fleet of lorries.

Now where, Bobby wondered, had the money come from for this new venture?

A puzzle, but on the face of it nothing to do with the murder near the Conqueror Inn. Gloomily enough Bobby perceived that once again, as so often in this affair, he was running up against curious, unexplained matters that yet seemed unconnected with the only thing with which he was officially concerned, the identity of murderer and of victim.

He found it interesting, too, that the report ended with the remark that everything tended to show that in spite of the fierce competition in the road transport business, in which anyone can start who can scrape together enough to buy a lorry, in spite of all war-time difficulties, in spite of a start entirely from scratch without any of those connections that count for as much in road transport as in other businesses, the K. and K.M.T.C. appeared to have been highly prosperous from the very beginning, even though rumours were current at the moment of a recent severe loss.

"And that," Bobby told himself, "is interesting, too, especially if it should turn out that the 'severe loss' amounts to £2,000."

But to follow up that idea was once more to become lost in a bog of mere conjecture, a bog in which Bobby was painfully aware he had more than once in this case risked losing himself entirely.

He picked up the 'phone and rang up K. and K.M.T.C., to ask if Miss Kram could possibly spare the time to see him for a few minutes, and would she prefer that he came round to her, or would she rather come to him.

After some hesitation Mr. Kram, who answered the 'phone himself, said he thought that Maggie would prefer to come to Bobby's office and promised that she would do so without delay.

"There's been enough talk already," Kram said sourly over the 'phone, "without police showing up here any more."

Bobby said he was sorry and he always tried to carry out an investigation as inconspicuously as possible, but all the same, people who might have information to give had to be questioned.

Nor was he much surprised to find, when Maggie arrived, that she was accompanied by her father, who seemed to take it for granted that he was to be present at the interview. So Bobby had to explain that that could not be permitted; Miss Kram was of age and fully responsible. She was of course, entitled to the presence of a solicitor if she so wished.

Kram protested angrily that that was absurd—she could have a lawyer's help, but not that of her father? Preposterous, he declared, and tried to argue the point, till Maggie cut the discussion short by declaring she was quite willing to talk to Bobby alone. Why not?

She seemed inclined, however, to make fresh protest when she found that Sergeant Payne would also be present, but on that point Bobby was firm. No police officer but takes care always to have a colleague present when he has to question a woman.

Safety first, in fact.

In the end, Maggie withdrew her objection when she understood that Payne was not going to take a verbatim shorthand report, an idea to which she seemed strongly to object.

"I have asked you to call," Bobby explained, all this settled, "because, from information we are now in possession of, we have learned of your recent marriage."

"I don't know what you mean," Maggie retorted, looking straight at him. "I'm not married."

For answer, Bobby, who had anticipated this denial, handed her the copy of her marriage certificate he had procured.

"How did you find out?" she asked angrily, apparently unaware, or forgetting, that marriages are matters of public record. She tore the document in half and threw the pieces on the floor. "What's it to do with you?" she demanded.

"Nothing," Bobby answered, "unless, as we are beginning to believe, the dead man we are trying to identify is Larry Connor and your husband."

She made no answer for a moment, but her eyes were fire in a face like death.

"I don't believe it," she said harshly with a kind of desperate energy. "It isn't true. It isn't, I tell you."

"You would wish to be sure, wouldn't you?" Bobby asked. "Is there any way in which you could identify the body? Any scar or birthmark? Anything at all by which we could make—certain?"

She shook her head.

Bobby said:

"The body has not been buried yet. That will have to be done soon. Do you wish to see it? I must ask you that. You know from the papers that the features are unrecognizable, but if you wish—"

She shook her head again.

"I think I must go," she said. "I think I must go."

She got to her feet and stood for a moment so unsteadily that Bobby thought she was about to collapse. He jumped up and put out his hand for her support. With an effort that was almost visible she rallied all her forces, turned, and went away, walking slowly, with stiff, careful steps. Nor did Bobby try to stop her, for he felt she had reached the very limit of her endurance. If there was anything she knew and was willing to tell him, she would return, he thought. From where he had been quietly sitting at a side table, Payne said:

"By God, she has guts."

"Yes," said Bobby. "So she has."

Payne said again:

"She knows and she won't tell, though it's tearing her in pieces."

"Why won't she?" Bobby asked.

"Because she thinks it was her father did it," Payne said.

"I suppose so," Bobby agreed.

CHAPTER XXI
MICKY BURKE AT HOME

IT SEEMED CLEAR that the next step indicated was a further talk with Micky Burke. Better perhaps, Bobby thought, for him to call at Burke's address rather than ask the Irishman to come to headquarters. For one thing, useful knowledge of a man's character and disposition can often be obtained by observation of him in his own home. Micky lived alone as Bobby knew, for that had been inquired into as a matter of routine, in a small house of the 'two up and two down' variety in one of the working-class districts of Midwych. The housework Micky did himself; and it was apparently admitted in the neighbourhood that he did it as well and kept the house as clean and tidy as any woman could have done. He was too silent and reserved, kept himself 'too much to himself' as the neighbours put it, to be much liked, but his general reputation was that of a respectable, hard-working man; and if he didn't wish to be friendly, and if he wasn't the sort of neighbour you could go to to borrow an odd pot or pan, or half-a-crown on the eve of pay day, still he interfered with nobody. If he could get along without you, just as well could you get along without him. The city police in the district knew nothing against him. A minor but rather curious point was that though certainly no teetotaller—indeed a steady drinker—he never 'used,' as runs the common expression, any of the public houses in the neighbourhood. What drink he required was delivered from an off-licence establishment.

Fanciful perhaps, Bobby told himself, to see anything strange or suggestive in the contrast between this somewhat drab, self-contained, hard-working and monotonous existence, and the reputation his employer had given him, and that Bobby had since verified, for a kind of fierce recklessness in his handling of the giant lorries he drove on the roads. Possible, Bobby supposed, that he found a way of release from the inhibitions that seemed to govern his everyday life, in the risks he took and the skill he showed in crashing those great vehicles at such speed round corners, past other traffic, through every peril and danger of the high road.

An unblemished road record, though.

An interesting character, Bobby thought, and wondered again, remembering those still, cold eyes of his, whether the restraint he so clearly exercised upon himself in his everyday life—or why this avoidance, for example, of public houses?—did not come from a knowledge of a hidden strength of passion and of purpose that had of necessity always to be kept under watch and ward lest it should break from restraint.

The district of the city in which Micky lived was some distance away and not one Bobby knew well. So he stopped at the nearest of the city police stations, asked for directions and for permission to leave his car there, and completed the journey on foot.

A well-kept little house he found, with clean, well-laundered curtains at the windows—Bobby wondered whether Micky's housewifely skill extended to starching and ironing or whether the curtains went to a laundry—and a knocker and doorstep plate that shone like the buttons on a guardsman's tunic in peace time. The house stood at a corner where there crossed each other two long drab streets of working-class houses, built in days when two rooms down and two rooms above were thought ample accommodation for any working-class family. At the back of each house a microscopic yard took the place of a garden, and, as a concession no doubt to the amenities, there was a bare open space behind to serve as a sort of communal drying ground for the weekly wash.

The back door opened on this, the front door on one street, the kitchen window directly on the long cross street; and Bobby supposed that only the suspicious mind of a policeman would notice that thus was provided three separate and distinct means of access and departure in three separate directions.

Bobby knew that Micky had finished his day's work and would probably be at home. When he knocked Micky came at once to the door. He did not speak, but a flicker in his pale eyes, gone in an instant, showed recognition and perhaps even unease. Bobby said:

"Oh, good evening, Mr. Burke. I wonder if you could spare me a few minutes?"

Still without speaking, Micky drew aside. Bobby accepted the silent invitation and entered the kitchen on which the street door opened directly. It was a clean, well-kept, bare-looking room, with no concession to comfort—a hard, chill room of one who neither knew ease nor sought it. The only armchair was of the high-backed wooden variety. There was no covering on the floor, but the boards were scrubbed clean; well scrubbed every week at least, Bobby guessed. The walls, distempered in a plain self colour, were bare, except for a calendar cut from a religious newspaper, and for a representation of the Sacred Heart. On the mantelpiece, as bare otherwise as the rest of the room, stood an alarm clock and two large photographs—one of a young and good-looking man, the other of Burke's employer, Merton Kram. Before each of these a candle burned. A kettle was beginning to boil on a small fire in the grate and on the table was Micky's supper. It consisted of fried fish, fried potatoes, greens, and looked appetizing. Taking no notice of his visitor Micky went back to his meal and Bobby asked pleasantly:

"May I sit down?"

"You needed no asking to come," Micky said. "Why wait for it to sit?"

He continued his meal. Bobby sat down and watched in silence. Micky was finishing his fish. Rising, he cleared away the remnants of this first course and then produced a baked pudding that had been keeping warm by the fire. Not the work of any amateur, Bobby reflected, as his thoughts turned, somewhat sadly, for it was long since he had eaten, to the dinner probably slowly spoiling at home and to Olive darkly brooding over its ruin.

"Mr. Burke," Bobby said, "I am very anxious to get in touch with your nephew, Mr. Larry Connor. Can you help me?"

Micky shook his head, helped himself to a liberal share of his baked pudding, and began to eat.

"Have you heard from him since he left here?"

Micky shook his head again and then deviated into language.

"Never any hand at writing, wasn't Larry," he said briefly.

"Miss Kram had a letter from him, I believe."

"It's what she told me," Micky answered. "Why not?"

"Mr. Burke," Bobby said, "did you know that your nephew and Miss Kram were married?"

Micky laid down his fork and spoon and looked long and hard at Bobby. For the first time he seemed really moved and Bobby noticed how a slow, dark flush spread over his features.

"No, nor were they," he said at last. "What's put that into your head?"

"I have seen their marriage certificate," Bobby said.

"There's a lie," Micky said slowly. "A police lie. An English policeman's lie. You have not."

Bobby did not answer. Micky got to his feet. He had forgotten now his supper to which before he had so stolidly and so ostentatiously devoted his attention.

"There's a black lie," he said again, but this time with less conviction. "A lie, a trap."

Bobby gave him briefly the place and date. Micky said:

"At a registry office? That's no marriage."

"As legal and as binding as any other," Bobby answered. "Do you see any objection—?"

"And her an English heretic," Micky said, "and him vowed and sworn—"

He checked himself abruptly, and Bobby said:

"Yes? Vowed and sworn—?"

Micky sat down and spoke more quietly.

"It was too much to say, vowed and sworn. It's an Irish girl I was thinking of, a true Irish girl and no heretic either."

He began to eat again, stuffing his mouth so full that Bobby felt sure he was seeking time for thought. Presently he said:

"Well, if it's wed they are and legal and all, what's that to do with the police? Is it English law now that a lad can't wed without asking the leave of the police?"

"No," Bobby answered, "but it is the law that a lad can't die with a bullet in his heart without it having to do with the police. Come, Mr. Burke, you must realize that until I can get in touch with your nephew I shall have to go on thinking that it may be his body we found buried that morning near the Conqueror Inn."

"Then you must wait," Micky countered, "till Larry turns up again and that'll be in his time and not in yours."

"Why should he choose to leave a wife he married so recently?" Bobby countered in his turn.

"That's for him to say and not for me," Micky retorted. "It's a thing that's clean out of my understanding—his marrying Miss Kram, I mean, if it's the truth it is and no lie. It'll be that she talked the lad into it, the way a woman can talk any man into any folly, and now he has come to himself, he sees there's nothing for him but to run for it. I reckon that'll be the way of things."

"Strange," Bobby said, "that should happen at the very time we find the dead body of a man of about Larry's age, of about his size and height and weight—we've made sure of all that. The same coloured hair, too. Had Larry any mark upon his body, a scar or birthmark or anything, by which he could be identified?"

"No," answered Micky, "none, for he was perfect from the sole of his foot to the crown of his head."

"So was the dead man," Bobby said quietly, and Micky made no comment. Then Bobby said: "He lived with you, I think. May I see his bedroom?"

"You may," Micky answered, "seeing there's no way I can stop you and you being police. But if it's fingerprints you have in your mind, I gave the room a thorough cleaning from top to bottom after he had gone; and if it's clothing or papers, there's none; for what he had, he took, and he travelled light at that. It's the room at the back that was his, so go you and look for yourself."

Bobby did not avail himself of the invitation. He was very sure it would not have been given unless every precaution had been taken first. Micky was busying himself clearing the table. Bobby said:

"The body is not buried yet, though that must be done soon. Will you see it in case you are able to recognize it?"

"I will not," Micky answered, "for it can be no one I know, and Larry it can't be, when I was with him long after the poor man you found was dead and his soul with the blessed saints."

Micky crossed himself and went on with what he was doing. Bobby watched him in silence for a time and then said:

"You would have objected to the marriage if you had known of it. Would Mr. Kram have objected too, do you think?"

"Ask him that," Micky retorted, "and tell him if you will, that it's too good for her was Larry."

"I see you have a photograph of Mr. Kram there," Bobby remarked, glancing at the mantelpiece.

Micky turned, stared at it, and then turned back to Bobby again; and again Bobby thought he could see a flicker of some unknown emotion in those still, cold eyes of his.

"What about it?" Micky said. "He gave it me the other day. You ask him."

"I see there's a candle burning before it," Bobby observed.

Micky turned on him in a cold fury.

"There's too much you see," he said, almost hissing the words through tight lips. "There's too many questions you ask. Maybe it's better you should be going now."

The threat in his voice was evident but Bobby took no notice, though he could see how the little, dried-up man was quivering with the intensity of some obscure, deep-rooted passion. Difficult to tell why his emotion should be so great, or why it should seem to have been brought to a head by this reference to his employer. Unless it was that he shared the belief that Sergeant Payne had attributed to Maggie. Partly to put this idea to the test, Bobby continued:

"You see, what's in my mind is this. If Mr. Kram objected strongly to any marriage between his daughter and Larry, could that have led to a quarrel ending in Larry's getting shot? Perhaps in self-defence. I have to consider every possibility, you know."

"There's no sense," Micky said slowly, "in pestering me with questions when I've no knowledge I can answer from. Get on with your hangman's job, get Mr. Kram hanged if you can, and leave me be. For now there's the washing-up to be done and then I'll be for bed. For I've work to do if you haven't."

"My work," Bobby answered, "is to try to bring to justice a murderer—of your nephew, I think. You don't seem inclined to help."

"I'll take no help or want it from English police," Micky snarled.

He lifted the kettle from the fire, and, going into the back kitchen, set to work washing up his supper dishes.

No good, Bobby decided, trying to extract information or help from a man making it so plain he intends to supply neither. He gave a final glance round, a final look at the photograph of Micky's employer on the mantelpiece. A significance in its presence there, he thought, and yet what that significance might be, he found it difficult to guess. He called a farewell to Micky, drowned perhaps in the clatter of the plates and cups Micky was busy with, for he got no answer, and let himself out. Before he had gone more than a step or two a woman came up to him. He recognized Maggie Kram and halted, surprised. She said to him:

"Micky hasn't told you anything, has he?"

"Mrs. Connor,' Bobby answered, "telling the police nothing sometimes comes to much the same as telling them a lot."

"Has it this time?" she asked in a low voice.

"It has made me feel more sure than ever that the murdered man is your husband and I think you know it," Bobby answered. Then he said: "Why did you follow me?"

"I didn't," she answered, "but it was easy to guess where you would be going next, so I came too, and waited till I saw you. Are you going to tell my father?"

"That you married Larry Connor?" Bobby said. "I expect it will be necessary."

"I have told him now," she said. "I knew you would. Did you notice if Micky had a photograph of my father there?"

"There is one on his mantelpiece," Bobby said. "There is a lighted candle before it. What does that mean?"

She answered him only by a long, strange look and then turned and walked away quickly. He hurried after her; he had almost to run to reach her side, she went so quickly. He said to her, for he believed that he had interpreted aright what lay behind, that last long look of hers:

"Mrs. Connor, will you not tell me what you are afraid of and why?"

"Of another murder," she answered in a voice that he could hardly hear, "and that it will not be me."

CHAPTER XXII

CONSIDERATIONS AND CONJECTURES

BOBBY WAS IN gloomy mood when he arrived at the office next morning. Forebodings were dark in his mind with the memory of that candle on Micky Burke's mantelpiece, burning inexorably away before Mr. Kram's photograph, symbol perhaps of a life doomed also soon to be extinguished.

Responsibility is heavy when there is question not only of a murder to be avenged but also of a murder to be averted.

Leader, too—what fear was it that made a man of his character and record well pleased with the close supervision of an officer of police?

Nor was Bobby's uneasiness diminished when he heard that Mr. Kram had made application for permission to obtain a new revolver on the ground that the one previously in his possession had been stolen. Impossible, declared Mr. Kram in his letter, that it should have been lost or mislaid, and it must therefore have been stolen.

"Well, Kram's not going to get his permission, not if I can help it," declared Bobby crossly to Sergeant Payne who had come in for instructions. "Can't give permission to buy a revolver to suspected murderers, for it's pretty clear, Payne, you were right in thinking Maggie Kram believes it was her father. And what's more, she is afraid Micky Burke knows it."

"Means," said Payne, "she thinks her father killed her husband?"

Bobby nodded.

After a pause, both men heavy with their own thoughts, Payne added:

"Bit tragic."

Bobby nodded again. He was remembering Maggie's coy giggles the first time he had seen her. He suspected now that she had been told at the time that Larry had gone away and that her giggles and her readiness to flirt had been her way of showing her resentment at such a secret departure so like a desertion. Then, hearing of the unidentified dead man found near the Conqueror Inn she had begun to grow uneasy. Later on her suspicions had turned towards her father.

But were those suspicions well founded? Bobby asked himself.

Was it going to be his duty, he wondered distastefully, to try to use a daughter's testimony against her father?

He supposed that if she volunteered such testimony it would have to be used. But he would not try to force it from her. He would rather throw up his job—only, of course, in war time, he would not even be allowed to resign. Already he had sent in his resignation two or three times, in the hope of being able to join the army, only to be told with some asperity that his duty was to stop where he was.

As if suddenly deciding that his former comment had been inadequate and that it ought to be emphasized, Payne added:

"Hard luck on the girl."

"Can't be sure that it is like that," Bobby said, rousing himself from his own thoughts. "Can't even be sure that that's what's in her mind. Can't be sure of anything till we are sure who the dead man is."

"No one else missing, no one but Larry Connor," Payne said.

"No one that we know of," Bobby corrected him, "and being missing isn't proof of death. I've sent a wire to Cork," he added, "to ask for inquiries to be made in the village where Larry comes from."

"Well, of course," agreed Payne, "if Larry turns up there all alive and kicking, then it has to be someone else got himself killed that night."

It was in no expectation of any such result that Bobby had dispatched his telegram. His reason had been entirely different, but he did not explain further. He felt it was too much of an imaginative effort for it to be exposed to Payne's criticism unless the event justified it. Olive had not wanted telling, though. She had seen the idea at once.

"If it wasn't Larry Connor—well, who was it?" Payne went on as Bobby remained silent.

"There's another man we've heard of but never seen," Bobby said. "Perhaps because he doesn't exist. But I think quite likely he does—or did till that Monday night."

"Young Christopherson?" Payne asked. "You think perhaps he wasn't killed at Dunkirk but deserted instead when he got back and they've been hiding him at the Conqueror Inn?"

"I put that to them," Bobby said. "It seemed to account for things that puzzled me—like not wanting too much custom and the music stand and the violin put out all ready though neither Christopherson nor Miss Rachel play. I made sure that's what it was when I saw someone dodging about the outbuildings. Only it wasn't, it was Leader instead. Threw me off my stride altogether. What was Leader up to?" he added abruptly, for that was a question to which at present he saw no reasonable answer.

Payne did not try to answer it. Instead he said:

"Christopherson's the type would go a long way to protect a son of his if he thought it right."

"Yes," agreed Bobby and went on thoughtfully: "I suppose you could almost excuse any man who had been at Dunkirk not being too keen on facing it again."

"Most of them were keen enough," Payne said. "All most of them wanted was another go to get a bit of their own back."

"Yes, that's true," admitted Bobby. "All the more credit to them. When you've been in hell and got out, it can't be much fun going back."

"Of course," admitted Payne in his turn, "this chap seems to have had it as bad as he could if it's true he was actually blown up by one of those dive bombers."

Incidentally Payne himself had been blown twenty feet into the air by a bomb during one of the raids on Midwych. But that had always seemed to him merely a piece of somewhat disagreeable routine duty. As Bobby, deep in thought again, made no comment, Payne asked:

"I take it, sir, you've thought of getting a search warrant?"

"Oh, yes," Bobby answered, "but would they give me one? It's all conjecture, you know. Deduction from given premises. That's all, and the deduction may be quite wrong. Magistrates are pretty sticky about giving search warrants. I call it deduction. A magistrate might call it guessing and say guesses weren't good enough. Besides, Christopherson has the official notice of his son's death. Another thing. Would a search succeed? It's an old warren of a place with outbuildings like a young town, and I shouldn't wonder if it isn't provided with a few secret hiding places—priest's holes and so on. No. I think the search warrant must be a last resort."

"Another thing, sir," Payne said. "If it was young Derek Christopherson who was killed—well, why?"

"There's another possibility," Bobby said. "One that would link up the two of them—Larry Connor and Derek Christopherson, I mean. Suppose Larry had got to know about Derek and was threatening to give information. You said just now Christopherson was of the stuff to kill to protect his own?"

"So he is," Payne declared once more.

"I think so, too. And Rachel—what about her?"

"Her too," asserted Payne, "her as much as her father—or more. There's nothing either of them wouldn't do if they thought it right. And it wouldn't bother either of them what other people thought."

"Their own judges," Bobby said. "Their own judges once they made up their minds. Only—did they?"

"No real evidence," Payne said. "There's the snag."

"There's still another possibility to consider," Bobby went on. "Captain Wintle was very emphatic about there being no firearms at the Conqueror Inn. Said he had asked. Why did he ask?"

"Now that," said Payne, "that takes some thinking out."

"Is it a fair argument," asked Bobby, who had been trying hard to accomplish that same 'thinking out,' "to say that Wintle would not have asked such a question, unless he had been afraid of firearms being used?"

"Yes, I see that," agreed Payne.

"By whom and why?" Bobby continued. "No apparent reason why he should suspect either Christopherson or his daughter of wanting to shoot anyone. But suppose a deserter were hiding in the inn?"

"Resisting arrest," Payne interposed, looking quite excited, for, as the authorities wouldn't let him join the army, what luck if there was going to be a chance of a scrap on his own doorstep, so to speak.

"That was my first idea," Bobby said, "but only a man off his head would try a trick like that. So then it struck me: Suppose this imaginary deserter of ours is off his head in actual fact? Suppose his Dunkirk experience threw him off his balance? It has happened. Shell shock. That sort of thing. It might be another reason why father and sister are hiding him. Not so much to save him from the army as to save him from an asylum. They might think his best chance of getting over it, getting normal again, was with them. Suppose, too, he had fits of violence. Thought he was back again, fighting at Dunkirk, thought he had still to hold the Germans off." Bobby paused, hesitated, and then added in a very apologetic tone: "I suppose you think it's a devil of a lot of conjecture all built up from Wintle's saying that about firearms."

"Well, yes, sir," agreed Payne, "but it does seem to hang together and all very carefully reasoned out. We do know from the dabs on the cut-out window pane that the dead man, whoever he really is, was up to something there at the Conqueror Inn. It seems quite feasible that if young Derek Christopherson was that way, crazy like, he might have thought it was the Germans after him again. A service revolver was used and he could easily have had one he picked up over there, at Dunkirk."

"There's still another possibility," Bobby said. "It might have begun like that but ended differently. Even if something of the sort did happen, it doesn't follow it was Larry Connor who got killed."

"No," agreed Payne. "No, I see that. It might be the other fellow, it might be Larry who killed Derek if it did come to a scrap. Only then, if the Christophersons knew Derek was dead, because of having made an attack on Larry, why were they the first to call us in and yet now won't say a word?"

"Possibly," Bobby answered, "Christopherson put the call through before he knew what had happened. Or he may have realized that the loss of two thousand pounds was bound to cause inquiry and he wanted to divert suspicion."

Payne was beginning to look worried.

"My head's fair buzzing," he complained. "If there's only one line to follow up, you know where you are. But that makes two quite new ones, and how many is that altogether?"

"Four, isn't it?" Bobby remarked. "First, Merton Kram killed Larry as a result of a quarrel following Larry's secret marriage to Kram's daughter. Plausible, and accounts for that candle burning on Micky Burke's mantelpiece and means Maggie's suspicions are correct. Seems inconsistent though with the murder occurring near the Conqueror Inn and doesn't explain the breaking and entering. Or the careful Christopherson secrecy. Second, Derek Christopherson, suffering from shell shock, killed Larry, thinking himself back at Dunkirk, and Larry a German attacking him. Plausible in itself, but doesn't explain Micky's belief and Maggie's. Nor does it seem to account for the mutilation of the features so carefully carried out. Thirdly, Larry knew about Derek and was threatening to give information. Blackmail possibly. So the father and the sister made sure he didn't. Plausible in itself, but only if you leave out a good many other little details. Nothing we know about Larry to suggest he was a blackmailer. Fourthly, Captain Wintle caught Larry hanging about the inn, gave him a thrashing the first time and the second time ended in a killing. Quite possible, but again a lot of other small points have to be left out."

"I don't see that that matters, sir," Payne declared, "because they may be all irrelevant. But with four contradictory theories, only one can be the right one. Well, which?"

"Perhaps none of them," said Bobby, looking as discouraged as he felt. "What we want is a theory that covers the whole ground. That two thousand pounds must have something to do with it, but I can't bring it into any theory I've thought of yet. If it's a true picture, everything ought to fit. Then there's Leader keeps dodging in and out of the picture. You haven't forgotten what I told you about him?"

"No, sir," answered Payne. "I suppose he ought to be theory number five. There's one thing. If it is Derek who was killed and buried out there by the road, that does explain why his face was smashed in. Nearly everyone in the district would have been able to recognize him only for that, and the Christophersons would have had something to explain. Son a deserter instead of a hero."

"It's a motive," agreed Bobby. "Speaking of Leader, I could bear to know a bit more about him and why, even before the murder, he was out on the moor, asking about eggs. Job for you, Payne. I want you to go along to that pull-up place Leader called the Ritz. It's somewhere on the main road north of here and it has the name up, Leader said. Try if you can pick up any gossip there, any crumb of information. Both Loo Leader and Micky Burke seem to have used the place, and, so far as I can see, it's the only point of contact between them."

"Very good, sir," said Payne.

"You'll have to get something to eat," Bobby went on, "as an excuse for being there, so you might order tinned eggs."

"Tinned eggs?" repeated Payne, looking puzzled. "What's that, sir?"

"Don't know," Bobby answered. "I asked my wife and she said she had never heard of them. Dried eggs, of course, but not tinned eggs. Leader said he got them there. I wondered a bit what he meant. You see," Bobby explained apologetically, "this thing's got me so tangled up, I've even wondered if 'tinned eggs' might be some sort of password or signal or something. I know it sounds silly, but so did Hitler sound silly till we found we had to take him a lot more seriously than we wanted to."

"Very good, sir," Payne answered. "I'll ask for 'em and see what I get," but it was plain from the tone of his voice that he wasn't greatly impressed.

"Oh, I know it sounds fantastic," Bobby admitted, still more apologetically, "but you never know these days and anyhow it'll do no harm to ask." Changing the subject he went on: "What I more specially want to know is how it happens Leader had the same idea as Kram about using the Conqueror Inn barns as a kind of central depot."

"Doesn't seem to fit, does it, sir?" observed Payne.

"It doesn't," Bobby agreed with gloomy emphasis. "Nothing— jells," he declared, using a word he had picked up from a housewifely spouse very much occupied with the local Woman's Institute.

Payne, having received a few more instructions, was preparing to depart, when the 'phone bell rang. Bobby answered it. A distant voice said:

"If you want the revolver that did the killing at the Conqueror Inn, dig in the north-west corner of the two-acre oat-field, under the thorn bush."

CHAPTER XXIII
BURIED REVOLVER

HURRIEDLY BOBBY POURED into the 'phone mouthpiece a dulcet request to be told who was speaking and an invitation to a personal meeting, anywhere, at any time. No answer came. Only too certainly had the unknown spoken, hung up, departed. An equally hurried though less dulcet request to Exchange to trace the call brought a tart reminder that the dial system was in use in Midwych. So Bobby hung up and told Payne what the message had been.

"A man's voice," Bobby added, "but probably disguised. Bit of a squeak that didn't sound quite natural. Anyhow, I didn't recognize it. It might be a woman for that matter. Quite likely," he added with the deep-seated pessimism that comes from long experience of such things, "only a hoax. Someone trying to be funny."

"Shouldn't wonder," agreed Payne, "the world's so full of such a number of fools."

"Practical joking," pronounced Bobby, "is the lowest form the meanest intelligence can take in its feeblest moments."

"Yes, sir, so it is," agreed Payne admiringly, thinking this sentence worthy of his favourite newspaper's favourite leader writer. "But I suppose we've got to sit up and take notice?"

Bobby nodded agreement.

"And if," he said, scowling fiercely, "I spot some fool sitting about there and grinning, I'll"—he paused and added, less fiercely—"I won't be able to do a thing."

"No, sir, so you won't," agreed Payne, and then the 'phone bell rang again.

Bobby, still scowling, answered, and as he listened a beaming smile replaced that dreadful scowl.

"Oh, good," he said, "good work, Briggs. Very good indeed. I shan't forget it. Carry on and thank you." He hung up and to the attentive Payne he said: "That was Briggs, the chap we told off to keep an eye on Mr. Merton Kram and the K. and K.M.T.C. He saw Kram come out and go to a 'phone box down the street. Briggs says he thought it a bit funny as, of course, Kram has a 'phone in his office and so why did he want to use a street box? So Briggs rang up to report."

"Means it was Kram 'phoned just now," said Payne, looking excited. "Hadn't we better have him round here right away and ask him how he knows?"

Bobby thought for a moment and then shook his head.

"He would only deny it and we've no proof," he said. "He could easily say he had been ringing up someone on confidential business he didn't want any of his staff to know about and we couldn't prove he was lying. I couldn't swear to his voice. No evidence," said Bobby; and remarked gloomily that when his expected fate overtook him and he died of a broken heart, on the shattered fragments would be found engraved the words:

"No evidence."

Payne made sympathetic noises. Bobby, cheering up a little, remarked that if the information did come from Kram, and if it proved correct, it was interesting, very interesting indeed.

"But for the present we'll keep it up our sleeve that we know it was Kram," he added. "We'll tax him with it sometime and see how he takes it."

"Anyhow, it isn't just one of those tomfool attempts to be funny," Payne observed. "If you ask me, sir, I should say the revolver will be there all right."

Bobby agreed. Payne departed on the errand already assigned him, and Bobby sent another plain-clothes man to relieve Briggs, whom he had decided to take with him in token of appreciation.

"I thought you might like to be in on the job," he told Briggs when the man reported. "It may come in very useful, knowing that that message was from Mr. Kram, as it's quite certain it did, though unfortunately we can't prove it."

"No, sir, I see that," Briggs admitted. "If the post office would only record all messages, it would help us a lot."

"So it would," agreed Bobby, "but also hinder us a whole lot more. Can't have Gestapo methods and the trust and help of the public as well. Two incompatibles. And two-thirds of police work depends on the public co-operating."

Before long he and Briggs were on their way in the little Bayard Seven that was Bobby's private property but that on account of the petrol scarcity he now used almost exclusively for official purposes. He had told Briggs to put spade and pickaxe in the car; and in the hope of escaping notice, for he well remembered how in its solitude the Conqueror Inn seemed like a lonely sentinel on watch over all that countryside, he left the car, duly immobilized and as far as possible hidden in a fold of the moor, nearly two miles from their destination. The rest of the journey they completed on foot, though to do so necessitated making a wide detour.

So far as they could tell, their arrival in the two-acre oat-field in the corner by the thorn bush passed unobserved. They began work, taking it in turn with spade and pick, though the latter implement was not really required. It was not difficult to see where recent digging had taken place, for indeed the archæologists tell us that a hole in the ground is the one thing that can never be concealed.

The task was neither long nor difficult. Barely a foot below the surface they found the revolver, wrapped in soiled and dirty paper. On the butt was a stain that looked to Bobby very like blood, but of that, of course, he could not be sure. Very carefully avoiding touching it more than was absolutely necessary, he packed it in the prepared box he had bought. Then he turned his attention to the paper wrapping. With some surprise he found it was not a newspaper but a sheet of an ordnance map.

"The largest scale, too," he remarked. "Six inches to the mile. What do you make of that, Briggs?"

Briggs, eager though he was to confirm and if possible enhance his newly-acquired reputation for exceptional brilliance, could only look puzzled. Then he brightened up and said:

"Lorry drivers often have maps, sir. Useful if they get put on a fresh route."

"On the six-inch scale?" Bobby asked.

"Well, I don't know about that, sir," admitted Briggs. "It does seem a bit queer."

"So it does," agreed Bobby, "and I don't like things that seem a bit queer, not one little bit do I like them. I wonder who it belonged to? Not much chance of finding dabs on it now after it's been buried." He held it up to the light on the remote chance of perceiving some greasy stain that might have survived burial in the damp earth. A vain hope; but all the same he continued to look and the longer he looked the more interested and puzzled he appeared. At last he lowered it and said: "Someone has been making tiny holes all over it, pin pricks they look like. What do you make of that, Briggs?"

Briggs made nothing of it, and, admitting as much, looked so puzzled and downcast, and so much as if he felt that now he had lost all his previously acquired merit, that Bobby hastened to say that he made nothing of it either. But he added that he thought the map might repay more careful examination. This being safe ground, Briggs said with enthusiasm that he thought so, too, and had the inspector noticed that now someone had come out from the inn yard and was standing there, watching them?

Bobby, engrossed with their discoveries, had not seen this and turned to look. Rachel, he thought, though it was not easy to be sure, for whoever it was stood against the grey background of the old barn. But a woman he felt sure and then she slipped away and when she re-appeared it was in the company of a man.

"Watching us," Briggs said briefly.

"Come along," Bobby said, "we'll see if they have anything to say."

To the inn accordingly they proceeded. The two figures by the old barn stood for a time as if waiting and then first Rachel went away and next her father followed her.

Through the yard Bobby and his companion passed and on to the back door of the inn. It was open. Bobby knocked. A voice called to them to enter. They went into the kitchen. Christopherson and Rachel were standing there, side by side, their tense attitude, their strained faces, their air of a mutual support that each felt the other needed, that each gave to each as each from each received it, all alike declared their apprehension and their dread. Nearer the inner door Mrs. Christopherson was standing, but as Bobby and his companion appeared, she gave a low cry that was half a sob and went away at a sort of shuffling run. To the other two, the father and the daughter, Bobby said:

"I think you know what we have found. Is there anything you would care to say?"

Christopherson shook his head. Rachel made no sign. Bobby continued:

"If you will not speak, things must take their course."

They were silent still, but it was a silence more eloquent, more charged with deep emotion than ever could words have been. Bobby said:

"I have my duty to do."

"I would ask no other of any man," answered Christopherson.

"I take it," Bobby said, "you know this revolver I have found buried on your land is the one used in the murder?"

They still remained silent, but Bobby saw how Rachel's hand stole out and held her father's, held it in such a grip that the knuckles showed white with the unconscious strain.

"If you do not wish to make any statement," Bobby went on, "there is nothing more for me to do at present. Expert examination will soon make it certain whether this is the actual weapon used. If that is so, you can understand what conclusions will of necessity be drawn. I am sorry." He hesitated and then added in a lower voice: "I wish I could help you."

He turned to go. Christopherson sat down on a chair near by. Rachel stood by his side. She had drawn herself to her full height, her head high, in curious contrast to her father who seemed to have shrunk in upon himself as he sat, so that the giant of a man Bobby remembered appeared now as of less than ordinary size. As Bobby put out his hand to open the kitchen door to go, Rachel spoke.

"Thank you," she said. "I think you want to be kind. I think you were kind to come and tell us you had found—that. But there is no help that you or anyone can give us."

Bobby bowed slightly and went out of the room. Briggs followed. Bobby had a last glimpse of the tall young girl bending above the stricken form of her father. As they crossed the threshold into the inn yard, Briggs said:

"Do you hear that, sir? Do you hear?"

"Yes," said Bobby.

"It's a woman crying," Briggs said. "The girl's broke down."

"No," said Bobby, "she will not break while she lives. That is the mother."

He walked on and Briggs followed. Briggs said after a time:

"Wouldn't ever think those two were a pair of murderers, would you, sir?"

CHAPTER XXIV
CAPTAIN WINTLE'S STORY

DUTY CAN BE a harsh master, the search for truth a dreadful task; and back again in his office Bobby, hard as he tried to concentrate his attention on the events of the afternoon, found it wandering continually to the two strangely contrasted, tragic figures of Maggie Kram, torn by the fearful suspicion that her father was the murderer of her husband; of Rachel Christopherson, upright and protective by her father sitting bowed under some other, some different, some equally heavy fear.

"If only they, or even one of them, would trust me enough to tell me the truth," Bobby said aloud, "I might be able to do something to help."

But he supposed perhaps they dared not, and then no doubt, as he reflected a little bitterly, to them he seemed merely a policeman, an enemy, hot and eager in relentless pursuit.

He wrenched his mind from these thoughts and applied it to his work. Already he had communicated with his superior, Colonel Glynne, the county chief constable, now in London, where he was still wistfully hoping that on one pretext or another he might presently get somewhere near the fighting line. After all, a retired Admiral of nearly seventy had managed it and was now in Libya, and all the colonel's deepest instincts revolted from the thought that what the navy could do, the army could not. So he was pulling strings hard at the War Office and, knowing this, Bobby decided that he might as well pull them for police purposes, too. So he had rung him up, ostensibly to report developments, really to ask him to obtain without the customary official delays, all possible information concerning the service revolver bearing the serial number of that found on the Conqueror Inn land.

Then the weapon itself had to be packed with care and dispatched for expert inspection and report, and the large scale map in which it had been wrapped had to be given a meticulous examination.

Because to Bobby it seemed unlikely that all those tiny pin holes with which it was studded, plainly visible when the map was held up to the light, had been made merely to pass an idle hour. Almost certainly they had a purpose and a meaning, even though he had not been able so far to find any significance in their apparently random distribution.

The hour was late and he was still dissatisfied with the result of his long continued poring over the map when there came a call from London. This time Colonel Glynne's string pulling had been successful. His War Office friends, unable to dispatch him forthwith to the thick of the fight—and often they were sorry not to, and the thicker the fight, the better—had been glad in the faint hope of keeping him quiet for a time to help him to get the information he wanted. Every priority and urgent tag they could think of they had attached to his request. So now here was the reply to the effect that the revolver bearing the number quoted had been issued to Captain Peter Wintle, at that time a newly commissioned second lieutenant.

Bobby listened grimly, thanked the colonel for his assistance, and agreed with the suggestion that Captain Wintle should be asked immediately for an explanation. A call put through to Ingleside Camp brought the information that by a lucky chance Captain Wintle was in Midwych and could probably be found at the Central Station where he was on duty in connection with the dispatch of troops to the north. Thinking a personal message delivered by an inconspicuous civilian might be less likely to embarrass Wintle than would be the receipt of a police 'phone call, Bobby sent a plainclothes man to ask for an interview as soon as the captain was free. He was to ask, too, if Captain Wintle would come to police headquarters, or if he would prefer their chat to take place elsewhere? Just as the captain liked, any place he cared to mention would be agreed to, the plain-clothes man was to say. But he was also to make it very plain that no delay in time could be accepted.

The plain-clothes man came back with Captain Wintle's compliments and he would be happy to call to see Inspector Owen as soon as possible. Probably within the hour, as his duty was nearly accomplished. In less than half an hour in fact Wintle appeared, looking worn and tired and as if he had slept but badly of late, a result perhaps of army cares and worries, but, since he had a wary and apprehensive air as well, due more probably to other causes. He accepted stiffly Bobby's invitation to be seated, refused even more stiffly the offer of a cigarette. He would be glad, he said, if whatever business the inspector had with him could be dealt with as quickly as possible, as he was anxious to return to camp.

"I'll do my best," Bobby promised, "and I am sorry to have to trouble you again. The fact is there has been a grave development in the Conqueror Inn case."

He paused, watching Wintle intently. Easy to see the stiffened attitude, the increased nervous tension, the other showed. There was a quickened apprehension in his eyes, a tightening of the lines about his mouth, even his voice was less steady than usual as he said:

"Yes. Well. What is it and how does it affect me?"

"Can you guess?" Bobby asked.

"No," Wintle answered. "I don't deal in guesses. I prefer facts. What are they, if you have any?"

"This afternoon," Bobby said, "a service revolver was found buried on land belonging to the Conqueror Inn. It has been identified on official army information as having been issued to you in 1939."

Wintle stared at him blankly, shrugged his shoulders, made an impatient gesture with one hand.

"Oh, nonsense," he said. "Impossible," he added after a pause. "Some mistake," he added again when Bobby made no comment. "Or are you just trying some form of police trap or bluff?"

"Captain Wintle," Bobby said sternly, "please be good enough to understand that I am speaking as a responsible officer of the law, engaged in the investigation of what seems to be a cold-blooded and rather specially brutal murder. The revolver found to-day bears the serial number of the one army records show was issued to you. No doubt official records may be mistaken. I think it unlikely in this case. I think an explanation is necessary. Can you give one?"

"No," answered Wintle. "I should think it's impossible. I lost my revolver and pretty well everything else I had at Dunkirk. I don't see how you can possibly have found it where you say. Anyhow, I have no idea how it can have got there."

"There may be links," Bobby said. "It is my business to try to find them. In this case, Derek Christopherson."

"You know, I suppose," Wintle answered in a voice a little too unmoved, "that he was reported killed at Dunkirk?"

"I remember your telling me he saved your life there," Bobby remarked. "I got some details. Mr. Christopherson showed me letters he had received from the boy's C.O. From one or two of his comrades too. I wonder if you would mind telling me exactly what happened?"

"I don't see why you want to know," Wintle answered. "What has what happened at Dunkirk more than a year ago got to do with this story of yours about finding my old revolver here? Anyhow, there's not much to tell. I don't suppose it would sound anything at all to a man who has never been under fire."

"Not many of us in England, man, woman or child," Bobby reminded him, "but knows now what that is like. I should really be greatly obliged if you would tell me the whole story."

Wintle still looked very much as if he would have liked to refuse but apparently could think of no reasonable excuse to offer for any such refusal. Ungraciously enough he said:

"A shell burst upset my car. It was full of S.A. ammunition I was taking up to the firing line. When the car went over I was trapped. Couldn't move. The thing was lying right across my legs. It caught fire and the ammunition started popping off. Also the Jerries had a machine gun trained on me and kept it going pretty briskly. To make sure, I suppose. I started praying my hardest one of their bullets would get me. I could feel the flames beginning to bite. I could smell my trousers starting to singe. I thought a bullet would be a bit easier than getting burned alive. But they all missed and I remember cursing Jerry for a damned bad shot. I don't suppose you can guess what it is like to lie under machine-gun fire and pray that one bullet will score a direct hit because you can feel the heat of the flames increasing, watch the flames growing bigger and nearer and nearer and bigger. I remember managing to wriggle my revolver free and making up my mind that if Jerry's bullets wouldn't do the trick, I would end it myself. I know you ought to take what comes to you, but I didn't feel up to lying there and burning. And those damned flames were very close and very hot. Then young Christopherson came along and somehow—God alone knows how, he is not a big man or a strong—I shouldn't have thought it possible—sometimes I think it wasn't possible, even though he did it. He got his shoulders underneath and he heaved once and then he heaved again and I saw the flames all round him and the bullets flying by, and me praying now that they would miss. He gave a third heave and he held that car up in midair as I thought no man could have done. I crawled out and if you think I can remember—or cared—what happened to my revolver or anything else, you are mistaken. That's all. I know it doesn't sound much but it was a lot to live through."

"Yes," Bobby agreed. "Yes. I think I can understand how you feel. It was the act of a very gallant man." Slowly and thoughtfully he added: "You know I have been wondering a lot what might be the after effects of such an experience on any nervous, highly-strung temperament."

CHAPTER XXV
THE COST OF TRUTH

To THIS COMMENT or suggestion perhaps, Wintle only answered by a bleak and hostile stare, as if in some way he resented what Bobby said or else perceived in it some hidden menace. The latter, Bobby thought, and thought that such quick suspicion confirmed the theory that now was growing in his mind to a coherent shape.

"Well, if that's all you wanted to know—" Wintle said and made as if to rise and go, but Bobby checked him by an almost imperceptible gesture. Wintle frowned, sat down again, and said: "I don't know what it all has to do with you. I don't know why I told you, only I suppose you could have found out for yourself. I made a report. I wanted some recognition given. But there's no recognition they give a dead man—except the V.C. You can get that when you are dead. Nothing else. It was worth a V.C. what young Derek did all right. No independent witness though, so it didn't count. Besides, V.C.s were earned by the dozen out there on Dunkirk beach."

"Yes," said Bobby. "Yes," and again Wintle gave him that bleak and hostile stare in which so much of apprehension seemed to show as well. Bobby went on: "What happened after Derek released you?"

"What do you suppose?" growled Wintle. "Think we stopped to talk it over? I had to report back as quick as I could. I knew they wanted that S.A. ammunition in a hurry. I had to let them know I had been knocked out so they could send for more."

"And Christopherson, did he go with you?"

"No. Why should he? He was driving a lorry. There were two or three other men in it—wounded, mostly, he was taking down to the beach. He went back to the lorry. A Stuka came along and made a dive. I saw the bomb fall square on the lorry. A good size bomb. I was thirty or forty yards away but the blast knocked me flat. When I got up I ran back to see what had happened. There wasn't any lorry or any wounded men any longer—just a hole where the lorry had been and bits of it and of the men scattered all round. That's all."

"You didn't actually recognize Christopherson's dead body?" Bobby insisted.

"It's hard to recognize small scattered bits," Wintle answered grimly.

"Yes, of course," agreed Bobby.

"One of Christopherson's platoon N.C.O.s saw it happen," Wintle said. "He was driving another lorry just behind—man named Bradley, I think. If you want to check up, you can ask him. I know he reported it."

"It was your account I wanted," Bobby explained. "You see, what is in my mind is that all you can tell us of your revolver is, that you had it in your hand when Derek Christopherson started to help you out from under your car. Now it turns up here, buried on Derek's father's land. You see what that suggests? Obviously either you brought it back with you or it was someone else. I have to consider whether it was you, or, if not, who that someone else can be. You tell me you can't remember anything about it. The possibility does suggest itself, doesn't it? that Derek picked it up if you let it fall, as might happen very naturally when you were trying to get from under the car as he lifted it up. So it might have been in his possession when the bomb fell. After that anything might in theory happen to it, but does it seem likely that anyone but Derek Christopherson could have brought it back here to Derek Christopherson's father's farm? Isn't that a fair and logical conclusion?"

"Damn cold-blooded reasoning," Wintle said, "but there's a flaw in it. You are trying to prove that one of us must have brought the thing here—and I suppose buried it as well. But if you prove it was one of us, that shows it wasn't the other, and that applies to both."

"Isn't there a flaw in that reasoning, too?" Bobby asked. "That one of you two didn't do a thing, isn't proof that neither did it."

"Oh, well," Wintle muttered. "We can talk round and round like that all night. Anyhow, I didn't bury any revolver anywhere, and why should I?"

"Captain Wintle," answered Bobby, "the first instinct of a murderer is to try to hide the weapon used."

"You have got back to that now then?" Wintle asked. "Got as far as calling me a murderer?"

"I have not done so," Bobby said quietly. "I am pointing out certain circumstances, pointing out the suspicions they cause, and I am asking you if you wish to, or can, offer any explanation. At present I am obliged to accept your statement that you know nothing of what became of your revolver. But I am not at all sure. What they call an open mind. Another piece of evidence may turn up and throw quite a new light on things. But I do know very well that blast has very funny results. I have seen some even here at home in Midwych. Sometimes even more strange non-results, if I may put it that way. I remember two A.R.P. wardens. In our first blitz. They were standing close together at a street corner. One was blown to bits. The other was hardly hurt. The idea was the blast had made a kind of whirlpool so to say—a cyclone rather. With a comparatively calm centre, where the one warden had been standing, while the other got the full force of the blast, though only a yard or two away. Only theory of course. No one seems to know much about how blast acts. Anyhow, everyone thought both those men must have been killed. One was. The other man just picked himself up and began to brush the dust off his clothes. So then everyone thought he was all right. He wasn't. He was in a sort of mental haze. He was in a kind of dazed condition for some hours, didn't seem to know where he was or what had happened. I am asking myself if something of that sort may have happened in this case, to Derek Christopherson. A musician, I understand. More sensitive than most of us perhaps. More easily thrown off his balance. Shell shock. That's what they call it for want of a better name. Suppose in that sort of dazed condition he got back to England and then made his way home to the Conqueror Inn. I have seen and talked to Mr. Christopherson, the boy's father, and I don't much think that without very good reason he would give shelter to a deserter—even though his own son. But if Derek were in that kind of mental condition I think he might, he and his wife and Miss Rachel. Especially Miss Rachel. I think she is a strong character. I think her father is a strong man but I think she is stronger still. If that is what happened it was foolish of them, I suppose. They may have feared for his reason. They may have thought that if the army authorities got to know and arrested him as a deserter it might complete his mental upset, drive him permanently insane. Would the army have understood quickly enough or would they only have found out that highly skilled medical care and attention were necessary when it was too late? When the balance of the boy's mind had been destroyed for good? I think that was the danger Miss Rachel saw and I think she made up her mind it was too great and she would not let her brother face it. I think she would tell her father they were justified, since Derek was plainly unfit for military service. I think they—she and her parents—were caught between two duties. There was the duty to their country at a moment of deadly peril, at a moment when men and women worked at their machines till they dropped and rose up again from where they lay to go on working, at a time when old men and boys were drilling side by side on every common and village green in the land. Against that was their duty to brother and son, to save his sanity they saw in danger. I don't think it was an easy choice, but I think I know which choice they made."

"Why are you telling me all this?" Wintle asked.

"So that you may tell it to Miss Rachel," Bobby answered. "She does not trust me. She sees me merely as the official, the policeman, the man whose duty it would be to pounce on her brother and hand him over to a court martial. If she would trust me, I think I could help. That is, if I am right in what I've been saying and it has happened like that."

"Who put you on to it?" Wintle asked.

"Do you agree it is more or less the truth?"

"Who put you on to it?" Wintle repeated, ignoring Bobby's question.

"No one," Bobby answered. "It is merely what I think is a logical reconstruction from the facts. I had to ask myself why the Conqueror Inn didn't seem to want custom. Why an attic was occupied by someone who according to Mr. Christopherson was himself, though it didn't seem he was the type of man likely to be occupying a separate room from his wife, more especially a room on another floor. Why there was hidden on his farm a revolver, lost you tell me, where at any rate Derek could have picked it up. I don't know whether you will feel willing to repeat what I have said, and why I have said it, to Miss Rachel. Before you do, and if you do, I think I must warn you of one thing though I am not sure that, as a policeman, I ought to. But all this does not seem to be quite the ordinary crime. I know I am not dealing with ordinary criminals. I want you to understand this—that my duty must always come first. I have this in my mind. Is it possible that Derek Christopherson, still more or less mentally unbalanced, believed he was still at Dunkirk, still in danger of being attacked by German soldiers? If so, is it possible—I take it he would go out for fresh air sometimes after dark—is it possible that if someone came upon him abruptly in the dark one night, that his mind flew back to Dunkirk, that he thought a German soldier was attacking him, and that he drew the revolver he had in his pocket and fired and killed?"

Wintle had taken out his handkerchief and was wiping his face and forehead.

"I don't believe you are being straight with me," he muttered. "I don't believe you've built all this up just by adding one thing to another. You must know more, someone must have told you something."

"Oh, yes. Naturally they have," Bobby answered. "But not intentionally and sometimes more by what they failed to say, rather than by what they did say. The most important thing I learnt, the so to say key word to the puzzle, was from something you yourself told me."

"I did? What was that? Rubbish," Wintle exclaimed. "What do you mean?"

"You told me you had asked whether there were any firearms kept at the Conqueror Inn."

"Well, what about it?" Wintle asked. "Why shouldn't I? What could you get out of that? What do you mean, key to a puzzle?"

"So much the key that it seemed to open the door to everything I've just been saying," Bobby answered. "Why should you ask that unless you were afraid of firearms being used? And why should you be afraid of that unless you knew there was someone at the Conqueror Inn who might use them dangerously? But that someone wasn't likely to be either Mr. Christopherson or his wife or Miss Rachel. So who could it be? I had to think that out. You see, the whole of my—speculation—follows in logical succession from that one remark of yours."

"You build a lot on one remark," Wintle said.

"Yes," agreed Bobby. "Yes."

"You've no proof of what you say."

"No," agreed Bobby. "No."

"I suppose this means my commission goes," Wintle said. "I suppose I might be able to join up again in the ranks."

Bobby said nothing. He did not see that there was anything he could say usefully. Presently Wintle said:

"If all that's true, can you blame them?"

"It is never for me to blame anyone—except myself," Bobby answered. "My duty is to get at the truth and that I must do and will to the best of my ability, no matter at what cost."

"Oh, well," Wintle muttered. "Well, now then, there it is."

"The cost of truth is sometimes high," Bobby said. "In this case it may mean destroying a man's reason, it may mean breaking a girl's heart, it may mean wrecking a soldier's career."

Wintle gave Bobby another of those long stares of his, but one in which now curiosity and doubt seemed predominant.

"You see all that," Wintle asked, "and yet you mean to go on?"

"Yes," said Bobby.

"Oh, well," Wintle said and grew silent again, deep in thought. "Is truth worth all that?" he asked presently, though a little as if speaking to himself. "Not a question for us to answer, I suppose, either for you or for me. Well, can I go now? I have told you all I know and apparently a good deal more than I knew I had told you. Well, I would like you to believe that anyhow I have never deliberately lied. I had no real knowledge that anyone—either Derek or anyone else—was hidden there in the Conqueror Inn. They never told me. I never asked. The first time I went there I felt there was something—I didn't know what. Just imagination, I thought. The second time I went I got there late, after dark. I heard someone shouting in the yard, something about Germans. I thought I knew the voice but I wasn't sure. I looked out and I thought I recognized the figure. But it was dark and I couldn't be sure. All Rachel said was that it was a man who was suffering from the shock of what he had been through. I didn't ask who the man was and she didn't say. I expect you think these are pretty feeble excuses."

"No," said Bobby.

"If it was young Derek Christopherson," Wintle went on, "he had saved my life. If he was a deserter, if Dunkirk had been too much for him—well, what had happened to him was because he had stopped to help me. If he had driven straight on, he would have missed that bomb. It may have been my duty to report that I thought a deserter might be hiding in the Conqueror Inn. I just couldn't do it. I knew I ought. I didn't. It'll mean my commission—cashiered probably. I take it you'll make a report at once?"

"Not till my case is more complete," Bobby answered. "Not then unless I have to. I suppose I'm like you. I ought to report that I think a deserter may be hidden at the Conqueror Inn. But I'll make that subsidiary to my first duty of discovering the truth about the killing there. In the meantime don't you think that if the military authorities knew, they might take a sympathetic view?"

"After they had established the facts and by that time the mischief might be done," Wintle answered. "You don't know our brigadier. It would have to go to him first. One of the old school. To him a deserter would be just a deserter. Only that and nothing more. And shell shock just a sissy word—nothing more."

"I mustn't give you advice," Bobby said. "I merely mention that if the Press got hold of such a story as you have told me and if the chief actor in it didn't get sympathetic treatment—they would kick up a shine that would rock the Government itself. Imagine one of the sob writers in the Sunday papers letting himself go about it."

"Yes, I know," Wintle answered. "But it might be too late. That's what Rachel says." Bobby noticed this use a second time of the Christian name. "That's always the snag—long before the Sunday papers got to work, the mischief might be done and the boy's mental balance upset for good. What are you going to do?"

"I don't know yet," Bobby answered. "Even if the theory I have built up is correct as far as it goes, there's still a lot unexplained. No theory is satisfactory till it covers the whole ground and there's a lot left out in this one. I am afraid there are still a good many questions I shall have to ask you yourself—for instance what happened outside the Conqueror Inn the night you tell me you ran into a door and got a black eye, the same night the dead man cut out a pane of the kitchen window and broke into the Inn. Two nights that was before the killing."

"Whoever it was hiding there," Wintle said, "and I don't know for certain he isn't there now. That's the truth—Derek or another, they have not seen or heard of him since that night, the night Rachel heard the pistol shot."

Bobby wondered gravely if this was true. He thought so, or rather he felt sure that Wintle believed it to be true. He said:

"Does that mean the dead man is Derek Christopherson?"

"I have never dared to ask," Wintle said.

CHAPTER XXVI
THE FORGOTTEN MAN

AN UNSATISFACTORY INTERVIEW, Bobby told himself; and so he told Sergeant Payne when Payne reported next morning on the apparently equally unsatisfactory and uninformative evening he had spent at the little wayside snack bar that called itself the Ritz.

"Nice little place," Payne said, "clean and tidy and all that. Popular, too. I asked for tinned eggs, same as you said, sir, and it seems a sort of private joke there for sardines on toast. Goes back to Micky Burke. Some other lorry bumped into his parked outside, and he got into a panic and yelled out to be careful, he was loaded up with eggs, he said."

"Eggs?" repeated Bobby.

"Yes, sir," Payne answered. "I did prick up my ears a bit at that, seeing how often eggs have been spoken of, incidental like. But there was nothing to it. It wasn't eggs at all. One case was knocked off Micky's lorry and burst open and it was sardines, inside. Micky said he called out it was eggs just to make the other chap careful, so they all got chaffing him about his eggs and calling sardines tinned eggs to tease him like. Sort of family joke, sir, if you see what I mean. Funny to them that's in the know but not to anyone else."

"No," agreed Bobby. "No, doesn't sound first-class humour, does it?"

"Sorry I hadn't better luck, sir," said Payne apologetically.

"As good or better than mine with Wintle," Bobby remarked consolingly. "If you get a man talking, nine times out of ten he'll tell you something you want to know. Wintle did tell me a lot but not a thing that matters. Now, is that because he knows nothing or because he knows so much?"

Payne shook his head, looked doubtful, and said he didn't trust Wintle any further than he could see him after blackout and Bobby agreed. He remarked that he had seldom met a man about whom he found it more difficult to make up his mind than he did about Wintle.

"A difficulty in this case," Bobby went on, "is that you can't help feeling most of them are up against it pretty badly, and most of them have reasons you can understand for not wanting to tell what they know. Tough on a detective if he can't get any co-operation. The Maggie Kram girl won't tell us what she knows or suspects about what's happened to her husband for fear of implicating her father. A father hanged for the murder of a husband doesn't bear thinking of. But her suspicions do mean Mr. Kram is lying when he says he was at home the night of the killing and what's the good of our knowing that? The girl would certainly commit perjury in the witness box to back him up. Then there are the Christophersons— father, mother, and daughter. They had to choose between what seemed like sheltering a shirker and deserter or risking the sanity of a son and brother. Even now they won't tell the truth for fear of the consequences to him. Perhaps they don't even know the full truth."

"I think they know all right, only they aren't saying," Payne interposed. "If you ask me, there's nothing they would stop at to help that boy. They are the conscientious type and once you are up against a conscience—well, you are up against it, aren't you?"

Bobby nodded in full agreement.

"So you are," he said. "Sound psychology, Payne. A thoroughly conscientious crime is the hardest of all to deal with."

"If this Larry Connor spotted there was a deserter hidden there," Payne went on, "and tried to make trouble—perhaps to use it as a lever for having his way with the girl if there was any real cause for the other girl's jealousy—well, I wouldn't put it past them to finish off Larry to save Derek."

"It's an idea," agreed Bobby thoughtfully. "It would fit in with the attempt to break and enter by the kitchen window. But would it be in the Christopherson psychology to carry out that mutilation of a dead man's features?"

"When it's a case of conscience—" Payne said and left the sentence unfinished. "Good enough for an arrest, sir?" he suggested tentatively.

"Nowhere near it," declared Bobby with emphasis. "We've not a shred of proof that Derek Christopherson got back from Dunkirk, much less that he was ever hiding in the Conqueror Inn. Official records show him as killed in action and official records count. Our whole theory is an exercise in logic and can you imagine putting an exercise in logic before a British jury?"

Payne turned pale, aghast at the horror of such a thought.

"Then there's Captain Wintle," Bobby went on, "put to a choice between what he owed to his duty as an officer and what he owed to the man who saved his life."

"Do you believe his story about his revolver?" Payne asked. "Because, sir, I don't much think I do."

Bobby was sitting back in his chair with his hands thrust resolutely into his pockets because he was trying to break himself of a growing habit of rubbing his nose hard in moments of perplexity. Recently it had received domestic comment of some severity and he had promised reformation.

"I don't know," he said finally. "I hoped to get some pointers out of talking to Wintle. I didn't. We don't even know the revolver we found is the one actually used."

Payne looked startled.

"Oh, come, sir," he protested. "It's sure to be—certain."

"Nothing certain in this case," retorted Bobby. "I wanted to see if Wintle put that idea forward. He didn't. I talked as if it were established that his revolver was the weapon used. He seemed to accept that. Ignorance or knowledge? What do you think? It might be either if you ask me. Wintle may be the man we want. There is the quite good theory to work on that he killed Larry Connor in a jealous quarrel. Snag. We don't know that the dead man is Larry.

Evidence. Wintle's black eye and Maggie Kram's belief that Larry was somehow mixed up with Rachel."

"Slighter clues have led to the gallows," Payne said.

"Often," agreed Bobby. "But then there's plenty of evidence to suggest that the Christophersons did the killing, even though Christopherson himself gave the first information."

Payne nodded. He thought reasonable the suggestion that that might only mean that the alarm about the bank-notes had been given before the shooting occurred, or, alternatively, that Christopherson had realized that the loss of so much money was bound to lead to inquiry, investigation, and an almost certain discovery it was the part of wisdom to anticipate.

"Or again," Bobby continued, "there's the possibility that young Derek Christopherson, taking his exercise at night, ran into Larry Connor prowling round the Inn for his own purposes, got a shock, thought he was back at Dunkirk, and went for Larry, taking him in his disturbed mental state for a German soldier. Or if that happened, it may have turned out the other way with Larry killing Derek. You see we are up against a fresh complication now. At first we thought that as soon as we heard of a missing man, identity would be established—dead man and missing man sure to be the same. But now we have two missing men—Larry Connor and Derek Christopherson, and which is which?"

Payne didn't know and said as much with both haste and emphasis.

"But there is one thing," he ventured to suggest. "If there are two men missing and one dead, it's a safe bet the second missing man is the killer."

"No safe bets in this business," retorted Bobby, also with haste and emphasis, "not in this tangle of disconnected facts, uncertain motives and emotional complications."

Payne had produced his notebook and was consulting it.

"It's like this," he said. "First. Mr. Merton Kram is the killer and his daughter knows it and so does Micky Burke. Evidence. Maggie's doubts and fears and she ought to know. The candle burning before Kram's photograph on Micky Burke's mantelpiece."

"Yes, I could bear to know what that means," Bobby interposed.

"Secondly," continued Payne, "one of the Christophersons is the killer—father or daughter. Or the two of them together perhaps. Evidence. The revolver buried on their land. Motive. Keeping Derek hidden."

"The report hasn't come in yet from the gun expert to tell us for certain that that revolver is the one used," Bobby reminded him.

"Oh, well, sir, I think we can take that for granted," Payne answered. "Or why was it buried? And who else can have buried it but the Christophersons?"

"Yes, I know," Bobby agreed.

"Thirdly," Payne continued. "There's Captain Wintle. A downy bird if you ask me. Evidence. His black eye and the revolver used by the killer traced back to him. Fairly conclusive. So there's three lines to follow up and all of them good and promising."

"Nothing for us to do but make our choice," observed Bobby, "even if they do all contradict each other, and if two of them are certainly wrong, why not all three? And don't forget Loo Leader popping in and out in a way that wants explaining rather badly. What's his game?"

"Nosing round," said Payne with confidence. "Trying to find out anything he can use. Spot of blackmail."

"Might be," agreed Bobby. "Why was the revolver wrapped in a large scale map before it was buried?"

"Being wrapped in paper would keep it in better condition," Payne answered, a trifle surprised by the question.

"I meant its being a large-scale map," Bobby explained. "Was that something that was better hidden, too? And why the pin holes all over it?"

"Well, sir, are pin holes relevant?" Payne asked, respectfully contemptuous.

"Don't know," answered Bobby, "but anyhow I've rung up the Regional Commissioner's office and one of the staff is coming along to have a look. Those pin holes interest me somehow."

Payne managed to indicate it was an interest he could not share. Pin holes and murder seemed far apart, he thought.

"Then there's that business of eggs," Bobby went on. "Why did Maggie Kram, when she was trying to find out what was interesting Larry in the Conqueror Inn, hit on eggs as an excuse for making inquiries and why was Loo Leader talking about eggs as well? And why had Loo Leader the same idea as Merton Kram about using the Conqueror Inn outbuildings as a depot—to avoid cross journeys, they said, didn't they?"

But here they were interrupted by the arrival of the report of the expert to whom the dug up revolver had been sent for examination.

"Just another little snag," Bobby said with a sigh as soon as he had given the report a glance, "the bullet used in the killing did not come from this revolver. It has been fired quite recently but it didn't fire that particular bullet."

Payne said with great annoyance:

"But, sir—hang it all—well, I ask you. Weapon carefully hidden on the scene of a crime and you are to believe there's no connection?"

"I don't know about 'no connection,'" answered Bobby slowly, as his eye travelled down the long report. "The stain you remember we noticed is blood, fairly fresh, very likely dating from the time of the killing, though they can't be precise. Also they've found three fingerprints they've brought up clearly enough for identification. Photos enclosed. Prints on record as those of a man named Alf Hall. Remember the name?"

"Not at the moment," Payne confessed. "I'm trying to think."

"Pal of Loo Leader's, the forgotten man, I suppose," Bobby said. "Works for him as a lorry driver. So there is Loo Leader back in it again, and why Hall's dabs and not Loo's? I'm afraid we have rather forgotten Mr. Alf Hall."

"What was he in for if his dabs are on record?" Payne asked.

"Murder charge," Bobby answered. "Charge reduced to manslaughter. Sentence five years. Been out three years and some months. Nothing since known against him. Interesting."

CHAPTER XXVII
FIFTH COLUMN

IN THE AFTERNOON there arrived a member of the staff of the District Regional Commissioner—a retired major of the Indian army, as pleased to be back again at work as twenty-five years before he had been happy at the thought of retiring. He had with him a large-scale map of the district marked with a number of tiny circles in red ink. When the two maps—this one and that in which the buried revolver had been wrapped—were compared, complete coincidence was at once apparent between the red ink circles on the one, the pin holes pricked in the other.

"Means," said the major, "that every munition factory, all the new ones recently built, every factory engaged in war work, and that means practically every factory in the district, and in addition every dummy factory as well, all plainly marked here. Fifth column work. They are secret. What?"

"Hardly secret, are they?" Bobby suggested. "You can't hide a factory—even a dummy—from people living in the neighbourhood. Or from anyone passing near. You can keep secret the work being done, but the building itself has got to be visible."

"Fifth column work," repeated the major. "That map would give valuable information to any Hun bombers."

"Couldn't they get much the same information from aerial reconnaissance?" Bobby asked. "We've had machines over several times, flying high."

The major explained in some detail that photographs, though showing every detail of a building, often gave little indication of the building's exact location.

Bobby said, yes, he understood that; and did the major think it likely that a lorry driver, engaged in road transport, might mark in this way the position of the different factories, simply and wholly for his own convenience in delivering his load.

"If any lorry drivers," declared the major with some vigour, "are doing anything of the sort, the sooner they are put somewhere safe, the better. What?"

"Yes," agreed Bobby. "Yes." He had already explained the circumstances in which the map had been discovered. "And while," he said, "we think we know who tipped us off where to find the revolver, we can't prove it, and there's no telling if he knew anything about the map. Nothing to show."

"Map much more important, much more disturbing," declared the major. "A murder only means one more man killed. What? But we've had cases of bombs aimed at factories we thought no one knew anything about. Aerial reconnaissance, perhaps. You can't be sure. What? Is that all you know?"

"Well, we've found dabs—fingerprints," explained Bobby in case the word was not understood. "Not on the map. Nothing distinguishable there. On the revolver. We know whose they are and I am having the man brought in for questioning as soon as we can find him."

"He must be found at once—at once," the major insisted, and looked dissatisfied when Bobby, who knew well the difficulty of finding those who did not wish to be found, would say no more than that he would do his best.

The major suggested calling in Scotland Yard. Bobby remarked that that cost money and the Wychshire police rate was already a subject of bitter comment. Besides Scotland Yard had its own work to do, and plenty of it, and would probably display small gratitude if offered more. In the major's view these were mere excuses and poor ones at that. He said firmly that he expected the Regional Commissioner would want Military Intelligence informed. He made it plain that he considered it all much too dangerous and disturbing an affair for it to be left in the hands of local police. Bobby's murmur that in this country there are only local police, and Scotland Yard as local as any other, was received with some disfavour as having about it a distinct aroma of insubordination. It was added, not so much as a suggestion but as a definite order which Bobby would disregard at his own risk, that until the Home Office, Military Intelligence, and the Regional Commissioner, and probably other important officials as well, had been informed and consulted, no definite action was to be taken. That, said the major, was definite.

"Means, I suppose," Bobby reflected after the major had departed, "that my man is to have every chance to get away while the bigwigs are 'passing to you' for suggested action. Oh, well."

A discouraging prospect, he thought, and then he sent for Payne to whom he explained the official brake put upon their movements.

He added thoughtfully that it was, he supposed, a result of the odd way in which the case had continued to broaden out.

"Begins," Bobby said, "with the murder of an unidentified man and now reaches back towards Dunkirk and outwards towards Ireland and forwards to Lord knows where and what."

"Example," suggested Payne, "of not being able to see the tree on account of the wood."

"It does seem like that," agreed Bobby, "but all the same I think one can start now to pick out the really significant facts from the whole lot of incidents and information we've got together. And I do think if you do that you can see how they begin to make sense. There's the money Christopherson picked up."

"But we've never heard a thing about it," Payne protested. "Two thousand pounds left in the road and not a hint of a claim put forward. It doesn't make sense."

"I think it does," Bobby said. "It makes sense exactly because it doesn't make sense."

"Yes, sir, if you say so, sir," answered Payne, his voice full of a deeply contemptuous deference.

"Then," Bobby continued, "there are the dead man's dabs we found on the glass cut out of the kitchen window at the Conqueror Inn and in that connection the further fact that Leader had the same idea as Kram of using the Conqueror Inn outbuildings as a depot—to save what they called cross loads, wasn't it?"

"But what's the connection?" Payne asked, looking doubtful now.

"Add," continued Bobby, "the egg motive which was used both by Maggie Kram, calling herself Emma Jones, and by Loo Leader when they were dodging about the moor asking questions—Maggie because she wanted to know what attraction Larry Connor found at the inn, and was it Rachel? and Loo for reasons that are getting fairly plain, aren't they?"

"Oh, yes, sir," agreed Payne, firmly determined not to confess that for him they were anything but plain.

"Much more important," Bobby went on, "is the spanner Micky Burke says was taken from him by an army sergeant we can't trace. Practically that's proof, but proof we can't produce in court."

"No, sir," agreed Payne, wondering what the proof was, and, more especially, what it proved—or didn't prove.

"Add to that the discovery of the revolver buried on Conqueror Inn land wrapped in this map marked with factory sites and also showing Alf Hall's dabs, and—well, there you are, aren't you?"

"Yes, sir," agreed Payne, beginning to grow a trifle wildeyed as he wondered desperately where 'there' might be.

"Of course," Bobby concluded briskly, "I've always had a sort of vague suspicion of the truth. The double coincidence of Loo Leader and Alf Hall made one thing plain. I never feel much inclined to accept coincidences. Of course, they happen, and jolly rum ones, too, but not doubled. You may go to London for the first time in years and meet your old pal you haven't seen or heard of for years, and who is also in London for the first time in years. But it won't also happen that your old pal chances to know something you want to know and he is the only man in town can tell you. That's the sort of double coincidence I can't accept. In other words, coincidences aren't significant and if they are I don't believe them. Finally there's your discovery at the Ritz shack. That sort of clarified everything."

"Yes, sir, I see, sir," said Payne, his voice and manner making it quite plain he was very far indeed from 'seeing.' "Beg pardon, sir, but I didn't discover anything at all at the Ritz shack."

"You discovered that an order there for tinned eggs on toast was a joke for sardines on toast," Bobby reminded him. "It was when you told me that and how the joke started that I got the tie up I had been waiting for."

"Yes, sir," agreed Payne once more, and once more looking extremely puzzled.

"Now I feel sure we know," Bobby went on, too deep in thought to notice how Payne winced at that 'we,' "what it's all been about, we can go after the evidence we haven't got. It'll be a funny thing if now we can't squeeze some admission out of someone. Only there are 'definite' orders from the Regional Commissioner bloke to avoid 'definite' action. Only what right has a Regional Commissioner bloke, except 'in case of emergency,' to give any orders even to a back yard pussy cat—whether 'definite' orders or just ordinary common or garden orders. So far as I know a Regional Commissioner's powers are more or less dormant till he issues a proclamation that he is jolly well going to use them."

"I take it, sir, we are expected to co-operate," observed Payne, looking a trifle alarmed, for he had all a well-disciplined mind's respect for authority.

"So they ought to co-operate with us," Bobby remarked. "Blessed word—co-operate. Almost as blessed as Mesopotamia. Anyhow, I imagine my duty is to see that no murder goes unpunished. I think I shall continue to exercise my own discretion and you needn't look so scared, Payne. My responsibility, not yours. And I shan't rush my fences. One thing, when there's a war on, there's always the army if you get the sack. Hitler has cured unemployment all right, as all his pals in this country used to be so fond of telling us. No wonder he was so popular in the city of London when he cured unemployment in destroying trades unions—the perfect ideal, so seldom realized here below. No wonder the F.B.I. was so eager to—co-operate."

"Yes, sir," agreed Payne, realizing that with Bobby, as with others occasionally, a tendency to be nervous at the possible result of contemplated action was apt to show itself in a tendency to chatter. "There's that, sir. There's your pension, too, to think about," he added by way of reminder—a totally unnecessary reminder, too.

"A question for the B.B.C. Brains Trust," Bobby remarked. "Is a pension a curse or a blessing, good or bad, wise or foolish?—safety first, and is that O.K. in a universe that seems meant to be full of risk and change and peril? What do you think, Payne?"

"I never thought of it like that, sir," answered Payne. "I think you sleep better if you know there's a pension waiting when you have to lay off."

"I expect you do," agreed Bobby. "Some day I'll have to ask our philosophic landlord at the Conqueror Inn what he thinks."

The 'phone bell rang. Bobby answered it. He hung up the receiver and said:

"Talk of the Conqueror Inn and it's there. That was our local man we told to keep an eye on it. He says Captain Wintle has been there and has just left. Came for luncheon and now he's gone again. Driving. These military blokes never seem hard up for petrol the way we mere policemen are."

"What's he been up to?" Payne asked suspiciously.

"I hope," Bobby said, "he went to tell Miss Rachel what I said. I hope he has taken the hint to advise her to tell us all about it at last."

"Do you think she will?" Payne asked.

"Might," Bobby said. "And it might be a good idea to try to find out at once, strike while the iron's hot idea. If only we could get her to make a statement. The whole theory we've built up is a pure logical deduction—from observed facts certainly, but you can always put another interpretation on observed facts. That's why induction is a sounder method, only you can't often use it in police work."

"No, sir, you can't," agreed Payne firmly, making a mental note to consult a dictionary as soon as possible and find out the difference.

"Up to now," Bobby went on, "we may think we know it all—or know we know it all—but we've hardly a shred of evidence of fact we can plump down in court. Every single thing we've rooted out could be twisted to another meaning. I tell you what it is, Payne. There's nothing for the moment you can't deal with. I'll take a run out to the Conqueror Inn and see if I can get anything there—anything solid you can use to bang a jury's head with."

There were, however, one or two minor matters that cropped up and then the journey made at the economical speed officially recommended took some time. It was beginning to be late therefore when Bobby arrived, nor did he find Mr. Christopherson at the inn. Seldom now indeed that he was there. His frequent absences were already beginning to show their effect in signs of neglected fields and work postponed. To Rachel when she told him her father was not there, Bobby said:

"He is often away just now, isn't he? I think I can guess why."

Rachel's glance was grave and calm as ever, but she made no comment.

Bobby went on:

"He is searching for your brother, isn't he? And he has never found him?"

For once Rachel's habitual composure seemed shaken. She hesitated. Her lips quivered, her voice was less steady when she replied with the counter question:

"Who tells you all these things? How do you know? Who tells you?"

"Well, now then, look here," Bobby exclaimed in tones of extreme exasperation, "nobody ever tells me a thing. In this case, if I ask anyone the time, they look down their noses and say they don't know, and then if I look up at the sun in the sky and say it's about noon, they want to know who told me. It's true, isn't it?

Mr. Christopherson is out so much because he is looking for your brother?"

"I don't know," she answered. With a gesture that had in it something of despair, she said: "We don't even know if it was his body you found or another's."

CHAPTER XXVIII
RACHEL SPEAKS

AN ADMISSION AT last, Bobby told himself, though only an extremity of doubt and anguish had torn it from her. Yet the words she had used puzzled him as well and he said:

"You mean your father knew that morning, knew all the time we were digging there, that it might be his son buried in that grave?"

Rachel made a slight affirmative gesture. Bobby's mind went back to the grey morning when from its lonely moorland resting place they had recovered that naked, mutilated body. By no sign, by no word, by no least tremor of voice or muscle, had Christopherson disclosed the dreadful fear in his mind. A miracle of self-control Bobby could only think of with wonder, indeed with awe. Abruptly Rachel said:

"It was worse when still we did not know, when father said he could not tell."

"Surely there was something—some sign—something to show?" Bobby exclaimed.

"How could he tell?" Rachel asked. "Or I? Or mother?"

"Did you see—it? Did your mother?" Bobby asked. "Did you both?"

"Yes," she answered quietly. "We had to. I went first. Then mother went. The body was there in the barn. We had to see if we could tell."

Bobby said nothing, but again there was wonder in his mind as he thought of those two women going one by one to look on that dreadful corpse and still unable to tell whether or no it was that of the son and brother for whom they had done so much and risked so much. He seemed to see them standing silently in the great empty barn, looking, doubting, anguished, coming away unknowing and unsatisfied, doubting still.

"We did not know, we could not tell," she repeated. "It was a long time that night before we even knew Derek had gone. Sometimes he used to slip out at night. At first one of us would try to go with him, but he would not let us; and if we tried to follow or keep near, it made him so excited. Once he attacked father and father had to fight him off. But he never went far away and he always came back, so we gave up worrying. Lately he seemed so much better we came to think it was quite safe. We thought he was getting over it. When I told father what I had heard that Monday night, we thought at first it was only a lorry back-firing. We never thought of Derek. We didn't even know he had gone out. None of us had seen him go and we thought he was still upstairs. Father went to see. He said perhaps a lorry had broken down and he might be able to help. Or send for help or lend the driver a bicycle to go for help himself. We always tried not to have people at the inn more than we could help. So he went out and there wasn't any lorry, but he brought back the box he gave you full of pound notes. So then we thought he had better say so at once because there was sure to be an inquiry when it was such a lot of money. And then he went to look again and he found the revolver and the map, and we could see the revolver had been fired and there was blood upon it, and mother came to say Derek wasn't in his room. So when it was morning father went once more to look for him and mother and I waited, hoping he would come back. But he never did and father found a new dug grave instead and that is all we know. Nor have we ever seen Derek since that night, and perhaps it is his body that was buried there, and perhaps he is still wandering somewhere without knowing what has happened and perhaps he will never be right in his mind again."

"I wish you had told me all this before," Bobby could not help saying.

"How could we," she answered, "when all our hope was to find Derek first ourselves?" She added: "It was more than his life we were trying to save, it was his reason."

"You didn't give the army authorities credit for much understanding or sympathy," Bobby said.

"Would you have risked your brother's reason on soldiers' understanding?" she asked. "Captain Wintle," she went on, "said that, too. But Derek might have been driven out of his mind for ever before they did come to understand." After another pause she went on again. "If you knew my father's ideas, you would know what it meant to him to seem to be hiding a runaway." She lifted her head. "Derek wasn't a runaway but it looked as if he were. Father is a hard man in some ways and a proud man. He put all his life behind him when he put Derek first." Once more she was silent and once more added: "Mother said she would kill herself. I mean she said she would unless we helped Derek and hid him from everyone. Sometimes she used to carry a sharp knife about with her."

Bobby remembered that first morning he had been at the Conqueror Inn and the gesture Mrs. Christopherson made when she picked up a knife and went out of the room as he came in. Odd to think so much of this strange story was hidden in that gesture which at the time he had barely noticed and now only just remembered.

"You have all been through a good deal," he said.

Rachel till now had preserved a composure almost above the powers of ordinary humanity, but that simple, indeed conventional word of sympathy suddenly broke down, at least momentarily, her powers of resistance. She sat down and with the immemorial gesture of the stricken woman she flung over her head the apron she was wearing, so that her face was hidden, her sobbing muffled. Bobby went to stand by the window. A minute or two passed and Rachel was strong again and her voice hardly less steady than before as she said:

"Peter said it would have been better to tell everything, I mean Captain Wintle did. Perhaps we might have done so if we had known you better. None of us could think of anything but the danger that Derek might never be his own self again. Now perhaps he never will, if he is wandering about the country, and perhaps it is he who was killed that night for none of us could tell."

"If he is alive and wandering about anywhere," Bobby said, "we will find him and I promise if we do find him we will do everything possible to avoid any shock. I will see warning is issued of a possibly disturbed mental state and that medical help must be got before any action is taken."

He was going to leave then but there was so plainly something else on Rachel's mind that he waited.

"If you have any feeling you can trust me," he said as gently as he could, "tell me what else is troubling you. You know I must put my duty first. I remember your father saying he would not ask anything else. But I can see what a difficult position you were in and I am quite sure everyone will feel the same—even the hardest boiled sergeant-major that ever made a battalion tremble on parade."

He smiled as he said this, hoping for a return smile to prove that he had really won her confidence. No smile came, instead there was once more a full flood of terror in her voice as she said:

"Perhaps it is even worse, for perhaps the dead man isn't Derek but perhaps it was Derek killed him."

"Yes, I know," Bobby agreed. "Of course, I've felt for a long time that was a possibility, but there's nothing to show it was like that. I take it that was in your mind when you hid the revolver. What made you use the map to wrap it in?"

"It was the first thing handy; father picked them both up together," she answered, evidently quite unaware that the map was of any more importance than any other piece of paper. But there was a fresh tremor in her voice as she went on: "If it was like that, they would send him to Broadmoor, wouldn't they?"

Bobby had no reply to make, though he understood well that that dread had lain deeper than all other in their minds. Nor could he deny that if Rachel's fear turned out to be justified, then authority would very probably say that for the sake of the safety of others such a course would be necessary. All he could do was to repeat that the possibility was only one among others and certainly no more likely than another. He tried to explain that to his mind it was not the most probable explanation and not the one upon which he was working. All the same he knew how clearly she realized that it was one of the possibilities he had to take into account; and that if it proved to be the true one, there would be inevitable consequences. Impossible indeed to feel in any way sure of what might have happened in the confusion and the darkness of that tragic night.

Bobby departed then and when he got back to headquarters found a sulky, resentful and badly frightened Alf Hall waiting for him, brought in for questioning. So Bobby said how pleased he was to meet Mr. Hall again and Mr. Hall made it plain that the pleasure was in no way mutual.

"You haven't got no right to go and drag a respectable hardworking man away from his job," he protested and desired to be informed whether this was England or whether it was Germany.

Reassured that he was in fact still in England he remarked with sarcasm that he was surprised to hear it. He added challengingly:

"You ain't got nothing on me."

"Only a thumb mark," Bobby said.

"There you go," said Hall bitterly. "That's a cop all over. Once a bloke's been inside, coppers can't think of nothing but rising up his dabs against him. It didn't ought to be allowed. Call it justice when a bloke's done his time, to hold up his fingerprints? There's British justice for you," said Mr. Hall indignantly. "Give me Hitler."

"No great loss anyhow if instead we gave you to Hitler if he would have you," Bobby observed; and Hall, very much shocked and still more indignant, wanted to know if Bobby called himself an Englishman and was that his idea of patriotism?

So Bobby said that he did and it was, and could Mr. Hall explain how dabs on record as his had come to be found on a revolver buried near the Conqueror Inn and therefore near the scene of the recent killing?

Hall shook his head and looked Bobby straight in the eye, very straight in the eye indeed, in the manner in fact which Bobby had long learned to associate with a forthcoming downright and barefaced lie.

"I don't know nothing about that, guv'nor," he said. "I've never so much as touched one of them revolver things in my life. Never did like 'em, nasty things, the less you have to do with 'em, the better. Give me a broken beer bottle every time. So there can't be no dabs of mine where you say—except," he added, as if suddenly remembering what till then had entirely escaped his memory, "except that time in a pub when a bloke showed me one and asked me to give him ten bob, was it? for it. A bit too much he had had, not drunk, you understand, sober as a judge, only a bit jolly like, if you see what I mean, and he showed me this pistol he had and I had a look at it, and he offered to sell it me. But I wasn't having any and if you've got my dabs on any pistol, that's how it happened."

An ingenious story, Bobby reflected, and one difficult to disprove.

"What pub was it?" Bobby asked. "Who else was there?"

On both these points Mr. Hall's memory was a complete and unfortunate blank. First he suggested one pub and then another, corrected himself and thought most likely it was a third—at least unless it was a fourth. He couldn't be sure. But he didn't think anyone was present who knew him or whom he knew. He confessed that just possibly he himself, though sober as a judge, had perhaps taken enough to deprive his memory of its usual crystal clarity.

"What have you to say about the map?" Bobby demanded.

This time, however, Hall's denials were more convincing though less picturesque. He protested he knew nothing of any map; and Bobby, who from long experience believed he had developed a kind of instinct for telling when a man was lying and when he was speaking the truth, was inclined to believe him. Reverting to the question of the revolver, Bobby said:

"Have you any idea who the man was who tried, you tell me, to sell you a revolver?"

"Oh, yes" Hall answered readily. "Knew him all right. Course I did. Rather."

"Who was it?"

"Bloke called Kram, Merton Kram," Hall asserted. "In the same line of business as us, only bigger."

CHAPTER XXIX
STOLEN LETTERS

MR. HALL was allowed to depart then. Bobby was doubtful whether he had sufficient grounds on which to base a charge; and in any case knew it was generally wiser to defer arrest as long as possible, since so often under the threat of arrest the suspected person himself provides in panic the further evidence needed to make a conviction certain.

"I don't know if there is anything behind Hall's story," Bobby told Payne at the end of a long talk during which they had reviewed together the whole present position of the case, "but it may be worth while to wait a little to see how Kram reacts and what Hall does next. Anyhow, from what we know and can guess, Kram's part in the business is growing clearer. I think there ought to be every chance of getting a statement out of him."

It was late now and Bobby decided to postpone his talk with Kram to the morning, but he rang up the K. and K.M.T.C. to ask what hour would be convenient. A nervous voice asked the reason. Bobby said something vague about unexpected and important developments and rang off. He hoped Mr. Kram's slumbers would be uneasy and that he would arrive for the morning's talk in a state of nerves whence might emerge some of that positive and confirmatory evidence which was now Bobby's first need; now that he felt fairly sure that, from the various indications he had gathered, he could put together a fairly clear picture of what had really happened. Little use though to do that without what he called 'evidence of fact,' in default whereof any clever counsel could fill a jury's mind with such doubt and hesitation as to ensure an acquittal. And Bobby did not want an acquittal; for though a trial and acquittal may often serve that purpose of prevention and warning which is alone man's justification when he condemns to punishment his fellow man, yet this time Bobby felt there were far-reaching implications that went beyond even the primary duty of a police force—that of 'making sure to each his own,' whether that 'own' referred either to his life or to his possessions.

On his arrival next morning at county headquarters, however, he found there was another and equally unexpected development. Some days previously he had asked the city police to keep an eye on Micky Burke and the house where Micky dwelt alone, and now a 'phone message had been that moment received to say that Mr. Kram had a few moments before been seen to let himself into the Burke residence.

"And what," Bobby asked Payne, "what does that mean?"

Without waiting for a reply to what was after all a purely rhetorical question, Bobby rang up once more the K. and K.M.T.C. He learnt that Mr. Kram was out on business and that Micky Burke was on the road, having left early with an urgently required load of supplies for a bombed town.

"Now, I wonder," Bobby mused, "if that means Kram has taken an opportunity, or made an opportunity, to get Micky out of the way while he pays his place a visit. It might be as well to go along and see what friend Kram is up to. We can have our little chat there just as well as here and if he is prepared to make a statement, I can bring him back with me."

So Payne was left in charge; and in view of recent fervent official injunctions to save petrol, and not without a certain smug consciousness that an entry in the accounts—'To 'bus fare, in lieu of taking car for journey, 2d.'—would look very impressive, Bobby decided to use the municipal 'bus service that passed the corner of the street in which Burke lived. He arrived just in time to see the door open and Kram appear on the threshold on the point of departure. Bobby gave him a cheerful greeting and Kram, looking somewhat disconcerted, mumbled some sort of reply.

"I was coming on to see you," he said. "Burke's not here." He paused, looked doubtful, and then, with an air of having made up his mind, drew back into the kitchen, on which the door from the street opened directly. "Come inside a moment, will you?" he said.

Bobby followed him accordingly into the kitchen. It was clean and tidy as when Bobby had seen it before; and on the mantelpiece burned as before a candle, a freshly-lighted candle, before the photograph of Mr. Kram and yet another before that of Larry Connor. It was to his own photograph and the candle burning before it, flickering now in the draught from the open door, to which Kram was pointing with an outstretched hand.

"See that?" he said. "What do you make of that?"

Bobby had turned to close the street door and did not answer.

"Do you know what that means?" Kram asked again and answered his own question. "It means there is something he has sworn to do and until he's done it he keeps a candle burning there to remind him."

"Oh, yes," Bobby said. "Yes. Well, what is he going to do and why has he got to take oaths and burn candles about it?"

This time it was Kram's turn to make no reply. He looked pale and nervous, and Bobby had the idea that he regretted what he had just said and yet that it had relieved him, too.

"Why don't you get hold of Burke?" he asked presently. "Why don't you ask him a few questions? He could tell you a lot that would surprise you."

"Oh, I daresay," Bobby admitted. "I'm always being surprised. Ever since this case opened it's been one surprise on top of another. For instance, I was surprised to see you here when I was expecting you at our H.Q."

"So was I surprised to see you here," Kram retorted, "when I thought that's where you were waiting for me."

"Surprise general," Bobby agreed. "I wonder if there'll be a third surprise if Micky guesses why you got him off earlier than usual and if he turns up here instead to see what's going on?"

Kram looked startled and even more disturbed than before. The suggestion was plainly one he did not welcome.

"Priority load," he said. "Burke's got to deliver it. Well, I'll get off. Lots of work waiting."

"Oh, don't go yet," Bobby objected. "You haven't told me yet what you wanted here."

Kram looked at him gloomily and then even more gloomily at the candle and photograph on the mantelpiece.

"It was that," he said. "I didn't believe it. I wanted to see for myself. That's all."

"Well, now you've seen," Bobby said, "what's it mean?"

"You ask Burke," Kram said. "I'll be going," he repeated. "Work waiting. Sorry."

"Just a minute," Bobby objected again. "Burke's not here and you are, so we might as well have that little talk I 'phoned you about."

"Later on," Kram said, "later on, if you don't mind." He tried to brush past Bobby as he spoke. Bobby stopped him with a lifted hand. Kram said angrily: "You've no right to interfere with me."

"Oh, I don't know," Bobby answered with his most amiable smile. "I think I might charge you perhaps. Found on enclosed premises for a presumed unlawful purpose. That sort of thing."

"Oh, that's nonsense," Kram protested and began to laugh, but all the same looked none too comfortable. "Why," he protested, "Micky works for me, one of my men."

"Hardly a reason, is it?" Bobby asked. "And I wonder if that is all he is or if he is something else as well." He paused for an answer that did not come except in the shape of another sullen and disturbed look. Bobby nodded towards the mantelpiece with its photographs and burning candles. "I'm wondering a good deal about that, too," he said. "Interesting. Suggestive even. Unspoken evidence, you might call it." Abruptly he asked: "Do you know a man named Hall, Alf Hall, once a professional boxer?"

"He worked for me once," Kram answered. "I got rid of him. Quarrelsome. The other men didn't like him. He tried to bully them. I laid him off. He wanted to come back but I wouldn't have him. Why?"

"A revolver has been found near the Conqueror Inn," Bobby said, "near where the recent murder took place. There is reason to identify it with a revolver Hall says you showed him in a public house some time ago and tried to sell him."

"Oh, that's nonsense," Kram declared. "Hall trying to get himself out of a jam and telling the first lie that came into his head. So far as I know I've never been in any pub with Hall. I may have been, but not to my knowledge. Sometimes I have to go round pubs looking for men I want, if there's an extra rush on and I want more drivers or loaders. But not often and if I do I don't take revolvers with me or try to sell them either."

"Why should Hall tell a story like that; he must have known you would deny it at once?"

"To put you off, of course. Wants to make a fool of you and thought he would get one in at me because of my laying him off and not wanting to take him on again."

"I think perhaps there may be another reason," Bobby said. "Have you ever thought, Mr. Kram, that you may be in some danger yourself?"

Kram's expression made it clear that such a thought was very much in his mind.

"I had nothing to do with the killing," he said sullenly, "if that's what you are trying to get at?"

"It's one thing," Bobby agreed. "Conspiracy to defeat the ends of justice, a lawyer might call it. Judges hate the word 'conspiracy,' too. Puts their backs up at once. Red rag to a bull, conspiracy to a judge, same sort of thing. Or accessory after the fact. But that wasn't what I was thinking of. I feel sure now, you see, that the man killed that Monday night was Larry Connor. Micky's nephew and your daughter's husband."

Kram was mopping his forehead now. His voice was unsteady as he muttered:

"I knew nothing about that, nothing at all. I hadn't anything to do with anything that happened that night."

"Do you know I think you had?" Bobby said. "Or why has Micky Burke sworn something to himself? And why does he keep a candle burning before your photograph so he won't forget it for even one moment?"

Kram looked more disturbed, more uncomfortable, than ever, but did not attempt to speak. Only he got out a clean handkerchief to replace the one that now was too damp for use.

"An odd, primitive thing to do," Bobby continued. "But then I think Micky Burke is an odd, primitive character. Cunning mind. Violent emotions. Primitive ideas. Well, I told you I believe the dead man is Micky's nephew, Larry. I am waiting for a reply from Ireland. It ought to have been here before this. I suppose the Irish don't hurry themselves for a mere inquiry from England. When it comes, any minute now, if it is what I expect, I shall have the proof I want of his identity."

"How can you get proof in Ireland of an unidentifiable body found in England?" Kram asked, and when Bobby only smiled and made it plain he had no intention of explaining, Kram said angrily: "You are only trying to bluff. It's what you are doing all the time. You can't get proof here and you know it, because no one can swear to the identity of a body no one can recognize. So you pretend you can get it in Ireland. Bluff. Nonsense. That's all."

"As to that, we shall see," Bobby said quietly. "Of course, I mean proof of fact. Proof by inference is there on the mantelpiece, I think—the burning candle that proves Burke has made himself a promise about you he does not mean to forget. Why? It seems fairly plain—the inference, I mean. I don't think he thinks you fired the shot that killed Larry. I think if he thought so he would have killed you already. I think he is like that. But something else happened to Larry. His face was mutilated. Smashed till there wasn't a feature left by which even his closest friend or relative could recognize him. Who did that? Why? Not Micky himself, not to the boy he loved as his own son. Was it the man who told a long story to account for Micky's spanner having vanished? Did he invent that story in a hurry because the spanner was the instrument used and had to be got rid of—pushed down a rabbit hole perhaps or thrown into the canal—

because it was feared there might be traces on it of what it had been used for? You know, that spanner story always interested me. You went out of your way to tell it to me. A mistake. If you hadn't given me such a convincing explanation of why it was missing, I don't suppose I should ever even have known that it was missing."

"I don't know what you are talking about," Kram muttered. "Is all that rigmarole what you call proof of fact?"

"No," Bobby answered. "Oh dear, no. Merely deduction from observed facts—a dead man's disfigured face, a missing spanner unnecessarily accounted for, a candle burning before a photograph. Further deduction. Guess perhaps, but deduction sounds better. The promise Micky has made to himself is that he will do to your face what you did to dead Larry's."

Kram sat down abruptly, perhaps because his legs would no longer support him.

"He wouldn't ever dare," he muttered, without making any attempt to contradict Bobby's deductions—or guesses. "Never. I've made sure of that. He thought everything of Larry, Larry was all he cared for. But there's one thing he thinks still more of, one thing he cares for still more."

"What's that?" Bobby asked.

Kram looked at him but did not answer. Evidently he did not mean to say, and Bobby, since he thought he knew, did not repeat his question.

"I've taken precautions," Kram said. "Now he won't dare."

"We found a map," Bobby said. "Is it yours?"

Kram shook his head and did not seem interested. Plainly the question had not for him enough significance to rouse him from his other doubts and fears.

"What map? What of?" he asked.

Bobby did not explain, satisfied from Kram's manner that he knew nothing about any map. Instead Bobby went on:

"You told me once you had thought of renting the outbuildings at the Conqueror Inn for use for storage. Do you know how it is Loo Leader had the same idea?"

This time Kram looked interested but puzzled as well.

"No. Why? Had he?" he asked. "That's funny. No, I've no idea. Is there anything else you want to ask me or can I go now?"

Bobby considered for a moment. But again there weighed upon him the command—given by competent authority or not—laid upon him by the Regional Commissioner's representative to take no avoidable action until the map affair had been cleared up. He did not intend to respect that order of doubtful authority if he saw clear cause to disregard it; but also he had learnt enough prudence to know that only when such clear cause could be shown, would such disregarding action be wise.

"I think I should be justified in charging you as an accessory after the fact," he told Kram. "I feel pretty sure you know who killed Larry Connor and why it was you thought it necessary to do what was done to prevent identification. And I am very much inclined to believe that you are in considerable danger from Micky Burke. It strikes me that between arrest on one side and Micky Burke on the other, you are in a nasty spot and your only way out is to tell the truth. Then we might be able to help you."

"I've got my girl to think of," Kram said. "She's there, she comes first. She's had a hard time. I must do what I can. I've had to make too many fresh starts already. I'm getting old for that. I don't want to make another. I don't believe you can prove anything. I don't believe Micky Burke will dare do anything. I've trumped his best card all right. That's all right."

"Sure?" Bobby said. "Well, you can go now. But think it over. Before it's too late. Because next time I may be ready to lay a charge and once that happens, well, things happen, too."

"I'll think it over," Kram promised and went away, and after he had gone Bobby thought the opportunity a good one to make a quick examination of the rest of the house.

In the two rooms downstairs he found nothing to interest him, but in one of the two bedrooms upstairs he found on the small truckle bed there, pinned to the pillow, a note in Kram's writing. It ran:

"If you miss your letters, you will know they are in safe keeping and will stay so unless any accident to me makes my representative think it would be a good idea to hand them over to—you can guess who. M.K."

CHAPTER XXX

MANY QUESTIONS

Carefully Bobby removed this scrap of paper and put it in his own pocket.

"Who ever would have thought," he said aloud, "that Kram was such a fool?"

A closer search of the room revealed that one of the floorboards had recently been taken up and then replaced. Beneath was a small box, now empty. Bobby made sure it was empty, did his best to be equally sure there was no other hiding place, repeated to himself the reflection he had just made aloud concerning Kram's unexpected folly, and then returned to headquarters where he found waiting for him that message, at last arrived from Larry Connor's birthplace in Ireland, which he had been so long expecting. He sent for Payne and showed it him, saying:

"I think we may take it that gives us the proof we wanted."

"Yes, sir," agreed Payne. "Establishes identity all right. Good thing, sir, you noticed Burke had that picture of the Sacred Heart in his kitchen."

"Yes," agreed Bobby, "of course, seeing that made it plain at once how to make sure whether the dead man was Larry or Derek."

He added that effort must be concentrated on finding the missing Derek, who, it could now be taken for certain, must be wandering about the country in a confused mental state. A relief to the Christophersons, he said, to know that the identity of the dead man was finally established. Then he went on to show Payne the scrap of paper he had found pinned to the pillow of Micky's bed.

"A silly trick," Bobby said. "Asking for trouble. Asking for it the very worst way. Luckily Micky won't find out anything till he gets home; and as Kram has packed him off on a long trip with an urgent load, we have a bit of time on hand and I don't want to take action in a hurry. I must get in touch with the Regional Commissioner's lot and see what they think."

Arrangements were, however, made to intensify the watch being kept on the K. and K.M.T.C. office and yard. Then there were other matters to be attended to; and it was much later in the day when Bobby was informed to his surprise that Micky Burke had arrived and was asking for an interview.

"Now I wonder what that means?" Bobby said, checking himself only just in time from rubbing the tip of his nose harder than ever it had been rubbed before. "Looks as if things had come to a head. And how is it he has turned up so soon? Urgent load to deliver, I thought. Well, send him in, will you?"

Micky Burke appeared accordingly, and Bobby gave him a friendly smile, waved him to a chair, and offered him a cigarette, an offer which was not so much declined as ignored. The little wizened man looked older by far than when Bobby had seen him last. Red-rimmed eyes, dark hollows beneath them, suggested wakeful nights; and a nervous twitching of the lips, restless movements of the hands and feet, showed the strain the man was enduring and that now was beginning to appear through the fierce restraint so long put upon it. Perhaps the eyes revealed most—those cold, still eyes of the fanatic that were still no longer but restless, in them now a gleam of wild, uncertain light.

Near to cracking, Bobby thought, attentive and wary, telling himself it was an equal chance whether when the breakdown came it would come as breakdown or as explosion.

"Well, Mr. Burke," he said, "what can we do for you?"

"You were at my house this morning and there's no good denying what I know," Burke said; and his voice was low and uncertain, as if he controlled it with difficulty. "What right had you in another man's house? Isn't it the truth any longer that an Englishman's house is his castle?"

"Are you an Englishman, Mr. Burke?" Bobby asked, and Burke answered with violence:

"What's that to do with it? Am't I living in England? Haven't I my rights like anyone else? What's your English law for?"

"Not for those to break who wish," retorted Bobby. "You know, Mr. Burke, it really is like your countrymen for you to claim the protection of the very laws you are defying."

Micky waved this aside as entirely immaterial.

"It's the like of the English police," he said, "to come sneaking and prowling and prying when a man's away from his home. What right had you to break into a man's house? Where was your search warrant? Unless you had one, you were doing a thing clean outside the law."

"Oh, no," Bobby answered. "Because, you see, I was asked in."

"Now there's a lie would make a tip-top, long-accustomed liar blush," declared Micky indignantly. "For how could that be when the house was locked and empty?"

Bobby made no answer, for he was beginning to regret what he had just said. Micky might draw from that remark conclusions it was probably undesirable he should come to.

"Give me back the letters you stole," Micky went on, "and we'll say no more. Or I'll go straight from here to a lawyer."

"What letters do you mean?" Bobby asked.

"Well you know," Micky retorted, "and a fine scandal it'll make when it's blazoned out in all the world's press the things the English police do do."

He paused and looked anxiously at Bobby, apparently hoping that this alarming prospect would produce some effect. When it drew not so much as a word of comment, Micky tried another way.

"Nothing in them at all," he said, plainly trying to make his harsh, uncertain, anxious voice as smooth and persuasive as he could; "and how should there be, when there was no sense in them any way but only a deal of idle scribble and no intelligence to them anywhere? Give them back to me, Mr. Owen, sir, and if it's wanting me to leave the country you are—why, so I will."

"My dear man," Bobby assured him, "we are so far from wanting you to leave the country just at present that I am not sure I shall want you even to leave this building."

"There's no way you can stop me," Micky retorted sullenly. "There's nothing at all I have done you can bring up against me."

"Well, there are these letters, I suppose," Bobby observed, without thinking it necessary to explain that he had not even so much as seen them, much less ever had them in his possession.

"As harmless," Micky said, "as the day's newspaper when it's a year old, as innocent as his mother's milk on the lips of a babe new born, as clear of all wrong as the conscience of his holiness the pope of Rome."

"Well, now then, there's a testimonial," Bobby agreed.

"Let be that I see them," Micky said, "and I'll prove it to you, for I'll read you the meaning of them and so you can tell for your own self."

"Oh, we'll do our best ourselves," Bobby answered non-committedly; and noticed that Micky was looking at him with a new expression.

"Maybe it wasn't the thumping lie I took it for what you said before," Micky observed thoughtfully, "for if you've got them, why wouldn't you take an offer like that to have them read with no trouble? And why didn't they burn unless who took them knew beforehand?"

"Which means, I suppose," Bobby retorted, "you had tried to fix up one of those incendiary pencils the I.R.A. used to be so fond of, so that anyone who didn't know what precautions to take, would set a blaze going? Well, you know, we have heard of dodges of that sort."

Micky sat silent and scowling. Bobby said:

"There's a map, too. I think it once belonged to you. The map I mean you lost the night your nephew was murdered."

"I've lost no map," Micky said, staring at Bobby. "Any more than it's Larry was murdered that night. Isn't there the letter from him you've seen your own self? And haven't I a postcard from him only yesterday morning to say he was moving on to another job and how he would be writing again when settled? So how could it be Larry that was killed?"

"If it wasn't Larry that was killed," Bobby retorted, "if you are telling the truth about the letters and the postcards that you have had from him, why are you having masses said in the parish church where he was born for the repose of his soul?"

Micky gasped, looked very disconcerted.

"How do you know?" he asked. "How did you find out?" With a sort of desperate hope in his voice, he added: "It's only a guess you are making and a bad one too, for there's no truth or accuracy to it, none at all."

Bobby smiled and gave Micky details that showed his knowledge was complete.

"Easy to be sure," he remarked, "as soon as I knew you were a practising Roman Catholic—and there was a picture in your kitchen proved as much—that you would have masses said for Larry if it was in fact Larry who was dead, dead in a moment, with no time or opportunity for the last rites. If it was someone else, someone you had no connection with, there would be no masses said, least of all for a Larry from whom you were getting letters and postcards. But if Larry had died like that, then it was the first thing you would be likely to think of. So I got inquiries made where he was born and then I knew."

"God rest his soul," Micky said and crossed himself; "the soul of a poor lad that was cut off in his duty, all unsuspecting and unready, and him never been to confession since he left Ireland for fear of what the priests here would give him for penance. Back to Ireland they might have sent him or refused him absolution, same as was done to one of the best of our lads."

"Have you been to confession lately?" Bobby asked.

Micky shook his head.

"It's not safe to let out so much as a whisper to any priest that's here," he said. "It's all corrupted they are with living in this country and never understand it's all for Ireland, and no absolution will you get except under promise to desert the cause."

He stopped and stared again at Bobby.

"So that's how you worked it out about Larry," he said. "It's cunning you are to be sure. Sure, it's an evil thing to be so cunning as all that."

"Not so evil perhaps to bring the truth to light," Bobby said.

"Give me back those letters that you stole from me that'll tell you nothing nor make any sense," Micky said. "You had no right to take them."

"Hadn't I?" murmured Bobby, wishing very much it was he who had taken them and at the same time relieved to notice that Mickey had apparently forgotten now the doubts which he had seemed before to be beginning to entertain. The last thing Bobby wished was that Micky should guess who it was had in fact removed the papers. He asked: "How do you know I have been at your house?"

"There's little use your denying it," Micky retorted, "when it was seen you were and me told the same within the hour. Nor any trouble to know who it was by the account I heard and the likeness of you I could tell at once."

"You were on the road with an urgent load you were under orders to deliver at once," Bobby observed. He paused to reflect. "You must have been told on the 'phone. But you couldn't have been rung up because no one would know exactly where you were or how far you had got. It must have been you rung up first. That means you must have arranged with one of your neighbours to be on hand at some specified time at some place where there is a 'phone—a shop or a public house most likely. And that means you had arranged with one of your neighbours to watch your house and let you know anything that happened. You know, all that has its interest."

Micky crossed himself.

"It must be the devil himself," he said, "that gives you the help to work things out like that."

"Oh, come, Mr. Burke," Bobby protested, "be fair, don't give all the credit to the devil. Let me have some. I've worked out more than that. I've worked out why that map of yours was marked all over."

"Take more than working out," Micky retorted, "to bring it in the map was mine or that pin pricks on it were mine or had any meaning to them that I knew anything about."

"How do you know there were pin pricks on the map if it wasn't yours and you didn't make them?" Bobby retorted and Micky stared and frowned but made no other reply.

Bobby went on:

"I've worked out, too, that it was from you Mr. Kram got the money he needed to set him up in business again at a time when he was in very low water indeed. And I've worked it out that that business was in the black market, or why did you describe a case of sardines as eggs unless you didn't want anyone to know it was sardines you had in your load? In the black market you can sell a case of sardines for ten times the proper price. That's not a bad profit. Making money."

"There's no money comes my way," Micky told him. "Prove I've ever had one penny piece over and above my honest wage."

"No, I don't think it was money with you," Bobby agreed. "I've worked that out, too. Money made on the quiet is never spent on the quiet. It's always thrown about. But you never spent more than Mr. Kram might have paid any of his drivers. Well, if it wasn't money, what was it? A question. Another question. Was Kram pushed into black market activities so there might be a hold on him strong enough to make him keep his eyes shut? Was it the same idea that made you think of using the Conqueror Inn outbuildings as a depot, because you got somehow a hint there was a secret there you could use if you knew it to blackmail the Christophersons into keeping their eyes shut as well? Is that why Larry broke into the inn one Saturday night to find out the nature of that secret and who it was was hidden there and why? Did he see Derek, or speak to him perhaps, and is that what helped to excite Derek again and put him in a condition that helped to bring about the happenings of the following Monday? And was all of it a part of your plan for driving up and down the country unsuspected, delivering loads to factories and marking down on your map the exact position of them all? And was that map meant to go across the seas one day?"

"Now there's a deal of questions," Micky said calmly, "and not one of them you can prove an answer to and not one of them you'll get answer to from me."

"Here's another question," Bobby said. "Will you answer this one? Larry Connor met his death that night. Do you want his death to go unpunished or do you want his murderer brought to justice? Who killed him?"

"I don't know," Micky answered slowly. "I know no more than you. How should I know, and all happening on a sudden with no more warning than the stroke of doom, and the night that black there was no seeing anything but its own great darkness and the flash of the firing of the pistols."

CHAPTER XXXI
PROMISE OF FRIENDSHIP

ONCE AGAIN BOBBY found himself faced by that ignorance of event which had so often and so long hampered the course of this investigation.

"There's times," Micky was saying, "when I was sure as death maybe it was Christopherson himself to keep safe and unknown from all who it was he had hidden there, and then there was more times by far I was more sure still it was the girl."

"Rachel Christopherson, you mean?" Bobby asked.

Micky nodded.

"Then there was other times when it was Merton Kram I named in my mind; and times I could see how it might be Maggie Kram out of the black jealousy of her heart in the thought it was the Rachel girl drew Larry to the Conqueror Inn when there was only his duty took him there to find out their secret so that we could use it for getting the hidden employment of their great barns. But it wasn't Maggie, for I made certain and sure she rested at home that night; and it wasn't her dad, for his pistol wasn't of that high calibre and there were those that saw him far enough away at the time the shooting was done; and it wasn't Loo Leader, for Mr. Kram made sure of that, having seen him far distant like himself at the time; and I don't think it was the inn landlord, for there's no such look in his eyes as comes to a man when he has killed a man; and so it's there that only Rachel's left, and she with her quiet eyes that wouldn't change or alter whether it was the bars of heaven she faced or the fires of hell."

He paused and wiped his forehead which had grown damp as he talked. He said:

"Tell me, Mr. Inspector Owen, is that well worked out?"

"You know no more than that?" Bobby asked. He said: "Nothing is well worked out unless there are the facts behind it."

"It's the truth of it to my way of thinking," Micky said again; "and if it had been a man the long, wakeful nights I've lain and thought had brought so to my mind, there's a thing I would have done myself and asked no help from English law. But a woman there's no right or power in man born of woman to touch, and so let your English law take her and do the hanging that's her due."

"English law," Bobby observed dryly, "wants more than belief, even if it's a belief that's come from long, wakeful nights."

"If it wasn't her, who was it?" Micky retorted. "There's a question you've no answer to."

"A question to which I am still trying to find an answer, though," Bobby remarked. "Talking of hanging, does it ever strike you you are in some small danger of that yourself? Because, you know, in time of war, that map's a hanging matter."

"And for why?"

"Communicating to the enemy information likely to be of assistance to him."

"Where's your proof," Micky demanded, "that that map's mine or that ever I set eye on it?"

"You knew it was marked with pin pricks before I said a word about them," Bobby reminded him.

"Prove it was me spoke of them first," Micky retorted. "It was talk in a pub I heard of a tall man seen sticking pins into a map that put that into my mind. Prove even then that the pin pricks were more than a lorry driver's guide to find the way for quick delivery. Prove that anything was ever done to take that intelligence to any one outside the country. Prove all that or try to in the way and manner your English law and justice says you must, Mr. Inspector Bobby Owen."

"I notice," Bobby could not help observing, "you seem to put great faith in English law and justice and the high degree of proof it requires rather than run any risk of doing wrong to any man, even to the secret enemy in our midst. I wonder, Mr. Burke, if the sort of courts the I.R.A. set up at one time had the same ideas and never took any action, except when the proof was absolute by rule and precedent."

"Praise be, they had better knowledge of their duty," Micky answered. "They took the risk the other way and let none go there was a breath against, for fear of doing wrong to Ireland that comes first. If you in England have another way of thinking, then there's your duty and an evil thing on your part if you went against it."

"A bit squiffy, your logic, isn't it?" Bobby asked.

"Logic," repeated Micky with immense contempt. "What's logic? It's the heart and feel of a thing a man must go by. I'll tell you another thing, Mr. Owen. You've got it all wrong if you think there's any Irish is an enemy to your country. We're neighbours and neighbours should be friends. That's all we want and none want it more than the I.R.A."

"Glad to hear it," Bobby said, slightly surprised, "but haven't you rather an odd way of showing it?"

"What's there odd about it?" demanded Micky, surprised in his turn. "If your neighbour had up and grabbed a field of your farm, then before you can be friends the way you want, you've got to get him out. It's our best wish to see England win and for why not? Isn't England our best customer and always must be? We know what it is to do trade with the Germans—your best they take and send you concertinas and aspirins. But first is first; and what we need first is England's difficulty so big and hard she'll lie quiet when we march into Ulster."

"Oh, is that the idea?" Bobby said. "Suppose Ulster throws you out again?"

"They'll not even try," Micky answered confidently, "or none but a small little handful that'll maybe turn vicious till they've seen the plain good sense of the thing. Once your English soldiers aren't there any longer but fighting for their country same as they should be if there was any decency in things, then there's a great force in the six counties will rise up for the right. Maybe," admitted Micky reluctantly, "there may be a trifle of shooting when some are foolish enough to stand up against what there's no help for, but no more than that and less may be than in Dublin where the black-hearted traitors there that call themselves a Government must be put down."

"Good gracious," Bobby exclaimed, fairly startled this time, "you don't mean to start shooting your own government, do you?"

"No more than is proved necessary," Micky explained earnestly, "and not that if we can help it. But all must be done to make Ireland one again; and then we'll be able to give you our help in the war and you'll see for yourselves what it means to have Ireland on your side as a friend and ally, every man with you, the whole country as one man, all of the same mind."

Bobby fairly gasped, utterly overwhelmed by this picture of an Ireland with all its inhabitants of one mind.

"Well, well," he said, feeling slightly dazed. "You mean, all of you come to be of the same opinion as your own?"

"That's the way of it and maybe soon," Micky agreed. "It'll be a grand day," he added simply, and went on: "So there it is, Mr. Inspector Owen, and all my whole mind open as the day and clear as the bright dawn that even if any help was first intended to the Germans, and that's a thing you'll never prove and can't, it was only as a way to open the road for bringing bigger help to you for the winning of the war by Ireland's help. So isn't there a duty laid on you to let me have back those letters that you took from me beyond your right?"

"Well, anyhow," Bobby admitted, "you've given me an entirely original view of things. Let's come back to something more immediate. Will you tell me exactly what happened that Monday night?"

"There's little I know," Micky answered, apparently quite convinced that friendly and confidential relations had now been established. "There was a man we were going to meet who had let on he had great stores of stuff to sell, such as hotel and night clubs and their like are opening their mouths to buy that wide you might think they would never get them closed again. Two thousand pounds Mr. Kram did give me all in cash and one pound notes none could trace the way he always paid for safety's sake. But when we got to the meeting place there was no more than a note to say police was about and so the deal was off. So back we came with Larry dangling the box full of pound notes on his knees for safety's sake. Mr. Kram, being nervous like, for he had a word there was mischief afoot, drove out to meet us by the road he knew we were like to come back on. It was when we were past the Conqueror Inn and come to where no one lived, we had to stop by reason of a lorry drawn up across the road. I got down to see what the trouble was, thinking no harm, unsuspecting as the first snowdrop of the spring; and then were we held up at the pistol point as lawless as you please. A common thief it was who somehow knew about the load we had been to fetch and thought to take it from us against all common honesty, planning as like as not to sell it to those expecting it from us, and there was a treacherous thieving trick to make the worst blush, for what they put their scoundrel trust in was the thought we wouldn't dare make complaint or lay any information with police or lawyers."

"I suppose they were right about that, weren't they?" Bobby remarked.

"And how could we," Micky demanded, "seeing what our load was meant to be? And could the meanness of man go lower than to take and seek a cowardly advantage of the sort? Only there was no load we had, only two thousand pounds in a wooden box. It was that Larry thought the black scoundrels were wanting, and so he outed a small automatic he had with him for protection, and so the shooting started; and it was the bad luck was Larry's when he dropped with a bullet through his heart. Dead he was and when they knew it and all for nothing because we hadn't the load they thought, then the panic came upon them with what they had done and a dead man on their minds to the day they die. So off they went, and left me there by Larry, and him dead, and none other in the world I loved, and all around the darkness of the night like that in my own soul. Then came Mr. Kram driving to meet us, and when he saw what had happened he said how none must know or there would be such a deal of questions asked as would land us both in an English gaol; and that was what I knew was always a risk for me, but now it bore the meaning of all our mission here in England laid bare and betrayed and the secret business of the I.R.A. made plain. I wasn't for that to be, and Larry's life lost in doing it, and Mr. Kram and I, we dug a grave, thinking it so solitary a spot none would ever know. Then Mr. Kram said that was not enough, because of the singular danger the grave might be found; and we must take all clothing away, so we undressed the boy on the cold bare road and bore him to his grave and no priest to say a word but only Mr. Kram telling me again it was not enough for safety. And what he meant I did not know or ask, for there was a sorrow in my mind for Larry dazed me so I knew not rightly what he said. Mr. Kram came back with the big spanner from my lorry, and with it he broke up my boy's face, till not the mother that bore him would have known him from another. But while Kram was doing it, and me thinking of my great lonely loss, there was another came on us suddenly from the darkness and stumbled on my poor dead Larry; and who it was who came like that I had no knowledge then, but now I think it was Derek Christopherson they had hid away as a deserter from the army. And I think it was a great upset to him, for he let out a great cry and he began to run, and as he ran he let out a pistol shot that did no harm, only to himself, for in the hurry and rush of it he fell down as he was running and then got up and away again across the moor."

"What happened to the box of money?" Bobby asked.

"Of that we never thought again," Micky answered. "When a man dies as Larry died, there's little else you think of. Afterwards we read a piece about it in the papers but we didn't dare say a word for fear of having to tell what was best kept hid. If there was any pistol you found, it would be the one the man that came upon us, Derek or another, threw down as he ran. Most like Larry had the money box still in his arms when the bullet struck him and it fell when he fell, and if there was a map you found, maybe it came from his pocket when we were taking off his clothes, the poor lad, and the night all dark and cold."

CHAPTER XXXII
ATTRACTIVE BUT DANGEROUS

THIS NARRATIVE, VIVID though it was, had in fact added but little to what Bobby already knew or guessed. To the solving of the two main problems to which for so many days he had devoted all his energies, Micky's tale gave no help. Bobby's belief that he knew, as he had always felt he knew, who was responsible for the death of Larry Connor still remained no more than a belief founded on evidence too weak to take into a court of justice, too weak indeed, too much merely deductive reasoning for him himself to find it entirely convincing. Certainly he had confirmation now of his earlier theory that the black market activities of the K. and K.M.T.C. concern had been both planned and used as a camouflage for the even more dangerous activities of Irish revolutionaries. But then that much had been fairly certain ever since the first interview with Mr. Kram, who had talked to Micky in Bobby's presence with so odd a mixture of familiarity and hostility as to make clear that they were not merely employer and employed, master and man. At the time indeed Bobby had been inclined to think that might mean complicity in the Conqueror Inn crime but he had soon realized the greater depths beneath. Little help then that now Micky himself had confirmed their existence.

Bobby rose from his chair and said:

"Well, Mr. Burke, all this has been very interesting and I am very much obliged to you for being so frank. I have not," he went on with more exact regard for truth and fact than Micky realized, "had any opportunity yet to examine your letters you kept under your bedroom floor. What is interesting me most at the moment is how far you are directly responsible for all this and how far you have been acting under the orders of others?"

Micky nodded.

"I know," he said. "Well I know it. It's what you would wish you had the truth of, isn't it? But you'll not get it from me, for I'll say no word and haven't either, beyond what you knew already from its being set down plain in my own writing in my private papers for them to read that wouldn't have a scruple in their souls about another's property or privacy." When this thrust left Bobby quite unmoved—Micky seemed even yet not to have given up all hope of seeing Bobby burst into remorseful tears and return with apologies the missing documents—Micky went on: "And what's left is in secret hidden writing no man will ever read one word of, except them that know the way of it."

"In cypher, you mean?" Bobby asked, reflecting that Micky had evidently small idea of the skill now attained in the unravelling of such puzzles.

"I'll make you an offer as fair as man can make," Micky said. "If that's your wish I'll read you out the exact precise meaning there's in those letters for you to write down in plain English words and keep by you, if you'll let me afterwards take them away with me for the refreshment of my memory."

Bobby looked thoughtfully at Micky. He guessed what lay behind this apparently innocent suggestion. There had come into Micky's attitude as he sat there a new tension, in his eyes a new and fiercer light. Bobby felt this was Micky's last card he had now played and that his purpose and intention was to throw himself upon the letters the moment they were produced in an effort to tear them and destroy them beyond all hope of reconstruction. A little tempting, Bobby felt, to produce an envelope or packet supposed to contain them and watch the dash to seize and destroy that Micky would be sure to make. Tempting, Bobby told himself, but unofficial in the extreme nor serving any really useful purpose, and though Bobby was occasionally unofficial in his methods, it was always with a useful end in view. He shook his head.

"Can't do that, I'm afraid," he said, and was glad Micky did not know that the 'can't' was not conventional this time, but factual.

Micky got to his feet, too.

"Well, if that's the way of it," he said, "and you are going, I'll be going, too, if your mind's made up I'm not to have what's my own property and I've a lawful right to."

"I'll get you to wait a little longer if you don't mind," Bobby answered. He went to the door and called in one of the constables on duty. "Mr. Burke's waiting here for a time," he said. "I want you to stay with him. Understand?"

"Yes, sir," said the constable.

"You'll keep me here only by force," Micky exclaimed and moved towards the door.

"That's all right," said the constable, who was about twice Micky's size and weight, and he put up a large, restraining hand.

"It's false imprisonment it is," Micky said gloomily, reseating himself however. "There's whacking big damages you'll have to pay when I get you in the courts."

Still unaffected by this final threat, and indeed Micky himself had plainly lost hope in the efficacy of the assortment of threats, cajolements, and stratagems he had tried in succession, Bobby went into another room and rang up the Regional Commissioner's office, giving a very brief account of his talk with Micky.

"Rather an attractive little man," Bobby said, and the line spluttered with such indignation Bobby half expected it to fuse.

"Fifth columnist," said the line, crackling as if all the atmospherics in the universe had concentrated on it.

"Oh, yes," Bobby agreed, "dangerous little man, dangerous as any rattlesnake but attractive all the same. And apparently quite anxious to come in on our side as soon as he thinks we are sufficiently near drowning for us to be grateful to him for diving in to save us—which he is quite ready to do and quite convinced he can do."

Here the telephone line became simply indistinguishable from an electric storm of the highest and best variety.

"Yes, sir," said Bobby soothingly. "Quite so, sir. The difficulty is, I'm not sure if I've enough to hold the man on. Yes, sir, I quite realize that we can hold anybody for anything under the defence of the realm act. But there is always a right of appeal, and some of the courts set up still go all stuffy about evidence. Yes, sir, more's the pity, but there it is. Worse off than we are now if we had to let him go again. I'm holding him for the present. Would your people like to interview him? My own feeling is he will say no more than he has said already and he only said that because he thought I had it all in the letters he believed I had taken from his hiding place."

The voice at the other end of the line began to sound less indignant and more worried. Bobby reminded it that his own primary duty was to investigate a case of murder. The voice said the murder had become unimportant, almost irrelevant. Bobby did not contradict this, though it was not his conception of his duty. The case, said the voice at the other end of the line, had broadened out far beyond any question of private killing. That was merely the unimportant start. It had gone beyond even black market activities, serious as those were, more serious than murder since murder was but private and personal and the black market a public crime. This new development touched the safety of the realm, since the possession of a map showing the position of factories engaged in war work would be of immense assistance to the enemy, incalculable assistance since this is largely a war to be won on the factory front.

"Once that map's in Ireland," said the troubled voice at the other end of the line, "easy enough to get it to enemy hands—through the German Ambassador so comfortable and handy there in Dublin for such a job. Or direct to one of the submarines that we know touch the Eire coast sometimes."

Finally after more delay, after much further telephoning, after consultation even with High Authority in London, it was decided that Micky should be allowed to go for the present, though he was to be kept under close observation. In that way some knowledge might be obtained, it was thought, about his associates. Little attention was paid to Bobby's expression of opinion that this was not likely, since, in his view, Larry Connor had been probably the sole medium of communication. The danger, Bobby also foresaw and mentioned, that Micky might carry out whatever scheme of vengeance was symbolized by the burning candle on his mantelpiece, was waved aside as an inevitable and necessary risk. Bobby was inclined to think that in some quarters such a development was regarded as likely to have useful results, an opinion he himself was not much inclined to share. Everything else, including the murder, now plainly regarded as of merely minor interest, was to be put aside for the present, and all effort was to be concentrated on securing the papers which it was to be supposed were in Mr. Kram's possession.

All this took considerable time, and though Bobby did remember to give instructions for Micky and his attendant constable to be provided with their tea, none the less Micky was in a very sullen and indignant mood when at last given permission to depart.

"A long time it'll be," he said, "before ever I come to tell what I know to police, thinking that so I might help, and the world's own fool I was ever to come near the place."

"Well, you know, Mr. Burke," Bobby remarked, "the only reason why you came was your rather cheeky hope that you might be able to bamboozle or bluff me into giving you back these letters you've lost. Can't blame me, can you, if it didn't come off?"

"And isn't it the smarty of all the worlds together that you are, Mr. Inspector Owen," Micky snarled, "the way you work it out what's in a body's mind, and may the ill luck of the unluckiest man that ever lived be a drop in the wide oceans to the ill luck that'll come to you."

"Now, Micky," Bobby protested gently, "if you say things like that, I shall almost begin to think you don't quite like me."

Micky looked as if he were going to say a good deal more, but the large constable uprose and looked so longingly, so yearningly, at Bobby that Micky judged it prudent to retire. Bobby was still occupied with the necessary arrangements for keeping him under close observation when he was told that the man detailed to watch the K. and K.M.T.C. had reported over the 'phone, first, Micky's arrival there—which Bobby had expected since presumably Micky would want to offer some explanation concerning that urgent load for the bombed town he had apparently deserted half-way to its destination on hearing of Bobby's visit to his home—and, secondly, his departure again, driving an empty lorry at a speed as high as so heavy a vehicle could well be driven at in the tangle of streets and crossings and other traffic that made up the busy quarter where the K. and K.M.T.C. had its head office. This departure, the report continued, had been followed by signs of bustle and excitement in the K. and K.M.T.C. yard. Then a car had appeared, driven by Maggie Kram, and she had started off, possibly in pursuit and certainly at as high a rate of speed as was consistent with escaping the attention of the city police.

This time, domestic disapproval quite forgotten, Bobby rubbed the end of his nose very hard indeed. He felt uneasy. The news seemed ominous, ominous both in regard to Micky's departure in such haste and to Maggie's equal haste to follow.

Sufficiently ominous and doubtful indeed for him to feel that prompt and personal inquiry was desirable. He sent for his small Bayard Seven he used now so much on official business, to be brought round; told the big constable, a man named Peel, who had been guarding Micky, to come with him; and with Peel at the back of the car—he filled it so completely he had rather the air of overflowing here and there—he set off for the K. and K.M.T.C. premises.

There at first it seemed no one knew anything beyond the bare facts already reported. Micky had arrived, had asked for Mr. Kram, had been told he was out, had said he would wait for his return, had refused to answer inquiries concerning his own unexpected return. Then, suddenly, without warning or known cause, he had jumped on an empty lorry standing in the yard, and, before anyone realized his purpose, he had driven off at a breakneck speed. One of the men had then gone to inform Miss Maggie in the office of such eccentric behaviour. Whereupon she, offering no word of explanation, ran into the yard, seized on an old car, long unused, its licence surrendered some time previously, and so had driven off herself in the same great haste.

With growing unease Bobby listened to this story, getting it from the not highly articulate tellers by quick, imperious questions, for somehow he too seemed to feel that the need for haste was great.

"Didn't Mr. Kram say where he was going?" he asked.

One of the men didn't know. The other said that the boss had left word in the office that if anyone wanted him, more especially with regard to one bit of business about which he was expecting a call, he was to be rung up at the Conqueror Inn. If he wasn't there, a message was to be left with the landlord. When Bobby remarked that the Conqueror Inn had no telephone, it was explained that the message was to be given to the post office in the nearby village, with the promise of a liberal tip for anyone who would take it up to the inn. Bobby's informant added that apparently Mr. Kram had gone to meet Loo Leader with whom he had some business to discuss. At any rate he had tried to ring up Leader at Ingleside camp, where Leader had a load of dannert wire to deliver. Failing to make connection he had decided to try to catch him at the Conqueror Inn by which Leader would have to pass on his return.

Bobby found this information but little reassuring. It sounded to him as if Kram, anxious to place Micky's stolen letters in safety, had decided to hand them to Loo Leader. Did that imply, Bobby asked himself, that in some way Kram felt sure of Leader's loyalty and obedience? He asked if the message had been put through and was told that had been done. The postmistress was alone when she received it and had replied that it must wait the arrival of someone able and willing to deliver it to the Conqueror Inn. Later on, she had rung up to say that Captain Wintle had driven by with a friend, and, as she knew him as an occasional visitor to the inn, she had stopped his car and asked him, if he was going there, to deliver it for her. He had promised to do so.

Bobby thought that things seemed to be converging on the Conqueror Inn in a somewhat curious way. Only coincidence, he wondered, or was there at work some cause of which he knew nothing?

"Did Micky Burke know where Mr. Kram had gone?" he asked.

"Oh, yes," the other answered. "It was when I told him where the boss had gone that he said he would wait."

"It wasn't then that he went off in such a hurry in the lorry you say he commandeered?" Bobby asked again.

"That was afterwards," replied the man. "I just happened to say my sister what lives in the same street as Micky told me she had seen the boss there near Micky's house, as if he was coming away. She thought maybe Micky was ill and the boss had been to see him, so she asked me on her way to work—she's on second shift. When I told Micky, he let out a sort of yell and grabbed the lorry and off before any of us suspicioned what he was up to."

"Left us both," confirmed the second of the two men, "standing with our mouths open, staring after him."

Once again the pair of them were left open-mouthed and staring, as Bobby without a word ran out to where he had left his Bayard Seven by the kerb with Peel sitting, or rather overflowing, inside. Leaping into the driver's seat, off he drove at a speed such as Micky Burke first of all and then Maggie Kram had shown, all three of them at utmost haste for the Conqueror Inn.

CHAPTER XXXIII

CHASE AND PURSUIT

So NOW HERE upon the road to the Conqueror Inn were Bobby and Maggie Kram and little Micky Burke, that dangerous but attractive man; each driving at a speed increasing to its utmost as one by one in succession they passed beyond the limits of the town and came to the long bare road across the moor, where neither other traffic nor police nor control of any kind hindered them or delayed their furious progress.

It was a dangerous road on which they drove so dangerously; a difficult road, in bad repair, for under war-time conditions it had been neglected, made slippery by recent rain, with many sharp turns and hairpin bends where those who in ancient days had traced its course had striven to avoid for themselves or their pack-horses the swampy places and the steeper slopes or the patches of tangled brushwood or other obstacles long since vanished.

First of this odd procession then thundered Micky in his great empty lorry that for lack of a balancing load leaped skittishly and bounded like a ball thrown by a child. Indeed only by the favour of good fortune and the application of a skill Micky himself might perhaps have been less able to show in moments of less tension, did it hold its place on the road.

Next came Maggie Kram, hatless and coatless, as she had run from her office desk, driving every whit as recklessly; and she had gained a little, so that now she was not far behind. But though her car had been built and designed to travel at a very high rate of speed, higher than that ever intended for any lorry, it had been out of use for some time and was in poor running condition, so that twice the gain she had anticipated would enable her soon to overtake Micky she lost by minor defects. Micky, too, looking behind, had seen her car racing in pursuit; and though he could not at that distance distinguish the occupant, yet he took alarm when he saw such speed to match his own, and set himself to tear a yet greater energy from the lumbering vehicle he drove.

A strange thing it was how in some way he seemed to inspire the wood and iron and steel of the lorry with something of his own fierce resolve as he set it roaring round corners, crashing along the straight, bounding and leaping over ruts and holes, tearing up steep slopes as if still upon the level ground.

Finally, far behind, for the others had had a long start, yet gaining steadily, drove Bobby, his little Bayard Seven jumping along at a speed of which the makers had been wont to boast as well within its power but had never much expected to see tried out upon the open road. Yet it was better suited for the conditions of this queer chase and race than either the huge, lumbering lorry Micky controlled or the ancient car Maggie was sending along at a speed beneath which its long disused mechanism was protesting at every yard.

It was beginning to run better though, to gain more rapidly, and Micky, looking back, saw how much nearer it had grown. Bending low in his driver's seat, he tried still to force more power from his engine.

Uselessly now, for it had no more to give. The big old car was close now, very close, and close behind them both scampered the little Bayard Seven rather like a lively kitten chasing a couple of tigers. And each of those two in front far too intent upon the other to have any heed for the third behind.

The Conqueror Inn was well in sight now, and here a cottager from the nearby village, brought by some errand of the season to cross the moor, leaped only just in time from the road to leave it clear and to watch aghast while lorry and great following car and the little one behind went screaming by like the wind in torment. It was a tale he often told, of the sight they presented as they fled by so madly and so wildly across the slow, bare moor where haste and speed seemed such exotic things as to have no place there.

Closer still now to the Conqueror Inn. Aloof and still, like a solitary watchful sentinel it waited tranquilly their coming, as heedless of the frantic, nearing rush as always it had seemed to the passing of the years.

Now the big car, running ever more smoothly with use, like an athlete out of training beginning to find his muscles responding to old habit, was so close to the lorry as to make plain it soon would overtake and pass its rival. Seeing this Micky adopted different tactics and began to swing his lorry from side to side, so that on that narrow road the pursuing car could not pass without the certainty of a collision in which it, the lighter vehicle, must receive the greater hurt.

But Bobby, in his small light car, well balanced by the weight behind of the unlucky Peel who by this time could show a bruise on almost every inch of skin, so had he been tossed and thrown about, saw presently an opportunity where an easier stretch of the road ran across a more level tract of the moor. Taking the risk of some hidden obstruction that might be lurking there to cause disaster, he left the road, taking the ditch at its side in a leap from which luckily his car descended on all four wheels and still upright, and so went bumping across the moor to join the road again in front of both lorry and car and with no worse damage done than an extra bruise or two to the unlucky, sadly suffering Peel.

A yell from Micky when he saw the manœuvre successful and the little Bayard Seven leap as it were from nowhere into the road ahead, passed unheard in the clamour of that triple race. Micky's attention thus distracted he forgot for a moment the reckless skill with which he had tossed the lorry from side to side to prevent the pursuer now close on his tail from passing by. As reckless as himself, Maggie saw her chance and took it, thrusting her car to the lorry's side so that they raced abreast, side by side, while in front Bobby kept his place ahead and Peel wished earnestly they were still in the rear, for he was keenly aware of what Bobby in the high flush of his pursuit had quite forgotten—that now if disaster came, the disaster so far so miraculously avoided, then it would probably strike them first as they were in the lead.

There entered a new element, for Maggie had brought a pistol with her, that pistol of which her father had reported the loss and of which she, for her own reasons, had taken possession. She began to use it now, firing at the lorry's engine and at its tyres. But the shots missed or were without effect on any vital part, and the small, sharp reports were lost in the roaring of the clamour of the chase.

By now the roar of so wild, so fierce a race, such as this lonely road across the moor never yet had seen in all its long existence since first skin-clad man of the Stone Age came that way, had penetrated within the quiet rooms of the inn. From it came hurrying Christopherson himself, followed by Kram whose car stood before the inn door. But within Peter Wintle and his companion the postmistress had mentioned and Rachel were busy with their own affairs and took no notice, and next Loo Leader, with whom Kram had finished his business, drove at this moment his heavy lorry from the yard where it had been standing, out into the roadway.

Bobby saw its nose appear and was just able to get by, suffering not even a scratch, cheating catastrophe by almost literally a hair's breadth, for in actual fact there was not a much greater distance between lorry and car. But the narrowness of that tiny space between the two was yet enough for safety. Behind a crash was inevitable, with Leader turning in his seat to shout after Bobby angry protests at so reckless an exhibition of speed and thus oblivious to the even greater danger thundering on him from the other side.

Both of them, Micky in his lorry, Maggie in her ancient car, as they still raced side by side, saw clearly the collision coming but too late to avoid it. Loo Leader's lorry was half across the road, sideways on. Micky struck it fair and square. Maggie wrenching her car sideways did save it from piling up on the tangled mass of the two wrecked lorries, but in the sharp turn at that great speed it failed to keep its balance. It overturned and somersaulted, threw Maggie clear, somersaulted again, came to rest upside down, while Maggie, by some miracle unhurt except for bruises and a broken rib or two that at the time she had no knowledge of, scrambled again to her feet.

She began to run towards the piled up lorries. She still held her pistol in her hand, though unconsciously. The lorries were beginning to burn, the petrol catching fire. On the road at some distance lay Micky Burke, crumpled and broken, thrown with such violence against the hard surface of the road, so shattered by the violence of that awful impact, that death must have come to him before he even knew it threatened.

Loo Leader had had better fortune—or worse. He was hurt, dazed, his head badly cut and bleeding, but he was still alive, on his feet again, still able to stand, even though uncertainly. Maggie, herself still so suffering from shock she hardly knew where she was or what had happened, came towards him, and he saw her and saw the pistol in her hand. At that, almost mechanically he drew a revolver from an inner pocket made for it in the lining of his leather driver's jacket. He took a step or two towards her, his pistol lifted as if he meant to fire first. Bobby had managed to halt his car and was running back up the road towards them. Peel, who in the general excitement had not even noticed a few more bruises gained when the Bayard was so abruptly halted, came pounding behind. Bobby, seeing Maggie and Leader, each pistol in hand, facing each other, shouted. They took no notice. Leader flung up his pistol hand and cried out to Maggie to keep away. Christopherson had run back into the inn for water to throw on the lorries beginning to burn. Kram, bending over the dead body of Micky Burke, no longer attractive, no longer dangerous, looked up and saw, too, how Maggie and Leader faced each other, pistol in hand—though in fact Maggie had emptied her weapon, firing at Micky's lorry, and it was now harmless. He shouted, too, his voice also unheard and unheeded in the general confusion. Leader shouted again to Maggie to keep off and still she came on, too confused and bewildered to realize clearly what had happened or what was passing. Leader fired. The bullet flew wide. Maggie did not even know it had passed not more than a foot or two away. Her father cried out again and began to run. Bobby flung himself forward, snatched at Leader's arm, by a dexterous, unexpected twist wrenched the revolver away.

He gave it a quick glance. He saw it was a service weapon, a point forty-five.

"The evidence I've been wanting," he said. He said to Peel who had come to his side: "Look after this man. I'm charging him with the murder of Larry Connor."

"Yes, sir," said Peel, unmoved, and laid a heavy hand on Leader's shoulder.

CHAPTER XXXIV
FOUND

By now Christopherson had extinguished the flames that had threatened to destroy the two wrecked lorries. He and Kram were standing by the dead body of Micky Burke. Bobby helped them to remove it from the road to the shelter of one of the barns. Captain Wintle had brought Rachel to look after Maggie who still seemed dazed and had begun to complain of the pain in her side that afterwards was found to come from two or three fractured ribs. Rachel took her upstairs to one of the bedrooms. When the three men had left dead Micky Burke lying in the barn where they had placed him, Wintle said to Bobby:

"I have found Derek Christopherson."

"It was he you had with you in your car, was it?" Bobby asked.

"Oh, you know that too, do you?" exclaimed Wintle, astonished.

Kram, who had not been listening to this, said to Bobby:

"What have you done with Loo Leader? He has some business papers of mine, way bills, and so on. I'll get your man to let me have them."

"They are in my pocket," Bobby answered. "I took them from him. He will be charged with murder. You will be charged as an accessory after the fact."

"Oh, that's nonsense, you can't do that," Kram protested, but looking startled and alarmed; and he made a move towards his car, as if he contemplated departing forthwith.

"I wouldn't try that if I were you," Bobby warned him. "It wouldn't do you any good."

"You can't do that," Kram repeated. "How could I be an accessory? I wasn't there. I didn't know anything about it."

"You held back information," Bobby reminded him. "I think you will also be charged with offences against the food regulations. If you wish to make a statement you can do so."

"What for?" demanded Kram, recovering a little from his first dismay. "I've nothing to make a statement about. You've got it all wrong. Look here. About those papers of mine Leader had. Way bills. That sort of thing. You might let me have them. They've nothing to do with it."

"If they haven't," Bobby said, "why did you take them from where Burke had them hidden under his bedroom floor?"

"Oh, you know that, too?" Kram muttered and looked even more disturbed than at first. "Besides, I didn't. You can't prove it."

"Well, I've the note you left in your own writing," Bobby told him. "A silly trick. I suppose Micky knew, too. Or guessed. When he found his papers gone and heard you had been there. At first he thought we had them, but when he heard about your visit he knew it was you. That's why he came after you in such a hurry. Just as well for you it's turned out as it has or it might be you that was dead, not Micky, and I might have another murder case to handle.

Didn't you know what a dangerous little man he was? I think you had better change your mind about that statement. I can't make you any promises. I have no power to. But the courts often take full confession into consideration. You are in a serious position, Mr. Kram. You may be charged as accessory to a murder, with illegal traffic in food and other supplies, and with treasonable activities in association with Micky Burke. Rather a big bill to answer."

Mr. Kram was looking more and more uncomfortable. He was not so much pale now, as a sickly green. His voice was shaky and uncertain as he muttered:

"Well, look here, listen, I hadn't any idea what Micky was up to. That's why when I got suspicious I went to his house to see if I could find out and I took his letters and things just to make sure. Look here. I'll make a statement if you like. Listen, Maggie knew nothing. I'll swear she didn't."

"I think anyhow she knew," Bobby said, "that Micky had sworn to himself to treat you as you treated dead Larry Connor when you made his features unrecognizable because you were afraid that if his identity were known, so would be his connection with you; and then your black market deals might come out. That's why she followed Burke, because she was afraid of what he might be going to do to you. She will be asked to make a statement, too, when she is fit."

"Oh, well," Kram muttered. "I suppose this is the end. You know it all, don't you? All right, I'll make a statement if you like. But leave Maggie out of it, she doesn't know anything."

Bobby took him into the inn and left him in one of the rooms with paper and pen and ink to write out his statement. When Bobby came out of the room Wintle was waiting for him. Wintle said:

"Does all this mean you know who was killed that night and who did it?"

Without answering this question, Bobby said:

"Where is Derek Christopherson?"

"In the kitchen, they are all there," Wintle said.

As he was speaking the kitchen door opened and Mr. Christopherson came out. Bobby said to him:

"You have found your son again."

"Yes," the big man answered. He looked slowly and doubtfully at Bobby: "Are you going to take him from us?" he asked.

"I don't think so," Bobby said. "I think there is no fear of that."

"I am going to ring up the doctor," Christopherson said. "Rachel says Miss Kram is hurt. Rachel doesn't think it is serious but a doctor ought to see her."

"I was going to ask you to do that," Bobby said. "Let me know when he comes. He must see Burke's body, too."

Rachel was coming down the stairs. She had left Maggie in one of the bedrooms. She was grave, composed, tranquil as ever, but her quiet eyes were shining, her calm features as it were illumined with happiness and relief. She saw Bobby and said to him:

"Derek is here, my brother. You will be gentle with him, won't you?"

"Yes," said Bobby.

"Thank you," she said; and put out her hand towards him and then towards Wintle, who took it and held it in his.

"He came to the camp," Wintle said. "They couldn't make out what he wanted. It was reported to me. They said there was a civilian talking about Dunkirk and so I went to see and it was Derek. He knew me, but he didn't know where he was or why. I reported it and asked permission to bring him here to be identified."

They all went into the kitchen. A young man was sitting there, Mrs. Christopherson at his side. He looked somehow a smaller, weaker, more frail, less tranquil copy of Rachel. There was a strong family resemblance, but one felt that there had not been bestowed upon him that strange serenity of spirit that was hers. He got up when Bobby entered and said:

"Up there they seemed never to have heard of Dunkirk. That's where I was when I lost my uniform—at least, I suppose I was, but I don't know how I got these civvy clothes."

"That's all right," Bobby said. "There'll be a court of inquiry about that. Perhaps they'll stop it out of your pay. Nothing to worry about very awfully even if they do."

"It'll be a shame to do that," protested Mrs. Christopherson.

"Oh, the army's full of shames," said Bobby cheerfully; feeling he had achieved his object of giving Derek something small to worry about that would keep his still disturbed mind from dwelling on any greater worry and so help it to a composure much more easily so attained than by any facile and not easily received assurances that everything was perfect.

"I think something must have happened," Derek was saying now, "I mean at Dunkirk. I don't seem to remember getting back. I bet we licked old Jerry at Dunkirk, but it was a bad show at first. If our chaps are there still, how have I got here?" He paused and looked puzzled again. "What did happen?" he asked. "I can't get it clear in my mind."

"We all came home again," Wintle said grimly; "at least not all of us. To make a fresh start," he said.

"Those chaps at the camp didn't seem to know," Derek complained. "I couldn't get any sense out of them. I thought perhaps the news hadn't come through yet. They keep things quiet sometimes. If we're going back I must report or I'll be getting left behind."

"You needn't be afraid of that," Wintle said, more grimly still.

"All you've got to do at present," Bobby told him, "is to go to bed and get a good sleep. You look as if you needed it."

"He must have his dinner first," said his mother firmly.

CHAPTER XXXV
CONCLUSION

LEAVING DEREK IN his mother's care, Bobby and Wintle went back to the front of the inn. Christopherson had just returned from calling the doctor who had promised to come along at once. Bobby said he would wait to see him and then went to speak to Peel, keeping guard over a sullen and silent Leader. When Bobby came back, Wintle said:

"I ought to get back to the camp. You don't want me any more, do you? Why have you arrested Leader? I never thought of him. Is there any evidence against him? I suppose there must be, but what made you spot he was your man?"

"I've known that long enough," Bobby answered. "I mean, I knew who was the killer. The difficulty was to know who had in fact been killed. That's what made this case so awkward to handle and so different from any other. Generally we know all right who has been killed. Our difficulty is to identify the killer. This time it was the other way round. Not much doubt who had done the killing but difficult to be sure who had been killed. There was always the possibility that the dead man was Derek. Even his father, his sister, couldn't be sure the body was not his. We had to remember there was official proof Derek was dead long before that Monday night. And if we went on the theory that the dead man was Larry, we had to face the possibility of his turning up alive and well. Both Miss Kram—Mrs. Connor really, his wife—and Micky Burke were saying they had letters from him. If you had told me exactly what you knew, Captain Wintle, it would have made things much plainer. It's a wonder I didn't arrest you and I'm rather sorry I never did. It would have served you right and there was a good case."

Wintle looked more than a little sheepish.

"Well, you see," he argued, "it's not as if I really knew. I didn't. Not a thing for certain. I told you so and it's perfectly true. I did see someone here and he did remind me of Derek, but all the same I wasn't sure. Honestly I wasn't. And the War Office said he was dead. You soon find out in the army that what the War Office says, goes. No good bucking against the War Office."

"You kept quiet about what happened the Saturday night before the killing," Bobby went on with undiminished severity. "If I had known for certain it was Larry Connor you saw—"

"How could I when I didn't know myself?" Wintle interrupted. "It's quite true I was near here that Saturday night and I admit I wasn't too keen on your knowing and I didn't see it mattered anyhow."

"What brought you here?" Bobby asked. "It was late, after dark."

"That was why," Wintle explained. "Training. You have to know how to lead your men in the dark. If you like to inquire, you'll find a good deal of stress is laid on being used to getting around in the dark."

Bobby did not ask how it was that this zeal for nocturnal training had led Wintle to the vicinity of the Conqueror Inn. He thought he knew. Lovers have been known before now to sigh in solitude beneath the loved one's window. And Wintle had become extremely red. So Bobby did not pursue the subject. Instead he asked:

"Well, what happened?"

"There was a chap hanging about. I asked him who he was and what he was doing. I had no idea he had been inside—broken in, I mean. I just thought it a bit suspicious. He didn't say a word, he just let out and caught me a whack in the eye. You noticed that eye. I suppose it did look a bit suspicious. Well, I went for him. I gave him a good hiding. I let him go when I thought he had had enough. Didn't know what to do with him anyhow, so I told him to get out. He went off in a hurry. That's all. I hadn't an idea it was in any way connected with the murder. Are you sure Leader's the man?"

"I've been sure of that long enough," Bobby repeated. He was a little excited to think that the long pursuit had come at last to an end and was inclined to be more talkative than his wont. By now the village policeman had appeared on the scene, and had gone off again with Peel, taking the prisoner with them. Bobby saw them go. He came back into the inn to wait for the arrival of the doctor. He sat down and said: "It was proof I wanted, the sort of proof you've got to give a jury before they will convict. I've got it now." He showed the service revolver he had taken from Leader. "I'm not going to believe," he said, "that two of the people on the spot that night had service revolvers and yet neither was the weapon used. The one Derek threw away didn't fire the shot that killed Larry Connor. So it must be this one."

"If it's a service revolver, where did Leader get it from?" Wintle asked.

"Plenty of them knocking about," Bobby told him. "Officers kept them after the last war as souvenirs and lost them; or died and the things were got rid of as lumber, or stolen, or anything. Batmen, too. Men were often in such a hurry to get back to civvy life they didn't care what became of their equipment, and their batmen took what they had a fancy for. Or any other soldier for that matter. I'll try to find out if Leader was ever a batman when he was in the army."

"What made you think it was Leader?" Wintle insisted. "If you knew, why did you suspect us others? Or did you?"

"Oh, yes," Bobby answered. "Very much so. I knew it was Leader all right. But also I knew I might know all wrong. Quite usual to know all wrong. Sometimes I was afraid it might really be Derek thinking himself back at Dunkirk, and very often I felt almost as sure it must be Kram. Or Burke for that matter. Besides the chance that it might turn out to be one of the Christophersons—father or daughter. Or both of them. I was never sure what they were thinking, but I was sure they were hiding something. And there was always Captain Peter Wintle. There was the strongest case of all against him and a toss up whether to make the arrest or wait a bit."

Wintle grinned again and even more sheepishly.

"There was more than once," he said, "when I could almost feel the handcuffs. I didn't expect to be hanged. I didn't see how you could prove I did what I knew I didn't. But I knew it would be the end of me in the army. I'm glad it was Leader you pitched on in the end. But I wish you would tell me why and why he wanted to murder Larry Connor."

"He didn't," Bobby answered, "either Larry or anyone else. It just happened. It grew out of what went before. Things often do. This is no static world. Easy to sow a seed but not so easy to tell what the harvest will be. All these things happened because some enemy agent in the Eire spite hole—some German or Italian or Japanese—offered Irish revolutionaries money for a list of factories in the Midwych district. I suppose it seemed a good chance to earn money they needed pretty badly to keep their agitation going. Larry Connor was one of their officers. He had always kept in touch with his uncle, Micky Burke, and with Midwych generally, and he knew about Kram. Kram had just emerged from a discreditable bankruptcy and wasn't likely to be troubled by any scruples. But they had to have a hold on him, so the first thing was to push him into the black market business. I don't suppose he wanted much pushing. He was always one of your 'get-rich-quick' merchants. Once he was mixed up in that sort of thing, he was in their power. He swears it was only recently he realized what Micky was up to or why he was so often taking lorries out in different directions. One of the conditions of the loan that had enabled him to start fresh was that Micky was to have a free hand. I expect Kram took good care to keep his eyes tight shut. In any case he knew very well that the moment he showed any sign of turning restive, his black market activities would be reported to us. That would have meant ruin—prison probably. They had him hard and fast. But then Leader came into the picture. Not at all as the first murderer, just on the make himself, just another of the 'get-rich-quick' merchants. He heard a story about Micky and eggs and at first thought that was all there was to it, just Micky collecting eggs on the moor to sell again in town at a profit. He soon saw more was going on than that. He heard about Kram wanting to use the Conqueror Inn barns. He wondered why and began to make guesses. Micky had picked up talk in the village, or at the 'Ritz' snack bar, about the Conqueror Inn and about the Christopherson family behaving strangely. Kram had been made sure of. This looked like a chance of making sure of someone else— someone whose occupation of an inn in that lonely spot would be very useful indeed. I think it was Larry Connor's idea. I think Larry was always the brains of the affair. He sent Kram first to have a look around. I don't know if he guessed young Christopherson was being sheltered there. What he did was to break in one night.

"There was an unexpected result. Derek, in his unstable mental condition, was thoroughly upset by Larry's nocturnal appearance. Another unexpected result was that Maggie Kram became violently jealous. She knew he was showing great interest in the Conqueror Inn and got it into her head that Rachel might be the attraction. So she started prowling round to find out if she really had a rival there.

"All this time Leader was watching. He found out that Micky was due to pick up a big load of black market stuff that Monday and he hit on the idea of holding Micky up on the return journey. 'Hi-jacking' the Americans called it in prohibition days, I believe. He reckoned Micky wouldn't dare lodge any complaint. I suppose it seemed safe enough. So he waited in ambush on the lonely road he knew Micky would use, a mile or two beyond the Conqueror Inn.

"Things didn't go according to plan though. In the first place Micky hadn't got his load. The man who was to deliver the stuff got a warning that he was under observation and didn't turn up. So Micky was running back empty. Then Larry showed fight. There was shooting and Larry was killed. Leader hadn't bargained for that. He and Hall panicked and cleared out at top speed. Then Derek, restless as a result of Larry's midnight visit, was out on the moor, heard the shooting and came along. Probably with a memory of Dunkirk and the fighting in France. Thought he was back there perhaps. What happened completed his mental upset and afterwards he wandered off. He wandered about till he happened to see soldiers at Ingleside. Then he remembered he was a soldier too and tried to join up again.

"But meanwhile his disappearance left it uncertain who the dead man was.

"Because Kram, warned by a code message that things had gone wrong, got scared and drove out to find Micky, and, if he had the load on board his lorry, tell him to jettison it somewhere instead of bringing it to their depot.

"What he found was Micky by the side of the dead body of the boy who had been to him like his own son. Micky was more or less dazed by what had happened so suddenly. Kram persuaded him to agree to a secret burial on the spot. He told Micky that not only would their black market activities come out if there was an investigation and Larry's connection with them was discovered, but that also Micky's own secrets would become known. If there was one thing Micky thought as much about, as he did about Larry, it was his connection with his Irish revolutionary friends. The young Nazi thought he would save Europe and the world by conquering it for its own good, for Hitler—and for himself. Gandhi thought he would save India by betraying it to the Japanese. Micky thought he would save England by seizing Ulster. People get these ideas. Like Torquemada, who thought he could save people's souls by burning them alive. Micky consented to the secret burial and to the removal of the clothing, but he hadn't expected the mutilation of the dead boy's face. That took him by surprise. He never forgave it. He swore to revenge it. The candle burning on his mantelpiece was there as a constant reminder.

"Only he decided to wait for a time till there was no danger of his revolutionary secrets being discovered.

"Something else didn't go 'according to plan.' Larry's disappearance had to be accounted for. A forged letter was sent to Maggie in his name. But it didn't deceive her and when she heard of the Conqueror Inn tragedy, she was at once afraid that the dead man might be Larry. She thought Rachel must know, she may have even believed Rachel was concerned in the murder. She took her father's pistol with her in an attempt to frighten Rachel into telling her what had really happened. Rachel's personality was much the stronger.

She quieted Maggie, took her pistol from her, refused to tell me anything. Later on I suppose she gave the pistol back to Maggie.

"At first Kram thought they had made themselves safe by making identification impossible. But in the excitement, the general confusion, the panic at the sudden death breaking in on all their careful plans, they overlooked the loss of the box filled with bank-notes Larry had been nursing on his knee. They didn't notice the map that had fallen out of Larry's pockets, perhaps while his body was being undressed. Nor did they know that Derek had thrown his revolver away and that it was lying there in the dark by the side of the road.

"When Christopherson came from the inn to see what had been happening he found the box of bank-notes and rang us up to tell us. Then they discovered Derek was not in his room upstairs. So he went out to look again and he found the map which he didn't think mattered at all and the revolver and—the grave.

"I don't know how they stood up to it—the strain, I mean, their ignorance of what had happened, their inability to tell whose the body really was. Somehow they seem to have some hidden, strange reserve of strength. I don't know where it comes from. A country innkeeper and his daughter."

"One man cracks," Wintle said, "and another holds, as all Britain held in June after Dunkirk. But I don't see what there was in all that to help you dig things up the way you did?"

"Eric," said Bobby.

"Eh?" said Wintle. "Who's he?"

"Little by little," explained Bobby, but Wintle still looked puzzled for he had not been brought up on Dean Farrar. Bobby went on: "Plain enough Leader was in it somehow. He was always hovering on the outskirts, so to say. I had to ask myself why. He admitted being not far away that Monday night. He had to. He knew we should find out. Might have been a coincidence. Other people were in the neighbourhood, too. But he was the only one who came back next day. Another coincidence? I don't like double-barrelled coincidences. And I thought he showed too lively a curiosity. Other lorry drivers went by without bothering their heads about what Christopherson and I were doing. He had to get down and see. I suppose he had to know what was happening and whether the man he had fired at and seen drop, was really dead or only wounded. He had to know if anything had been discovered. Possibly he had even thought the body might still be lying there and he might be in time to remove it. Or any other signs still visible. I expect it was a tremendous relief when he drove by the first time and could see nothing to attract attention. But when he returned, which he did as soon as he thought he could without making people wonder why he was driving up and down—then it must have been an even greater shock to see digging going on. Too much to suppose he, or anyone else for that matter, would have the sense and self-control to drive straight on. If he had, I shouldn't have known he had driven back the same way so soon and I shouldn't have wondered why. By good luck, Christopherson had mentioned seeing him go by that morning, so why had he come back again? And why did he want to know what we were doing unless he knew a good deal already? Those are the kind of little things that don't mean much in themselves but may be pointers to put you on the right path. I noticed, too, that both he and Hall seemed really upset and shocked when they saw how the dead man's face had been mutilated, and they seemed to know without being told that he had been shot. Not that that was much to go on. A natural guess perhaps. But it did seem probable that Leader might be the killer, but that the mutilation had been done by someone else. Why? Why should anyone but the murderer wish to prevent identification? Then when no one came forward to claim the money, it seemed clear the reason was the same. They daren't claim the money, they daren't allow identification. What else could that mean but something seriously wrong? Black market suggested itself at once. There are some people who seem to think that sort of thing is merely a kind of smuggling and no great harm. Quite surprised if they are told it's a kind of treason and they ought to be shot. Still more surprised now when they get a good stiff dose of imprisonment, instead of a smiling admonition not to do it again.

"Well, I was beginning to see light but there was still Micky Burke to be accounted for. If he were merely an innocent employee why was he helping to hush up his nephew's murder?

"And if he were concerned more deeply than an ordinary lorry driver, had he had anything to do with Kram's sudden and rather mysterious accession of capital that had enabled him to start again in a fairly big way?

"Again Micky was no teetotaller. Kram had described him as a steady drinker and yet he never went to any of the public houses near his home. Was that because he had his secrets and feared neighbours' gossip? When I told him of Larry's marriage he refused to believe it at first because Larry was 'vowed and sworn.' But when I asked 'to what?' first he wouldn't say and then he began to suggest Larry was promised to a girl at home in Ireland. But I could find no trace of any woman besides Miss Kram in Larry's life, and so I had to ask myself what else there was to which a young, eager man could be 'vowed and sworn'?

"There was still no proof of the dead man's identity, but it did become clear, though only slowly, that Christopherson had been concealing his son and that since that night he had disappeared. Equally possible that he was the murdered man or that he was a fugitive because he was the murderer. That he had disappeared without the knowledge of his family was plain, or why was his father neglecting his work to walk the moors as though in search, why was his mother sitting at the attic window of the inn as though on watch, why did Rachel rush away at full speed when I mentioned I had seen her father on the moor with a companion? She thought it might be Derek come back at last. If she had stopped to listen, I could have told her it was only the curate her father had happened to meet. Then there was the violin I saw in the old barn where they had encouraged Derek to play at times, beyond the hearing of any stray customer in the bar. Fair proof of identity when I knew Derek was a musician. And the story of what had happened at Dunkirk made it evident Derek might have survived after all, though possibly with injuries to the head or from blast shock that might have affected him mentally. Blast plays queer tricks on the human organism as I remember saying once before.

"Oddly enough, it came about in a queer way that Kram himself provided the evidence I was beginning to think we should never get. He rang up from a street box to say there was a revolver buried on the Conqueror Inn land. He didn't say who he was but luckily I had him under observation, so we knew all right though we couldn't prove it. Difficult to prove a 'phone call in the ordinary way, especially with the dial system. But Kram didn't know, no one knew, that when the Christophersons buried the revolver for fear it might implicate Derek, they buried it wrapped in a paper Christopherson had picked up at the same time. It happened to be the map that had fallen out of Larry Connor's pocket and it showed the position of war factories marked by pin pricks. It wasn't hard to draw conclusions, but it still remained to link up map, revolver, and murder. Not too easy, especially when it turned out that the revolver wasn't the one that killed Larry."

"How did Kram know anything about it?" Wintle asked.

"Leader told him. Leader trying to divert suspicion from himself. If criminals had sense enough to keep quiet and do nothing, say nothing, we should have a hard job to get them. I suppose it's too much for human nature, anyhow guilty human nature, simply to stand and wait and do nothing, when it knows it is under suspicion and in danger. It has to do something to try to make itself safe and then as often as not, what it does do, gives us the evidence we want. Probably Leader was on the watch, trying to reassure himself, trying to find out what was happening. Frightened. Badly frightened. Scared of developments. He must have seen Christopherson and Miss Rachel digging and guessed why. He may even have seen—I know he had a good pair of binoculars—what they were hiding. So then he thought that if he could get us informed and we dug the pistol up, we should assume the Christophersons guilty and that would make him safe. I daresay he has no idea how exactly it can be told which bullet comes from which gun. And he didn't know Hall had managed to get blood from the dead man on his hand and from it to the revolver he picked up when Derek threw it down and that then Hall had thrown down again in turn. I let them go on believing we thought we had the right weapon. I argued Leader would then feel safe and confident and probably start carrying his own revolver about with him. Once we could get hold of that and identify it with him, trace it to him in his possession, I would have the final link in the evidence that I needed to bring it all into order and relation. Perfectly simple logic. If he were guilty, then the revolver used must be his. I guessed he would have got rid of it immediately afterwards, because that is always a killer's first instinct. There was the risk it might be beyond recovery, at the bottom of the canal or somewhere like that. But there was a good chance it was only hidden, and that he could get it back; and I calculated he would want to begin carrying it again, once he believed we believed we were in possession of the murder weapon. He would want to feel himself protected against sudden arrest, still more against Micky. How scared he was of Micky I knew from the fact that he had been rather pleased at the idea of being under police observation. That meant police protection against Micky. I think he knew, I think Kram told him, that Micky had accused him to me, and he knew well enough what a dangerous little man Micky Burke could be. In actual fact, any suspicions Micky had of him, he had given up when Kram persuaded him it couldn't be Leader by pretending he had seen Leader somewhere else at the time of the shooting. Kram suspected Leader, more than suspected him, but he wasn't sure. What he was sure of was that if Leader were arrested he would tell what he knew about Kram's black market activities. All the time, all Kram did was with the one object of preventing any inquiry that might have that result.

"That was another of our difficulties. No one of them knew exactly what had happened. It all took place in a moment, in pitch darkness. Leader himself didn't know for certain whom he had killed—or at first whether he had killed at all. Neither Kram nor Micky Burke knew who was the killer. The Christophersons only knew that Derek had vanished. Maggie knew no more than that Larry had gone. Apparently you yourself knew even less. It was the sum total of all these ignorances I had to add together to reach the truth. Only when I saw Leader produce his revolver just now did I know my calculations were correct and that at last he had given me what I had wanted so long—final proof."

"What are the papers," Wintle asked, "I heard Kram talking about?"

"I don't suppose they'll amount to much," Bobby said. "They'll give proof of Micky Burke's fifth column activity but we knew that already. Both Kram and his daughter knew Micky meant to take his revenge for what Kram did to the dead boy. That had upset him terribly. He meant to retaliate in kind, Maggie feared by murder. Kram thought to protect himself by getting hold of Micky's letters. I expect we shall send copies to Dublin for the Irish police to act on, but I expect they know it all already. Even if they wanted to—and probably they won't want—not much they can do. No harm in one neutral in a neutral country telling another neutral where a British factory stands. And if the second neutral happens to mention it to the German or the Japanese ambassador, well, why not? One of the delights of being neutral. 'Ourselves alone.' The Eire motto and proud of it. Kram reckoned he could hold Micky off by threatening him with handing over the letters to us. But he didn't dare keep them himself so he gave them to Leader to keep for him. He thought he knew enough about Leader's complicity in Larry's death to make sure of Leader's loyalty. Leader played against Micky and Micky against Leader. A double game. A simple game. Kram always showed the kind of simple, obvious cunning you expect from a man of his type, the 'get-rich-quick' type, with always just the one idea— to find short cuts."

"I know," Wintle said. "You worked it all out to a fine point," he added.

"Detective work is like that," Bobby said. "You add one thing to another, one little thing to another, one here and another there, till at last all you want is the last nail to drive home to make the case complete, the last brick to lay to finish what you've been building up. And when you know that's all you want, you are almost bound to get it in the end."

"What will happen to Leader?" Wintle asked. "If it was like that, if he was only trying to butt in and never meant to kill, you can't call it murder, can you?"

"If you kill while committing an unlawful act, it's murder," Bobby answered. "The charge might be reduced to manslaughter. I don't know. That'll be decided later. Not by me. Thank God, punishment is no responsibility of mine. All my duty is to uncover the truth. Personally I always think English law ought to distinguish between degrees of murder. They do in some countries. Leader may get off with a long term of penal servitude. Better than hanging I suppose. Alf Hall will probably escape with a year or two in prison. As an accomplice. Kram will get off like that, too. And a fine he won't be able to pay, for I don't suppose there's much ready cash left after the loss of that two thousand and his Irish backers will have no further use for him. So he'll go bankrupt again. Two thousand is a big sum to drop at one go and now I expect the Treasury will pinch it, unless we can hold it for the benefit of the Wychshire police rate."

"Not a hope in the world," Wintle told him, "not if I know our Treasury."

And with that Wintle went back into the inn where he had caught sight of Rachel moving slowly in the background.

THE END